Bruce Aiken was born in Kent but has lived and worked for most of his life in a small village within the Exmoor National Park, Devon.

NINE OUT OF TEN MEN

BRUCE AIKEN

Copyright © Bruce Aiken 2024

All rights reserved. No part of this publication may be reproduced, distributed, or transmitted in any form or by any means, including photocopying, recording, or other electronic or mechanical methods, without the prior written permission of the author, except in the case of brief quotations embodied in critical reviews and certain other non-commercial uses permitted by copyright law.

ISBN: 9798879197723

For permission or requests, contact the author at bd.aiken@icloud.com

To everyone who has displayed
amazing patience with me.

PROLOGUE

Jenkins was the first at the scene of the crime, only to discover the lifeless body of a woman in the lounge. He purred for a few moments, rubbed his head against her cool legs, and meowed twice. Receiving no response, he moved on. Jenkins' main preoccupation was to see if there was any fresh food in his bowl. As he walked away, he left a trail of red paw prints in his wake. Jenkins' path had taken him through the pool of blood, still oozing from his mistress's neck, and spreading across the polished floorboards.

Carol Williams, Juliette du Colbert's cleaner, was the one who first alerted the wider world to her employer's murder. First by screaming at the lifeless body, which was oblivious to her distress, then by screaming again at Jenkins when he returned from the kitchen. Getting no response from either, she ran out the house, only to scream at an unattended lawnmower. Carol's shrill voice roused the couple next door, who had been involved in an illicit overnight liaison. The gentleman made a hasty retreat via a gate in the back garden which led to a little-used public footpath. The woman, after ensuring her friend was clear of the scene, phoned the police.

It took some time before a semblance of normality returned to the house. Even then, it was only the sort of normality that would be recognised by forensic pathologists or scene of crime officers.

A stiletto heel, buried deep in the dead woman's neck, had been plunged in so hard as to become partially detached from the rest of the shoe. The sole of the shoe, exposed because it was now tilted at an unusual angle, was bright red, an almost perfect match to the sticky, congealing blood.

The attending detective inspector recognised the trademark colour of the shoe's sole as that of a leading fashion brand.

"Manolo Blahnik, if I'm not mistaken." DI Colin Gilroy remarked.

"I think you mean Louboutin, boss," his sergeant replied with a resigned sigh.

"Exactly. One of those posh, expensive brands. So, is there a husband? And has anyone located him?"

In many respects, DI Colin Gilroy was a good copper, with a lot of experience under his straining belt, but he never liked to own up to his errors. Somehow, he always managed to adjust his memory to place himself in the right. DS Maryam Chandra was used to his idiosyncrasies, but they still irritated her. And he never got her name right, always calling her Miriam, or Mary, in front of everyone. It had become a standing joke in the pub after work. All her colleagues would order an orange juice for Mary Miriam. She never touched alcohol, which was almost a social error in her line of work.

"Not yet, boss. There is a husband, one Jonas Moon, though we're not sure if that's just his stage name. We've been trying to get hold of him, but he's not answering his phone."

A doctor had been summoned to pronounce the victim dead, a formality, but a necessary one. It wouldn't matter if a body had been dismembered, it still required a medically trained official to declare all parts of the body deceased. The sergeant looked to her boss, who was rubbing his chin and nodding slowly, as though he had already solved the crime.

"Do you want to talk to the cleaner sir? It was her who discovered the body."

"I'll leave that in your capable hands Miriam. She might be more forthcoming if she's processed by another woman."

There was only a limited amount the police could accomplish until forensics had checked for fingerprints, recorded the scene, and bagged any trace evidence they found.

The cleaning lady was outside, in the garden, being assessed for shock by paramedics. Maryam's interview with her took place in the back of an ambulance.

Carol claimed she had been cleaning, upstairs, wearing earbuds, and had heard nothing unusual, not even anything usual.

"I play my music quite loud; it makes the day go quicker."

She gave the interviewing officer the playlist she had been listening to – just in case it helped.

"I normally do Monday afternoons," she managed between sobs. "But this week I couldn't because I've got to take my mum to the hospital tomorrow." At which point, she burst into tears again.

Maryam closed her notebook to prevent it being splattered with tears, or contaminated by the handkerchief Carol was waving around after dealing with a runny nose. A paramedic put a comforting arm round Carol's shoulder, looked at Maryam, and shook his head slowly. There was nothing to be gained by extending the interview.

Maryam left the ambulance, and lingered on the half-mown lawn, wondering why the task had been abandoned. She studied the front of the house, the like of which she would never be able to afford on a police officer's salary and resigned herself to the loss of a lazy Sunday afternoon. She should have been eating biscuits, drinking tea, and watching a favourite film.

Jenkins had been taken in by the neighbour and was enjoying a rare feast of smoked salmon, originally intended for the gentleman who had departed rather suddenly.

CHAPTER 1

Some two months earlier, Oliver had come home from work on a Friday evening to find his wife, Hollie, slumped at the kitchen table. Her head was resting on a rush placemat, arms hung limply by her sides. She looked like she might be dead, but this was not the first time he had found her in such a pose.

"Are you okay?" he asked.

She opened one eye to look at him. Oliver was pristine, looking as precisely tailored as when he had left for work that morning. Clothes liked him. Even as students, after three days at a festival, he would still appear freshly laundered, hair unruffled, fingernails spotlessly clean.

"I hate my job," she mumbled.

Hollie had been teaching for five years. Her initial enthusiasm had waned, due to an ever-increasing avalanche of paperwork, mostly on computer now, but still paperwork, still tedious.

Oliver had come home to find her in this mood before, but it was becoming more frequent. A collection of what looked like essays were stacked in an untidy pile beside her head, an empty wine glass had left a stained imprint on the top sheet. If they were students' work, the topmost entry was probably the only one to have gained a mark that day.

"Okay, well, we've been here before, haven't we." Oliver adopted his most sympathetic tone.

"I don't actually hate the students, at least, not all of them."

"Another glass?"

"Please."

"So, is it time for a change?"

"No, the Malbec's quite nice."

"I meant your job."

Hollie had known what he meant. She also knew she could leave her job any time she wanted to, they could pay the mortgage and maintain their lifestyle solely on Oliver's salary; he was ridiculously overpaid. But she had been brought up by her mother to be independent. The idea of not having her own career, and her own income, was unconscionable.

"But I can't do anything else," she mumbled, as she lifted her head from the table.

The rush place mat had left a pattern on her cheek, along with an unidentifiable dark item. Oliver pointed to his own cheek.

"You have a little something stuck to your face."

Hollie touched her cheek with her index finger and retrieved a small, dark brown blob. She looked at it for a moment and then popped it on her tongue, chewed it a couple of times, and swallowed.

"I presume you know what that was?" Oliver asked, eyebrows raised.

Hollie nodded. She had bought a Chelsea bun on her way home from school. It was almost certainly a stray currant; it had definitely tasted like one.

They discussed the possibility of her changing career at least once a term. Hollie always maintained that a degree in classical literature would not open many doors in the worlds of commerce or industry. Oliver sat opposite her and reached for the jotter pad she had been using. He turned to a fresh page and took his fountain pen from the inside pocket of his jacket. She had never made up her mind whether the pen was a pretentious affectation or a rather sweet quirk. Oliver cleared his throat.

"Okay, no excuses this time, no prevarications, we are going to make a list of your talents."

Hollie groaned. He had threatened to initiate this process several times before, but she had always found the energy to swerve his analytical approach.

Oliver was now in full solution finding mode. Only those who knew him would expect a capital wealth management executive to be so inspiring. He divided the page with a vertical line and was only half-way down the 'pros' side when he ground to a halt. The ability to ski, poorly, and a childhood medal in tap dancing were already on his list.

"I'm quite good at crosswords and jigsaw puzzles, and Where's Wally," Hollie said, not convinced they were going to get anywhere.

"Problem solving and observational skills," he mumbled.

Oliver added both to the pros side of his list. Hollie put on an innocent girlish voice, partly because she knew it would annoy him when he was trying to be both serious and helpful.

"So, what new career would you recommend, sir?"

She felt sorry for Oliver and his quest for a solution. He was doomed to failure. Her abilities and experience were not applicable to anything other than teaching. And some days, she doubted that.

He tapped his teeth with the end of his pen. Hollie watched as a small drop of ink formed on the tip of the nib. It fell just where he had written 'excellent research and communication skills', making a sort of oversized, irregular, exclamation mark.

"Shit," Oliver muttered, wrapping the pen nib carefully in a tissue which Hollie had handed him. He looked at the list again. "You have a unique and valuable skill set."

Hollie groaned and let her head drop back onto the table mat.

"Are you looking for more currants?"

"You're only jealous because I didn't share the last one with you."

"How about we go to Giovani's? Let's get you out of this pit of despair and into a pit of pasta."

She lifted her head at the mention of their favourite Italian restaurant, stared for a few moments at the pile of unmarked essays, and stood up. Her chair tried to fall backwards, but she caught it.

"I'll need to change first. Give me five minutes?"

They both knew it would be more like twenty, but at least Hollie was up and motivated.

It was over coffee, after a very good Penne con Fungi, that Oliver once again brought up the subject of a change of career. Hollie sighed and repeated the fact that she realistically had no viable alternative to teaching.

"But you've always liked problem solving and puzzles, haven't you?"

"Please don't suggest any sort of role at your place. I think I would get more depressed in finance than I have in teaching."

Oliver looked down at his empty plate.

"I'm sorry," she added. "I know you love your job and are very good at it, but it's not for me."

Oliver looked up at her, smiling. Sometimes that smile was a warning. It usually meant he had an idea which she would not be expecting, and that she might not like.

When he told her what he was thinking, Hollie had just taken her first sip of her espresso. She tried to laugh, swallow and gasp all at the same time. Achieving none of those, she choked and had to put her cup down while trying to control her coughing. It rattled on its saucer and fell over, spilling the remaining coffee on the tablecloth. A waitress hurried over to see if she could help, and when Hollie tried to say she was okay, her throat caught again, and she couldn't breathe.

By the time she finally recovered, her face was red, and Oliver was still grinning.

"So, what do you think? Sounds like you're quite excited by the idea."

Hollie thought he might possibly have lost his mind. How he had come up with the idea of her becoming a private investigator defied all logic. The waitress reappeared, bringing with her another cup of coffee, compliments of the house. A kind gesture for regular customers. Hollie thanked the waitress.

The interruption, exchange of cups and the mopping-up process, gave her time to compose herself, and she wondered if she might have misheard her usually sensible husband.

"Did you really just suggest that I become some sort of amateur crime buster?"

Oliver offered his amoretti biscuit to Hollie which she took and nibbled slowly, while he continued to grin.

"Stella's idea actually," he said. "She's always going on about the investigators she has available and how they are all cloned from the same basic model. The last time we had supper with her and Jeremy, I had the distinct impression that she was fishing for you to offer your services, but you never took the bait."

Stella was Hollie's best friend; she had been ever since they were at high school together. Their paths had gone separate ways when Stella decided to study law, but they had remained close and still met regularly.

"But most of her clients are high-flyers, you know the type. They're usually in the throes of divorce, or suing each other, or suing a newspaper for suggesting they're getting divorced, or have forgotten who they're married to in the first place."

The waitress returned to see if there was anything else they would like. Hollie ordered a liqueur. She felt the need for a little fortification. Especially as that marking was still sitting on the kitchen table. The idea of being a private investigator was growing on her, in a curious way, even though she knew it was ridiculous. She was in no way qualified for the role.

"And you have the summer holidays coming up soon," Oliver added.

"In nine weeks and six days to be precise. Not that I'm counting."

"And you'll be moping about after the first week or two, complaining that you have nothing to do."

"I do not mope. And I'm quite happy to work on my suntan all summer. And I have lots to do, too much, it's practically a working holiday, you know that."

But Hollie also knew he was right. She did get restless when the weather turned grey or cool for any length of time.

"I don't mope," she mumbled.

"Give Stella a ring. Maybe I'm wrong, maybe she wasn't dropping heavy hints after all."

Hollie screwed her mouth sideways, obviously thinking about something.

"You know those detectives in old American movies," she said. "Do you think I'd look cool with a raincoat and one of those hats they always wear. What are they called?"

"You mean a gumshoe?" Oliver tried to affect an American accent but not one any American would be fooled by. "You have a raincoat already, and those hats are called fedoras, I think."

"So, what are gumshoes? Are they like gum boots, but shorter?"

"I have no idea."

The restaurant tablecloth was still a bit soggy with cold coffee. Hollie's excitement at the prospect of something new had waned, knowing it was never likely to happen.

"It won't hurt to call her, will it?" Oliver suggested.

Hollie didn't answer immediately. She had no idea what she might earn as an investigator, but it was not that important, providing she had some sort of income, and providing, of course, there really was a job on offer with Stella.

"But the summer holidays wouldn't really be long enough to know if I enjoyed it, or even if I was even any good at it."

"Then ask for a sabbatical."

"I could probably persuade Gordon to grant me one. He's a bit of a softie. But I'd need at least ten years under my belt before the governors would even consider it."

"Nothing to lose by asking, is there?"

Hollie thought it highly unlikely. Nobody she knew had ever been granted a sabbatical. Her sambuca arrived, brought to her by the same young waitress whose clothes looked like they had been sprayed onto her body. There wasn't an ounce of spare fat to be seen, except where it was spilling over the top of her blouse. Hollie noticed Oliver making a similar observation. She made a mental note to do a little more exercise and drink a little less wine. And maybe avoid biscuits. But that would all have to wait until the end of the school year, if only to allow her stress levels to subside first.

"You could always resign," Oliver suggested.

Hollie's mind had wandered back to her teenage years when, as now, Stella had been the taller and slimmer of the two of them. Bagging Oliver before Stella saw him had been one of her great strokes of luck. She often caught Stella looking wistfully at him.

She wasn't sure if she had heard Oliver correctly.

"What did you just say?"

"Resign. You could easily get another teaching post if it didn't work out."

Hollie knew that was true in theory, but testing it out in practice was quite another thing. Somehow her glass was already empty. They must be making them smaller than they used to be. The practicalities of changing career were already wafting around in her head.

"I'd have to give notice by the end of this month if I wanted to leave at the end of the summer break. And Gordon wouldn't be best pleased."

"He'll survive."

"I'm not saying I will resign, but I might ring Stella, just to see if you're right about her."

Oliver tried to get her to phone straight away, but Hollie resisted. She needed to get everything clear in her head before she spoke with her friend.

By the time they got home, she could easily have beaten Oliver to death and made the investigation of his murder her first case. He just wouldn't let it go. Once indoors, she put both hands up, palms facing towards him, just to stop him talking.

"Okay, okay, I'm going to ring her now. But the more I think about it, the more stupid the whole idea sounds. Stella is never going to let me forget this – and that will be on you."

Hollie went up to their bedroom. She didn't want Oliver listening while she made a fool of herself. She closed the door, sat on the bed, and stared at her phone as she speed-dialed her friend.

Hollie blurted it all out, barely taking a breath and not giving Stella a chance to respond. She blamed the whole idea on Oliver and said she wouldn't be able to start for at least two months, as she had to give her notice in at school.

When Hollie finally ran out of breath, Stella's reaction took her by surprise.

"Brilliant. A brain like yours is wasted in teaching."

"Well, I wouldn't exactly say it was wasted."

"You know what I mean."

"I'm not sure I do." Hollie sat up a bit straighter.

"Darling, if you stay in teaching, you're going to do the same thing every year until you retire. I would rather stick pins in my eyes than spend all my waking hours with those ungrateful oiks."

Hollie wanted to defend her profession, and some of her students, but Stella's generalisation rang true for a fair proportion of them.

"Anyway, if I did this, would the job be a sort of freelance thing, or would it be salaried?"

Stella's family were not unfamiliar with overseas bank accounts, so money had never been a concern for her when they were both at university, and it certainly wasn't now.

"Darling, don't worry, you will earn far more with me than as a state nanny to all those grubby little children."

After Hollie had once again defended her profession, they agreed to meet for a coffee the following morning. Stella said she would bring a file with her, for Hollie to peruse.

"You don't have to do anything yet, just familiarise yourself with the ins and outs of the case. Maybe not the best choice of words, given that the vacuous little fool in this instance has probably been cheating on his wife for months."

"Okay, but I'm not promising anything. I haven't given in my notice yet."

"When could you be free to work full time?"

"If I do quit, and I'm only saying if, I'll technically be employed until the end of August, but in practical terms, I suppose I would be free by the end of July."

The prospect of a summer without lesson planning, and all the associated bureaucracy, was appealing. But Hollie walked downstairs a few minutes later, realising that a summer of occasional sunbathing was also disappearing over the horizon. Oliver had made a pot of coffee and was carrying it into the lounge when she reappeared.

"Well," Hollie said. "You were right, I suppose. It looks like you might be living with a gumshoe by the end of summer. And I really ought to look up that word. It might mean something rude."

CHAPTER 2

When Saturday morning came, Hollie decided she would try to forget about school for two whole days. But she knew it would be evening by the time she had begun to relax, and by Sunday lunchtime, she would be thinking about work again. She wondered what it would be like to be a private investigator and whether, it too, would eventually involve repetition and form filling, the two aspects of her work she had come to dislike so much. The interaction with some of the students, and the support of her colleagues, would be a loss. She had a deadline of seven days to give in her notice if she was going to leave that summer.

When she left home to meet up with Stella, Oliver was mowing the lawn, in almost mathematically parallel stripes. On one occasion, she had caught him stretching string between two pegs to use as a guide. She had taken a few photographs on her phone before he noticed her. Hollie threatened to send them to his friends if she found him doing it again. Oliver had since settled for a finish slightly short of perfection.

She arrived at Kafé Klein a few minutes early, even though she knew Stella would be at least ten minutes late. It was a lifelong habit of hers, making a dramatic and tardy entrance. That morning was no exception.

It was a very small café, tucked away in a quiet square, but it was always a gamble to get a table, unless you arrived before ten in the morning. Hollie suspected the owner was English, even though her accent was vaguely East European, as were an ever-changing array of waif-like waitresses. She could have been a glamorous extra from any spy novel of the cold war period, doomed to die in some unusual manner. Stella was of the opinion the café was a front for people-smuggling. She always said it was interesting because of that aura of clandestine activity.

Hollie was already half-way through her coffee when Stella arrived. She appeared to be accompanied by her own personal wind machine. It swirled her lightweight coat around her as she swept through the door. Even on a Saturday morning, her trousers were perfectly pressed, her heels ridiculously high, and a blouse of expensive silk shimmered over her lean figure. She only had to raise a finger in the direction of the waitress to get her attention. Stella ordered two more coffees, and a slice of lemon drizzle cake, before she had even taken her seat. How Stella kept her figure so trim had always been a mystery, given the way she ate. Hollie only had to look at a biscuit and her jeans became tighter.

"I am so glad you are going to join us, darling." The phrase defined their meeting as if a decision had already been made. "I've brought a folder with me, outlining a particular case I want you to look at."

Stella fished in her cavernous leather shoulder bag and pushed a small silver pen drive across the table. Hollie had been expecting a bulging manila folder, holding surveillance shots and a variety of documents.

"Is it all on that?"

"What were you expecting dear, some antiquated pile of photocopies and a few grainy monochrome pictures?"

Hollie's fingers closed round the small cold object, and she wondered what secrets it contained.

"So, tell me, what's that gorgeous husband of yours doing this morning?"

"Probably stretching a piece of string across the lawn."

Stella frowned.

"Look," Hollie said. "Do you really think I can carry off this sort of investigating thing?"

"Of course, you'll be a natural, darling."

"And can I actually make a sensible living out of it?"

Stella said they would put her on the staff roster. She mentioned a salary significantly higher than her current teaching one.

"Of course, we don't offer quite the same holidays you enjoy now, but there would be other perks, bonuses, expenses and walking-about money."

"What exactly would I have to do to earn that sort of salary? Nothing illegal or dangerous? And what is walking-about money?"

"It's simply expenses you don't have to provide receipts for. Such a tedious business all that paperwork. Most of your time would be spent on quite run-of-the-mill research. But we need someone with intuition, rather than the ex-army, machismo plods we usually end up with. I think some of them might just as well drive around in a tank for all the subtlety they possess. We've been looking for a nondescript woman - no offence - but one who has a brain."

Hollie wasn't sure she liked the description, apart from the brain part.

"What exactly do you mean by nondescript?"

Stella apologised and said 'chameleon-like' might have been a better choice of words.

"I have long envied your ability to blend into any social gathering or situation. Your accent is good, without attracting undue attention, you can converse on a wide range of subjects, and I've always thought that you look equally comfortable in jeans or a ball gown."

Hollie tried to think of the last time she had worn a ball gown. It must have been at her university graduation party, and she hadn't looked that good after some loud-mouthed rugby type had thrown up over her. A pair of nail scissors had reduced the charity shop purchase to a somewhat overly revealing mini dress, but she had no idea what happened to it afterwards. Probably best forgotten. At least it had attracted the attention of Oliver that night.

"What sort of case is this?" Hollie asked, peering at the memory stick as though she could divine its contents. "Is it something urgent?"

"Just the usual sort of thing. We are acting for the wife. She suspects her husband may be one of the nine out of ten."

"Nine out of ten what?"

"Just an epithet we use within the firm. Taylor, our IT guy, read that nine out of ten men consider adultery at some time in their marriage."

"Is that a genuine statistic?"

Hollie was wondering whether Oliver might be one of the ten percent who never thought of straying.

"No idea. It may be ten out of ten for all I know. Jeremy has certainly thought about it. Totally open about it too. He has even made a list of his free passes should he ever catch me cheating on him. He thought I might find it amusing. "

"That could make interesting reading."

"Don't laugh. You're third on the list."

It came as no surprise that Jeremy had a wandering eye. He had wandering hands too, after a few drinks, and when he thought nobody was looking. Hollie was not sure whether she wanted to be on his list, but if she had to be on it, first or second would be a better ranking. She wanted to know who had beaten her to first place, and was about to ask, when Stella turned in her chair, distracted by some noise from a table the other side of the room.

"What are those juvenile idiots sniggering about?"

Hollie recognised three students from her school. You could never get away from them completely. Someone had told her once that, in a large city, you're never more than twenty feet away from a rat. She wondered if anyone had done a similar calculation for teachers and their students.

"So, if it's a divorce case. What will I be doing?"

Stella turned back to Hollie, still frowning at the disturbance.

"Well, this one is a bit more complicated than some. The husband is a B-list celebrity, although he thinks he's A-list, and if the newspapers smell a scandal, they might damage any case we build for our client. You would be following him, keeping a record of where he's been, who he sees. Getting into whatever clubs or restaurants he frequents. It's a bit of an open book because we don't have any solid information yet."

"How would any of that help your client? Other than confirm her fears."

"They have a prenup. She has the money. He has a pretty face and youth on his side. Of course, the prenup is not legally binding, but a judge will take it into consideration if the husband is shown to have broken the agreement. It's all in the file. It's quite simple."

"Okay, but you understand I can't start yet. My contract requires three months' notice, even though the last month or so is little more than a formality."

"But you're going to come on board? Please Hollie, you did say you would."

Hollie didn't remember making any promises, just that she would consider it. She glanced at the three boys again and one of them blew her a kiss.

"Definitely. Count me in."

Stella had also noticed the boy's gesture and turned to face him again. As sometimes happens in a small space, a silence settled on the room as she spoke. Even the coffee machine ceased its gurgling, so everyone heard Stella's offer.

"Have you boys ever considered a threesome?"

Two of the youths looked suitably embarrassed, but the ringleader rose to the taunt.

"Anytime you want gorgeous."

"Oh, I didn't mean with me," she laughed. "But I do hope the three of you enjoy yourselves. And do use condoms, heaven knows what grubby little infections you might all be carrying."

Laughter broke out from another table and the three boys, disgruntled but recognising defeat, made a noisy exit. On his way out their leader muttered, 'Bloody lesbians'. Stella didn't respond, simply separated a small piece of cake with her fork and made a show of savouring it.

"Thank goodness they're not in any of my classes," Hollie said.

"Well, you won't have to worry about schoolboys for much longer, just grown-up versions of them. So, tell me more about Oliver and this piece of string?"

Hollie explained about the lawn, the string, and Oliver's obsession with mowing perfectly straight lines. Stella had just eaten a morsel of cake. She had to cover her mouth to prevent herself from spitting it out when she laughed.

"Oh my God, please tell me you kept photographs of that."

Hollie picked up her phone and flicked through her photo files. She found three she had taken on the day she caught him. She handed the phone to Stella who squealed with delight.

"You have got to send me those, please."

"I can't, I promised Oliver they would never see the light of day unless I found him doing it again."

"Ooh, blackmail. Perfect. I think you have exactly the right mindset for this job."

"You're not going to ask me to blackmail anyone, are you? I assumed this was all going to be within the law?"

"Darling, have you forgotten, I am the law. Or, at least, a representative of it, and an expert in the finer details. But no, nothing I ask you to do will be illegal, not exactly, at least, not in any actionable way."

Hollie was wondering what she had let herself in for, but Stella was right about one thing, she had had quite enough of dealing with adolescent hormones for the time being. And, as Oliver had pointed out, schools in inner cities were always crying out for teachers, and she knew she was a good teacher.

"Now, I have to rush," Stella said, patting her lips with a handkerchief and pushing the half-drunk coffee to one side. "Can I leave you to pay, sweetie? I am going to miss an appointment at the hairdresser if I don't dash."

Stella's hair looked as though she had just come from the hairdresser. Hollie couldn't imagine what they could do to improve it. After adopting a bob style when she was fifteen, inspired by Anna Wintour, Stella had never deviated from it. The colour might subtly change with the seasons, the length varied a little, but the fringe was always perfectly cut so it just brushed her eyebrows.

Once alone, Hollie was conscious that she was gripping the pen drive rather too tightly, and that her palm was sweating a little. She had brought a soft leather satchel with her, having expected a bulky file of some sort. She tucked the pen drive into a secure inside pocket and made her way to the counter to pay.

"All taken care of," the waitress said, nodding towards two women who she said had enjoyed Stella's put down of the boys.

Hollie thanked the women but said they needn't have paid for her and Stella. They told her they had been the butt of those boys jokes the previous week and maybe now the young idiots would find somewhere else to go on a Saturday morning.

Stella had always had a way of winning friends and admirers without even appearing to try. That was maybe why she had risen so fast in her law firm. Stella had confided in her recently that she hoped to become the youngest ever, full partner.

On her way back home, Hollie pictured the pen drive in her bag. She visualised it glowing with secrets, gradually getting hotter, until it might threaten to burn a hole through the leather. She knew this was just her imagination, but when she heaved her bag onto the kitchen table, she didn't hesitate in retrieving the little stick that held her future, and some possibly juicy secrets.

"What's that then?" Oliver asked.

Hollie glanced out the window. She was almost disappointed

not to see a length of string stretched down the lawn. It would have given her the freedom to send those pics to Stella.

"Apparently, it's my first case."

"Do I get to see all the juicy details too?"

Stella had not specifically told her the file was confidential, just to be wary of the press. And Oliver was good at keeping confidences; he had to be in his job. Plus, she had no idea what demands this new career would place on her in terms of time and travel, so she needed to keep Oliver on her side.

"Why not? Providing you don't breathe a word about it outside this house."

"Cross my heart and hope to die or stick a needle in my eye."

"Where on earth did you get that saying from?"

Oliver shrugged. "We used to say it as children."

Hollie pulled her laptop towards her. It was still sitting on the table from when she had watched the news at breakfast. She pushed the memory stick into a spare port, opened the drive and clicked on a picture folder. The first image that sprung onto the screen was of someone they both recognised, someone who had been on the news that morning.

CHAPTER 3

Hollie had chosen to open the picture file first, simply out of curiosity. But both her and Oliver had been surprised by the image of the actor that popped up on the screen.

"That's Jonas Moon, isn't it?" Oliver asked, not sounding entirely certain.

"It is, but how do you know him?"

Oliver was not a television addict, often reading the news on his tablet while Hollie watched a crime drama or soap.

"He's married to one of our clients."

"I know you don't normally talk about your clients, but you could have mentioned you've met Jonas Moon?"

"It's easier not to say anything about them at all, or you'd be continually asking questions. As it happens, he's married to the Comtesse du Colbert, and everyone knows her, even you I suspect, because she's rarely out of the news."

Jonas Moon might have been a completely unremarkable actor if he had not married into money and fame. Hollie googled her, Juliette du Colbert was a multi-millionaire, probably a billionaire. Hollie wasn't sure which and was not especially interested. The Comtesse was sometimes referred to as 'the condom queen' in the popular press because her family fortunes were made from the production of natural latex. The plantations in Malaysia had long since departed the company's portfolio, but the nickname had stuck with her.

"Is he Stella's client?" asked Oliver, leaning nearer the screen.

"I think Jonas might be who I'm going to be following. But Stella didn't mention any names when we met this morning."

"So, you are definitely going to have a go at this thing?"

Until that point, a career as a private investigator had been little more than a fantasy, a wonderful but imaginary escape from the endless repetition of her chosen career. But the more she stared at the set of files on her computer screen, the more real it became. She was experiencing a frisson of excitement that she had first felt at a boyfriend's house at the age of sixteen. On that occasion, his parents had arrived home rather earlier than expected and the moment had been lost.

"Just tell me, I'm not mad to give up a career based on this offer. I mean, what if I'm useless at it?"

"You're not mad. And if it doesn't work out, you simply apply for another teaching post. Or do something else, look for a job in publishing or a literary agency. That's what you wanted to do originally, wasn't it?"

Hollie couldn't resist clicking on another file from the list on her screen. She started to read without answering Oliver.

"What a bastard," she muttered.

"Me?" asked Oliver indignantly.

"Not you, idiot. I mean Jonas Moon. The Comtesse is Stella's client. And she suspects Jonas Moon is actively having affairs with at least three different women."

"Admit it, you're hooked, aren't you?"

Hollie ignored him and kept reading. The more she read, the more certain she was that she would be handing in her notice on Tuesday. Oliver said he was going in the lounge to catch up on the lunchtime news. He had only just turned the television on when Hollie, laptop held in front of her, followed him in.

"I'm not mad, am I Oliver? Tell me I'm not mad."

"I already told you, you're not mad."

Oliver turned the volume on the television up a couple of notches.

Over that weekend, Hollie read everything in the folder, twice. She Googled both Jonas Moon and Juliette du Colbert, and frequently interrupted Oliver with snippets of information she had garnered from a variety of sources. On one occasion, she burst in on him in the bathroom.

"Oliver, this Comtesse du Colbert, did you know her real name is Julie Colby?"

"Yes. Of course I did. I told you, she's one of our clients."

"But why didn't you tell me earlier about her real name?"

"Because all our high-value clients expect a level of confidentiality. Now, do you mind if I finish my bath in peace?"

In a fit of pique, Hollie blew out one of his candles and left the door open as she trounced out. Oliver sighed, pushed the door shut with a long-handled loofah and relit the candle using a box of matches he kept on the windowsill.

Late on Sunday afternoon, Oliver was dropping off to sleep on the sofa. They had enjoyed roast beef with all the trimmings, which he had prepared, and the best part of a particularly pleasant bottle of Saint-Émilion.

The sofa suddenly bounced, waking him up, when Hollie flopped down on the edge of it.

"Move your legs a bit," she demanded. "Did you know Jonas Moon was married before, when he was eighteen?"

"Why on earth would I know that, or need to know that, or even want to know that?"

"It's interesting. And it's sad. His first wife was killed in a hit-and-run accident. They never identified the driver, but a witness said they thought the car was a pale green Porsche, an older model. His career was just taking off. He had a good part in a stage play and was signed to a talent agent. His life seemed to be in a perfect place. I wonder who his agent is now."

Oliver groaned and closed his eyes, guessing he was about to be immersed in yet another layer of famous-people trivia.

On Monday morning, Oliver breathed a sigh of relief as the front door closed behind him, but he did so a little too soon and Hollie heard him. She almost opened the door to ask him what the problem was, but she didn't want to start an argument. It was almost an hour before he would normally leave. Oliver had obviously had enough revelations about Juliette du Colbert and Jonas Moon.

Hollie was sat at the kitchen table, her laptop in front of her, a new blank document open on the screen. Her fingers were poised above the keyboard, motionless. There was no way of softening the message so, with teeth clamped together, she started to type her formal letter of resignation.

After sealing it in an envelope and addressing it to Mr Gordon Sheffield, Headteacher, Hollie put it into her messenger bag. She stared at it for a moment before closing the flap over it. It had to be done by letter; it would be cowardly to do it by email. And she would deliver it by hand, with an apology.

On the way to work, with her bag on the passenger seat, she thought she could sense the letter pulsing through two layers of leather, just like that pen drive had done. The bag had been an expensive present from Oliver on their first anniversary and was now a little worn, but it was never going to be discarded. After parking, the letter continued to shout its message to everyone she passed or greeted. It even blew raspberries at some of the more disruptive students she had had the misfortune to teach. Suppressing a giggle at one point, she shrugged her shoulders and composed her face.

The deed needed to be done as soon as possible, before she lost her nerve, so she walked straight to the headteacher's office.

"Hi Janet, is he free for a couple of minutes?" She was always a little afraid of Gordon's secretary, who doubled as sentry and bodyguard.

"I'm sorry. He is a bit busy this morning. Is it urgent?"

Gordon Sheffield's knuckles rapped on the glass partition which separated him from his front-line defence system. Although in the middle of a telephone call, he gestured for Hollie to come in. Janet pursed her lips and tried to reimpose her authority.

"I suppose you'd better go in, but don't hold him up for too long. He has a very busy schedule today."

Hollie turned her back on Janet and smiled at Gordon. Realising that she probably should be looking more serious, she straightened her face and opened the door to his office. He was still on the telephone but indicated for her to take a seat.

She opened her bag, slid the letter out and put it on his desk before she changed her mind about the whole crazy idea. Hollie had only ever felt more guilty when she had been going out with two boys at the same time. She had overheard their respective mothers comparing notes on their sons' girlfriends, the two of them unaware that they were both talking about her. To Hollie's delight, she had come out of the discussion rather well, but with a strong feeling of guilt. She ended both relationships later that same day.

Gordon the goldfish saw the letter on his desk and ended his call. It was an affectionate nickname, albeit somewhat unkind. Just because he had orange hair, and slightly bulbous eyes did not mean he really looked like a goldfish, merely a very close cousin to one.

"Is that what I think it is?" he said, not touching the envelope. "I hate the last couple of weeks of this month, I never know how many of these letters might appear on my desk."

"I'm sorry, it wasn't planned, it just happened."

"Have you had a better job offer? Not a health problem I hope?"

"Not really."

He looked up at her, eyes widening even more in anticipation of her next answer. "Pregnant?"

"No. Nothing like that. I just need a change, a break, maybe not permanently."

"I would hate to lose you, Hollie. Would a sabbatical help, unpaid of course?"

"I didn't think that would be an option as I've only been here five years."

Gordon sat down, leaned on his desk with both elbows and held his head in his hands. He spoke more to the envelope in front of him than directly to Hollie.

"I could talk to the governors." He looked up. "But I can't promise you anything."

Hollie was not sure whether that was her cue to leave or if she should say something else.

"Sorry," she whispered again. Hollie realised she was clasping her hands in front of her, head bowed, as though she were a child waiting for forgiveness.

"Can't be helped, I suppose. Anyway, thanks for coming to see me in person and not sliding the letter under my door."

She could feel a blush creeping up from her neck. That option had crossed her mind. She stood and went to offer Gordon a handshake but retracted her hand almost immediately. He did the same a fraction of a second later. On the third attempt, they managed to coordinate their timing.

"Listen," he said, still holding her hand. "I'll talk to the governors, maybe individually, and let you know asap if a sabbatical is on the cards."

"Thank you," Hollie said, freeing her hand and backing out of the office before her resolution deserted her. Gordon looked as though he was about to go belly up and float lifeless on the top of his tank.

The dragon, who masqueraded as his secretary, watched as Hollie crossed her office, possibly deciding which punishment she should inflict for anyone who deserts her glorious leader. Hollie was sure that fire and brimstone were in her armoury – although she was never quite sure what brimstone consisted of.

Out in the corridor, with the hubbub of an early morning bustling around her, the school looked different already. The corridors appeared shabbier with scuffed paint along the walls and the odour of over a thousand hormonally challenged teenagers lingering in the air. Other members of staff drifted through the building with an aura of fatality about them. Hollie wondered if familiarity and commitment made one blind to the monotony of the daily routine and the state of the buildings. There were pupils she would miss, mainly the ones who showed a real interest in her subject. But every year they left, just as they were developing independent thought.

A bell rang, echoing around the corridors. Hollie glanced at her watch and quickened her pace. She was late for her first class.

At home, after the school day, Hollie made a cup of tea and mooched around the kitchen, prepping the ingredients for a chicken and mushroom risotto. It could go on when Oliver arrived, usually around six. A bottle of wine had partly survived from the previous day, so she poured herself a glass. It was a bit early, but she was sure private investigators drank at all times of the day and night. Hollie sat at the kitchen table, staring out into the garden. After a few minutes, she rang Stella, expecting her call to go to answerphone.

"Hello, Hollie. Have you done the deed yet? Closed the door on those awful classrooms?"

"As it happens, I handed my notice in today. But do you honestly think I will be any good at this investigation thing?"

"Absolutely, piece of cake. Have you read the files I gave you?"

"I have, yes. The Comtesse is a rather unusual woman."

"Unusual and very, very wealthy - don't forget that important factor."

"I can't do much for the next couple of months. I need to tie up everything at school before I can spare much time on this case."

"No problem. We have an ex-army plod on the books. He has no imagination, but over the next couple of months he should be able to establish Jonas Moon's routines."

"Okay, that's good. I thought it might be a bit urgent."

"Not in this instance; it's very early days. Sometimes we need things checked in a rush, but the Comtesse has not yet decided which course of action she wants to take. It rather depends on what we unearth."

"I suppose we never refer to her by her real name?"

"No, not if we want to keep her as a client."

Stella told her to sit tight and keep up to date with anything she pings over to her.

A message arrived almost as soon as Stella had hung up. It was a new email address for her, only to be used for work. Strict instructions came with it about never sharing the address with anyone outside the firm and never, ever, to use her personal email for work or vice versa.

Hollie made up a new password based on her favourite detective, Hercule1920.

About an hour later, the first email arrived from Stella. She had booked Hollie in for self-defence classes, starting next weekend.

"Oh shit," Hollie said out loud. "What have I let myself in for?"

Oliver had just come home and asked her what was wrong. She showed him the website for the classes at a private gym and what they entailed.

"Oh dear," he said. "I suppose I'm going to have to behave myself from now on. But at least you will be able to defend yourself against Jeremy if he ever decides to act on his list."

"I told you that in confidence. If you ever mention it to him or Stella, I may have to terminate you with my about-to-be-learned deadly new skills."

Oliver poured her another glass of wine.

"Then I shall endeavour to stay on your good side – or learn to run faster if I can't."

CHAPTER 4

Over the remaining two months of her school contract, those months she was still required to teach, Hollie managed to keep the real reason for her departure a closely guarded secret. She didn't even tell Peter, a science teacher who had started the same year she had. They had both been equally as nervous in their first week and had formed a bond.

But nothing remains secret in a school for very long, and a few days after the news circulated, everyone was curious as to why she had handed in her notice. Many talked about getting out of teaching, but few were brave enough, or foolish enough, to take the plunge.

Peter managed to trap her alone in the staff room one day. He informed her there was a sweepstake running on the reason why she had quit.

"I got you as going into politics. I'm not likely to win, am I?"

"What are the other options?"

"Oh, the usual. Pregnancy, illness, divorce, emigration, prison, secret service, lottery win – one that you're not going to share with us – and someone even got gender reassignment. Not sure that one's going to be a winner."

"Why wouldn't it be?"

"Because you're…"

Peter struggled to find the word he was searching for.

"Because I'm too short? Too cuddly? Too boring? Or because I have a mixed ethnic background and a husband?"

"I was going to say straight, but I suppose sexy covers it. Anyway, who am I to make such judgements?"

Hollie smiled and winked at him. "Don't let Marcus hear you say I'm sexy – he'll only get jealous."

"That monster gets jealous if I look too lovingly at a pizza. Anyway, I suppose a hint is out of the question?"

"Let's say secret service is closer than any of the other tickets."

"Damn, that rules out politics I presume?"

"Sorry."

The exam season passed, and the majority of the teachers' conversations veered towards travel plans, suntans, and mental recovery. Hollie had managed to avoid all attempts to coax her into revealing her future, but eventually relented and told everyone that she had taken a position in a law firm. Judging by the general reaction, this news was far less interesting than most of the other options.

"As what?" Someone asked.

"Oh, just a general dogsbody, nothing exciting."

How can you tell your colleagues that you are going to become a private investigator. Even Hollie didn't really believe it.

The self-defence classes had proved fun and surprisingly interesting. Most of the time was spent in understanding how to avoid danger and dangerous situations, rather than the practice of physical combat. But she had learned how to break out of a hold or position herself to make an attack less likely. There was as much psychology in the course as physical training. One of the useful lessons was in making yourself less noticeable, and Hollie had been practising this at school.

She had learned to observe without staring, training herself to make use of peripheral vision, watch people by using reflections in windows. That was how she successfully identified the three culprits who had been taping small cut-out paper goldfish to the walls and furniture. The headmaster had thought it innocent fun, unaware that he was the butt of the joke.

There was nothing particularly malicious in the students' intent, and it was about as innocent as an end-of-year prank could be. Hollie chose to keep their identity secret but did slip a cut-out of a cat into each of their bags, inscribed with the words, 'thank you for the goldfish – but enough'. The paper goldfish ceased to make appearances and Janet was able to relax her daily hunt and removal of them.

In the first week after they had met to confirm her position, Stella sent a few snippets of information to Hollie. Two weeks later, she told Hollie that the Comtesse had requested the muscle-bound clod they had been employing should be removed from his duties. Jonas had mentioned that he thought a man had been following him, and rather than alarm him further, the Comtesse had suggested to Stella that a more subtle approach might be better.

Hollie had researched surveillance devices which could be easily procured and deployed. She had found how simple it was to download an invisible tracking app for a mobile phone and was surprised that several were available that would do the job perfectly. It was subtler than physically tailing someone, but it did rely on the Comtesse having access to Jonas's phone and his password.

She explained it all to Stella who passed the details on to the Comtesse. In the last week of the school year, the app had been successfully installed, without Jonas's knowledge. Stella had sent Hollie the website address and login details for her to track and monitor Jonas's location, his text messages and social media posts. She could even listen to phone calls if she caught them in real time. When she checked the app's log, there was very little activity showing on it. Hollie was beginning to wonder if she had got something wrong when Stella rang her.

"Hi, I was going to suggest we meet for a coffee and an update. It feels so long since we had a good chat."

"Only a couple of weeks, but yes, good idea. I have to say the last couple of months have been a bit weird."

"Why?

"I don't really feel like I'm doing anything useful for you, or for the Comtesse."

They agreed to meet on Saturday morning, in Kafé Klein. Stella said she had another client who was being rather demanding of her time, so if she didn't make it, Hollie would know why.

"There's no rest for the wicked," Stella added.

"I didn't know you were wicked."

"Don't you remember anything about our teenage escapades?"

"Good point. But I didn't realise you were still wicked."

Stella laughed heartily, told someone in her office that she was just coming, and said a quick goodbye, promising to tell all on Saturday.

Hollie was trying to decipher, and make a list of, who-was-who on Jonas's text messages when Oliver arrived home. He was carrying a box.

"Leaving present for you," he said, handing her the package. "Or starting present, depending on which way you look at it."

Hollie tore the wrapping paper off the box, as she always did, letting the shreds fall to the floor. Oliver would have carefully peeled off the tape, smoothed and folded the paper into a neat square, and put it in a drawer for re-use in emergencies. Hollie would periodically retrieve it from his hiding place and throw it away once he had forgotten about it.

They were shoes, trainers of some sort, not a brand she recognised and with thick spongy soles.

"Gumshoes," Oliver said by way of explanation. "Or the nearest I could get to them. I'm not sure anyone ever made anything that was specifically called a gumshoe."

Hollie was examining them carefully. She ran her fingers along the top of the bright pink trainers.

"What are they made from? Plastic?"

"Recycled bubble gum. I had to get our Amsterdam office to source a pair and send them over to me. They're not on sale anywhere I could find."

"Recycled bubble gum? I'm not surprised they aren't for sale. And they are very pink."

Hollie put them on. She was wearing cropped, pale denim jeans and white ankle socks. She stood, bent forward, and looked at them for a moment.

"I might stand out in the crowd a little too much in these. But thank you, it was a sweet thought. And I rather like them."

She gave Oliver a hug and a peck on the cheek. The shoes were surprisingly comfortable, but she couldn't get it out of her head that they were made from bubble gum - sticky chunks of discarded sweets which had been chewed and spat out. She shuddered.

"What's wrong?"

"Nothing. This job, it's all a bit new and daunting, and I'm not sure I'm going to be any good at it."

"Don't worry, you'll be fine. Anyway, what could possibly go wrong?"

On Saturday morning, Hollie had her first inkling of what could go wrong. Stella breezed into the café – several minutes late as usual.

"Oh my God, Hollie, you are never going to believe what's happened." She ploughed straight on without giving Hollie a chance to make a guess. "The Comtesse Juliette du Colbert is in hospital. She was attacked last night."

"Is she okay? I mean she's not seriously injured, is she?"

"Surface damage only, as far as I understand, and probably more damage to her pride than real physical harm. Of course, that didn't stop her being checked into a private hospital, surrounded by the best doctors money can buy. And, on top of that, she is demanding to meet you."

"Why? I mean, why was she attacked? And why does she want

to meet me? Have you told her about me?"

"First, she was at a fashion show. And you know what those events can be like."

Hollie had no idea. She had only ever been to one fashion show in her life, and that was when she was at university. It had been organised by art students, and she suspected it only remotely resembled the industry versions. The wine had been plenteous, but cheap, the fashion outrageous and largely created from plastic bags as far as she could remember.

"Someone accused her of stealing their designer, and a handbag war broke out. Probably very expensive handbags; some of those buckles can be quite vicious. I believe she has a cut just below one ear. Her plastic surgeons are assessing the damage today, two of them apparently, twins."

"Okay, but why does she want to meet me?"

"Because I told her you are starting work for us. And I also told her how brilliant you are."

Hollie reminded her friend that she had only finished teaching two days before, not even officially finished, and she had never investigated anything or anyone in her life.

"And you can't even officially employ me yet. I'm still salaried until the end of August."

"We can get round that, my dear. Not a problem. I'll have the boys in accounts work something out."

Hollie suspected the 'boys in accounts' could be much more creative in recording the details of her employment than the education department would be.

"So, when does she want to see me?"

"This afternoon. And, if you don't mind me asking, what are those strange monstrosities you have on your feet?"

"Gumshoes. A present from Oliver."

Stella raised an eyebrow but said nothing more about them. Hollie decided a change of clothes might be necessary before she met the redoubtable Comtesse. Her phone pinged. Stella had forwarded the address of the hospital.

One thing that had been at the back of Hollie's mind, was whether she would appear too amateurish for Stella's clients. She had no idea how to present herself in this new role. Teaching had been scary, but she had seen teachers in action all her life, so had always had a vague idea how to act and dress the part.

Stella had been babbling on about the other partners, and how much they were looking forward to meeting Hollie. Most of it filtered into her head, but a lot had wafted out almost as quickly.

"Sorry," she interrupted Stella in full flow. "But what am I supposed to do this afternoon? What is she expecting?"

"Just be yourself. I've been completely open with her. I told her this is your first job. She is on board with the whole setup. Fascinated by it, and by you."

Hollie tried to relax into the usual chatter and titbits she and Stella normally shared, but her mind was on the meeting with the Comtesse. The pink shoes had gradually retreated further under her chair, trying to hide from the prying eyes of other customers. She thought they might have been her signature look, like some detectives have a hat or a monocle or a raincoat. She was aware that most of her references were based on American television shows and dated films, but she had no idea what a private investigator looked like in real life.

"How should I dress?"

Stella had paused to cut her toasted tea cake into more delicate pieces. She looked up, frowning.

"For what?"

Hollie said she knew how to dress for teaching, for parties, for gardening, but what was a private investigator supposed to look like.

"Dress any way you want and in whatever is appropriate for the occasion. How would you dress if you were visiting me in hospital?"

"I don't know. Just whatever I was wearing I suppose."

Stella told her that it made no difference what she wore –

providing she didn't turn up to court in a bikini or follow Jonas while dressed as a clown.

"But I like my clown outfit. And what's this about me appearing in court?"

Stella said it was very unlikely, but she might be asked to make a statement in a hearing if she was a material witness to something.

"And I'm also slightly worried that you in a clown outfit might get Jeremy a little bit too excited. He has been acting very strangely lately."

Hollie decided that she did not want to know any more about Jeremy's desires, or how he was acting. She made an excuse about needing to sort her wardrobe out and see how much of it might be serviceable for a life outside the classroom.

"Well, you'll have an expense account too," Stella said offhandedly. "If there's something special you need, just run the receipt past the boys. I'll have a word with them on Monday, there shouldn't be any problem unless you start ordering designer outfits by the dozen."

Hollie had never had an expense account and was not sure what it might cover. Maybe she could emulate Stella's look. But following someone, while wearing five-inch heels might be a bit tricky – especially if they broke into a run. She also suspected that designer outfits probably didn't come in her size.

On her way home, Hollie mentally evaluated the options in her wardrobe for a meeting with the Comtesse Juliette du Colbert. She decided there was no point in trying to be anything other than she was, or trying to out-dress someone whose gardening clothes were probably better quality than her own party dresses. She suspected the Comtesse wouldn't even do her own gardening. Holly decided to stick with jeans, her new gumshoes, and maybe a bright blue sweater to distract from her pink footwear.

CHAPTER 5

When Hollie arrived home, the house was quiet, no television or radio was playing. She found Oliver in the back garden, reading the paper, a cup of tea perched on a low table beside his favourite director's chair - the one that had 'chief gardener' stencilled on the canvas back.

"Had a busy morning?" she asked.

Her touch of sarcasm was wrapped in a cheerful tone. It should have been her first day of doing nothing in the sun, not visiting someone in a private hospital. Although she was fascinated by what it would be like.

"Well, the lawn isn't going to mow itself, you know."

This was not strictly true. Oliver had, only that week, bought a robotic lawn mower. At that moment it was wandering around the garden by itself. It looked like some sort of confused metal tortoise who had lost its home.

"Well, at least your new toy is working."

"I've named it Mo."

"Is that short for Maureen or Morris?"

"Not sure yet."

Hollie ignored him and went back into the kitchen. She needed to grab a sandwich meeting the Comtesse. Oliver followed her in and helped prepare lunch or, to be more precise, got in the way.

"Why are we eating lunch this early?" he asked, popping a cherry tomato into his mouth.

"Because I have been summoned to meet the Comtesse Juliette du Colbert this afternoon, although I'm not sure what exactly the meeting is for."

Oliver nodded but said nothing. Hollie buttered bread, opened a can of soup, poured it into a saucepan, put two bowls in the sink to run hot water over them and put spoons and side plates on the kitchen table. Oliver filled the kettle and switched it on.

"I'll make a fresh pot of tea."

"Not for me thanks. No time."

"When are you meeting her?"

Stella had suggested early afternoon, straight after lunch. She had supplied her with an address in an expensive part of town. Hollie didn't know it well, but when she told Oliver, he whistled softly.

"Nice area. But I suppose she can afford it. I presume it's her pied-à-terre."

Hollie told him that it wasn't her house, but a private hospital, that they were meeting there because the Comtesse had suffered a minor injury in a fracas at a fashion show.

"I wouldn't want to be the one fighting with her. She is a serious force in the business world. I wouldn't be surprised if her opponent is in intensive care."

Oliver explained that the beautiful Comtesse does not take prisoners when it comes to any kind of disagreement, physical or financial. He told her that one of their advisers had suffered a broken tibia, just for calling her Miss Colby, by mistake.

"What did she do?"

"She kicked him. Hard. He hasn't made the same mistake a second time. In fact, we now keep him well away from her when she visits."

Hollie sipped her soup and wondered whether she might have been a little hasty in handing in her resignation. She was sure that somewhere in the loft were shin guards from her hockey-playing days.

"Oh, I forgot to say," Oliver added, launching a slice of bread and butter onto the ocean of his soup. "Jeremy called to invite us over for a celebratory barbecue tomorrow afternoon."

"That's strange, Stella never mentioned it. And why do you have to persist with those awful boarding school habits?"

Hollie was pulling a face at the bread in Oliver's soup as it began to sink.

"Because such idiosyncrasies cost my parents a lot of money to bestow on me. And, for your information, the French do it with onion soup and nobody bats an eyelid."

The differences in their childhood circumstances had never caused them any problems. Hollie's father had vacated the scene shortly after her conception. Her mother, an accountant, had brought her up to be independent and proud of her heritage, even though the details were a little vague in her mother's mind. There had apparently been a party, an amazing steel band, and a telephone number on a piece of paper, which had been accidentally used to roll a spliff. Her mother had never seen her father again after that night.

"What time is the barbecue?" she asked.

"Jeremy said mid-afternoon. Does that work for you?"

Hollie shrugged. She had nothing planned for the weekend.

By the time Hollie was ready to leave, Oliver was back in the garden, in his director's chair. He was keeping half an eye on Mo, as she continued to trundle around the lawn. Hollie had changed her clothes, trying to match a top to the lurid pink gumshoes, but with qualified success. A white cotton blouse had turned out to be a safer option than the blue top, and it coupled nicely with her pale blue jeans. At least she looked bright and cheerful, if a little like a first-year university student, trying to hit that sweet-spot between casual and smart.

When she arrived at the address Stella had supplied, Hollie found herself outside an imposing red brick building. A pair of solid oak doors were ornamented by large brass knobs and a discrete plaque, informing those who paused to read it, that it was the home of the Bergoff Clinic.

Hollie mounted the three marble steps and looked for a doorbell or knocker, there was neither option available. Without warning, one of the doors opened, revealing a young, slim woman in a smart black trouser suit and flat shoes.

"Can I help you?"

"I'm Hollie Parker. I have an appointment to see the Comtesse du Colbert."

The door opened wider, even before she had finished the Comtesse's name. The woman stood to one side to let her enter.

"I'm sorry, I couldn't see a bell," Hollie apologised.

"There is no bell."

The woman looked up and Hollie followed her gaze to a pair of security cameras above the entrance doors.

"The Comtesse is in the day lounge. If you would like to follow me, please."

The entrance hall to the clinic was spacious, even more grand than the exterior of the building. The floor was tiled but had Persian carpets softening the look. The only furniture was an antique desk which held an incongruous computer. An elegant staircase led to a mezzanine balcony and abstract oil paintings adorned the walls. Hollie looked down at her shoes. They were quite out of place here and she wished she had taken more care with her appearance. Stella's advice was not always to be taken literally.

Hollie followed the receptionist into another, much larger, side room. It was furnished more like a period house than any kind of medical facility. Three sofas were arranged around a fireplace which sported an elegant display of flowers. Fresh flowers, she guessed, probably replaced before they had a chance to wilt.

Relaxing at the end of one sofa was the Comtesse. She was not dressed like a patient in a hospital but in a two-piece lavender suit, and shoes with heels that could easily double as weapons.

"Do sit next to me, my dear. You are Hollie, I presume? Stella has told me very little about you."

She patted the sofa. Hollie chose the far end, more than four feet away from her client.

"I am, yes, Comtesse. I thought Stella had told you all about my history as a teacher."

The Comtesse ignored Hollie's words.

"Do call me Juliette. You will have already read my file, and probably all the scurrilous articles on the internet and in the tabloids?"

Hollie nodded. She was perched on the edge of the sofa, not sure whether to relax, just in case she fell into the soft cushions, maybe never to be seen again. She knew she was acting as though she was meeting royalty which was ridiculous, especially given what she had learned from her research.

"You must understand that much of what you read about me is malicious fabrication. My family has both a rich and diverse history. Those who are jealous choose fragments of my family's past to paint a portrait which suits their own agenda."

Her accent was difficult to place; it wandered somewhere between vaguely Mediterranean and East European, but Hollie guessed her mother tongue was English. The Comtesse paused and studied Hollie's shoes. There was no way to hide them, no table they could be slid under. Hoping to distract her, Hollie asked the first thing that popped into her head.

"How are you? Your injury, I mean."

"It was nothing, a mere performance. My acquaintance felt the need to be back in the headlines, poor dear, and I welcomed a chance to meet you far away from prying eyes. Also, my lovely doctors get to enhance their reputation for miracle cosmetic repairs, merely at the expense of putting me up for a night."

Hollie was beginning to realise how devious Stella's client could be, and how different the world was in which she lived.

"May I ask where your accent is from. I'm sorry if that sounds rude, but nothing in your file mentions an overseas origin."

"My father's idea." She was still looking at the pink statements on Hollie's feet when she answered. "Not inherited from him, but at his suggestion. Now, please tell me, where did you get those remarkable shoes?"

Hollie explained that her husband had bought them as a sort of joke, but she rather liked them, and they were surprisingly comfortable, not to mention waterproof. At least she assumed bubble gum would be waterproof, it was never washed away by rain. The Comtesse dragged her eyes away from Hollie's shoes and looked towards the door. Following her gaze, and seeing nothing of importance, she realised that the Comtesse, or Juliette as she had asked Hollie to call her, was staring into her past.

"When my father sent me away to school, he suggested I adopt an accent. He told me that the English upper classes judge everyone by the way they speak, and it would be a way to protect me. A foreign accent would be judged less harshly than his. We watched a James Bond movie, I can't remember how many times, and I learned my accent from a beautiful, dangerous spy. I never saw cause to revert to my former manner of speech, and now it is simply my voice. But tell me, where could I get a pair of those shoes if I wanted them?"

Hollie promised to ask her husband, and to pass the information on. She doubted the Comtesse had any intention of buying a pair. And that was obviously not the purpose of this meeting. The receptionist returned at that moment with a wheeled hostess trolley. It held both tea and coffee, plus an assortment of biscuits and small cakes. The Comtesse lifted one finger from her lap, which Hollie took as a sign to pause their conversation.

The woman poured a black tea with a slice of lemon for the Comtesse, and, after an enquiring glance, a coffee with fresh cream for Hollie.

"You may leave the tray."

The door shut with a precise click that Hollie suspected was quite normal efficiency within the clinic.

"So," the Comtesse said. "You will need to know all about my husband if you are to help me."

All Hollie had to do was listen and sip her coffee while the Comtesse, she could not yet think of her as Juliette, told her how she had met Jonas, fallen in love, and married. The story was unremarkable, other than the speed at which it had progressed, but Hollie came to understand that beneath all the glamour, the wealth, the fake accent and the confident appearance, there was a small girl who had been given everything she ever asked for except, possibly, love. A small girl who remembered being Julie Colby and was frightened of being alone. She was not that different to so many pupils Hollie had mentored over the years. But she needed now to put on her detective hat, not have a heart-to-heart about relationships.

"What makes you suspect he is having an affair? Stella told me that is what is worrying you?"

There was a brief silence from the Comtesse. She didn't move, she appeared not even to be breathing. Hollie wondered if she had drifted off into some sort of catatonic state – until the Comtesse gave a short, loud sniff, fished in her sleeve for a small lace-edged handkerchief, and blew her nose with trumpeting snort of which a lorry driver would have been proud. She mumbled from behind her hand, and the now damp cotton handkerchief.

"He comes home from rehearsals," she paused, looked at her handkerchief as though it had suddenly materialised in her hand, "smelling of cheap perfume. Please don't ask me to identify the fragrance, I am not familiar with high street brands."

She held the handkerchief by its corner and dropped it in a log basket next to the fireplace. Hollie suspected that the logs were only for show, maybe not even real. Regaining her composure, the Comtesse looked directly at Hollie.

"What have we learned, if anything, from his phone activity?"

In truth there was little of interest on Jonas's phone. There were long periods when he remained in the same location, near an innocuous area in a public park, and very few texts, other than those from his agent.

"I have been wondering if he might have a second phone." Hollie suggested. "Do you think that's a possibility?"

The Comtesse nodded her head slowly and took out her own phone. She scrolled through it and showed a message to Hollie.

Our marriage is about as real as your name. Neither will last. You will always be Julie Colby, the Condom Queen.

"I would like to think this was sent to me in spite, from someone I don't know. It is from an unfamiliar number. The sentiment is clear, although puzzling. Why would Jonas say such a nasty thing. Or why would anyone else pretend to be him. It simply doesn't make sense."

"Have you confronted him about it?"

The Comtesse shook her head and said that their paths hadn't crossed for a couple of days. Hollie took note of the sender's number and said she would try to find out who owned the phone. She promised to let the Comtesse know if they discovered anything and, after being reminded, to also let her have the contact details for the gum shoes. When they parted, the Comtesse offered three air-kisses to Hollie, just in time to prevent Hollie from dropping a curtsy – a gesture that would have been totally inappropriate, and extremely embarrassing.

CHAPTER 6

On Sunday morning, Hollie woke to hear Oliver snoring beside her. His rattling snorts were far too regular and made her smile. Oliver was pretending to be asleep in the hope that she would get up and make them each a mug of tea. Hollie turned over onto her side, facing away from him, raised her knees and slid her cold feet against his warm bottom. Oliver groaned.

"Okay, I'll get up. But how do you always know I'm awake?"

Hollie was not about to tell him he didn't snore, not after years of telling him that he did.

The letterbox rattled while Oliver was in the kitchen, followed by the thud of something heavy falling on the doormat. It was the weekend newspaper. Hollie ran downstairs to collect it.

She separated the sections of the paper. Oliver always had the news and the business pages, very thin on a Sunday. The sports section was discarded at the end of the bed, and Hollie had started to thumb through the magazine by the time Oliver returned. He was carrying two teas on a small tray with a shortbread biscuit for each of them.

Hollie found an interview in the magazine with Jonas Moon. She folded the cover back and slid down in the bed to read it in comfort.

"Something particularly interesting?" Oliver asked.

"Sort of. It's about Jonas Moon."

"Hmm, isn't that a bit like working on a Sunday morning?"

Hollie would have been tempted to accidentally spill her tea over Oliver, but she was too thirsty.

In the article, Jonas recounted his 'big break' in a television drama, which Hollie had heard of, but not watched. It had not been commissioned for a second series. As far as she could determine, he must have been cast in it at about the same time he married the Comtesse. She decided to check on those dates more precisely, maybe even ask the Comtesse, discretely, if she had ever invested in television or film production companies.

The various sections of the newspaper, holidays, lifestyle, and news gradually joined the sports pages at the foot of the bed. Oliver yawned and suggested getting brunch at a garden centre café they often frequented on Sundays.

They arrived well ahead of the lunchtime rush, so there were plenty of free tables. Oliver ordered waffles, bacon, and maple syrup. Hollie opted for poached egg on wholemeal toast, after assessing the waitress and her waif-like figure. Life was not fair once you turned twenty. She reminded Oliver that they were going to a barbecue, but he said he was hungry, and Jeremy's barbecues were always later than promised.

Hollie was gratified to see he was focussed more on the arrival of his heart-attack breakfast than the girl who delivered it. And she was probably young enough to be his daughter, had he been a precocious youth, which he probably had been.

When Oliver asked, between mouthfuls of waffle, whether the article on Jonas was of any help, Hollie explained the timing of his break-through part, and that it had coincided with his meeting the Comtesse.

"Does she have any interest in television or film?" Hollie asked, as though not really interested.

"I suppose I'm not giving away anything by revealing that the Colby Group has an extremely varied investment portfolio. It could possibly include a production company. But, if anyone asks, I didn't tell you that."

Hollie decided that she might broach the subject with Stella, rather than push Oliver further.

"I suppose it could be relevant?" Oliver said, before

devouring his last piece of bacon, chewing, and swallowing it. "Or are you just being nosey?"

"Me? Nosey?"

"Sorry. What was I thinking."

By early afternoon, they were on their way to Stella and Jeremy's for their barbecue. The house was only six miles away, but in another world if you judged it by property values. On their approach, two large iron gates swung open automatically, and the car tyres crunched as they ploughed through a deep gravel drive. Two vehicles were already parked outside the house: Stella's Range Rover Evoque, and a deep grey Bentley which neither of them had seen before.

Jeremy greeted them at the door, a flute of sparkling wine in his hand. He led them through a long hallway and into the lounge, where a sliding glass wall opened onto a large patio. Stella was there with another couple who were obviously the owners of the ostentatious car. Jeremy made an excuse that he had to get back to his cooking duties. Stella took over.

"Darlings, this is my boss Rupert and his wife Natalie. Rupert is one of our senior partners. He specialises in defending criminals."

Hollie estimated the man to be a well-preserved fifty-something, noting his manicured nails when they shook hands. His wife was much harder to assess. At first impressions, she could have passed for thirty, but whether that was the benefit of good genes or skilful cosmetic procedures, was difficult to determine.

"To be more accurate, my dear Hollie, I defend men accused of criminal activities, but not necessarily guilty. Every man is innocent until proven otherwise."

"What about women?" Hollie asked.

"Are women ever completely innocent?" Rupert laughed at his own well-worn joke.

Natalie apologised for her husband's sense of humour and

told him he should keep his rhetorical questions for the entertainment of juries, not friends.

Jeremy chose that moment to distract everyone by creating a minor fireball above the gas barbecue. A column of smoke rose into the still afternoon air.

"Men," Stella tutted. "A box of matches, a gas grill and they all turn into chefs - or arsonists - more often the latter."

"I hope you don't mind me asking," Hollie was still looking at the skirt where Natalie's hands were hiding in concealed pockets, "but is that Balenciaga?"

Natalie smiled and reached out to touch Hollie's arm. Slender hands, but lined skin, revealed her to be somewhat older than her face and figure suggested.

"It is. You have a good eye. Sometimes I think I could dress in rags and Rupert wouldn't notice. Ironic given my work."

Hollie only recognised the skirt because of Peter's fascination with fashion. For a science teacher, it was an unusual hobby. He had shown Hollie a picture of that exact skirt, a denim concoction with studs and straps attached to it. Sort of punk on steroids, but with a high price tag.

"Are you connected to fashion in some way?" Hollie asked. "Stella never mentioned what you do."

In truth, Stella had only ever referred to Rupert and his high-maintenance wife in slightly dismissive terms.

"Magazine publishing. Fashion, gossip, whatever sells."

"You're a journalist?"

"Goodness no, nothing so creative. For my sins I have a seat on the board. But it does come with passes to some of the more interesting fashion events and a few free samples."

Jeremy was busy burning burgers and halloumi kebabs while everyone else relaxed with wine. Rupert and Oliver found a common interest in railways and Stella recounted tales from her and Hollie's schooldays to the amusement of Natalie. The way Stella described their teenage years bore only a passing resemblance to the reality of a rather drab period. The bare bones of events were similar, but Stella blessed their escapades with considerably more panache than Hollie recollected. A phone trilled from indoors, interrupting Stella's flow.

"I'm so sorry," Stella said. "That's my work phone. I left it in the lounge. It had better be important to disturb me on a Sunday."

Within seconds of answering, Stella rapped on the glass doors and signalled for Hollie to join her indoors.

"I think work is beckoning you, my dear." Natalie pointed to Stella. "I'll supervise the boys and try to stop them from cremating our food."

As Hollie walked over to the glass doors, Stella hustled her inside and closed them the quickly behind her. She covered the phone with her hand, hissing, "It's the Comtesse".

"What does she want that's so urgent?" Hollie whispered so that the Comtesse wouldn't hear her.

Stella told the caller to hang on a moment.

"The Comtesse doesn't need anything unless you can perform miracles. She's been found dead. Murdered."

Hollie listened as Stella continued her conversation. Most of it consisted of short questions from Stella and long answers from the other party. Eventually, Stella hung up. She bit her lip, a nervous habit Hollie hadn't seen for years, and tossed the phone onto the sofa.

"Well, that wasn't part of the plan," she said, touching a finger on her lower lip where it was now a stronger shade of red.

"She's actually been murdered?"

Hollie hadn't heard the start of the conversation and was struggling to think who might have killed the Comtesse, and why. She was also beginning to regret handing in her notice at school. The divorce of the Comtesse was her only case. She wondered if it was too late to revoke her decision.

"It was earlier today. She was killed with a stiletto, so my contact said. Stabbed in the neck."

This was not how Sunday barbecues were supposed to go.

"How do you know all this? Was that the police?"

Stella didn't answer the question directly. She was as shocked as Hollie and repeated what she had been told.

"She was found this morning by her cleaner. The stiletto heel of her shoe was buried in her neck." Stella waved a hand in exasperation. "The Comtesse's neck, I mean, not the cleaner's neck."

Once she calmed a little, Stella explained the phone call had been from a contact, one with whom she had an understanding. Hollie didn't question what sort of understanding, but guessed there might be a reciprocal exchange of knowledge when convenient.

"The police are there, I presume," Hollie said. "Have they any idea who did it and was it a burglary or something else?"

"My friend couldn't say much more right now. Hopefully we'll get an update later. Although, from the little I know of these things, it is likely they will be looking at Jonas as their primary suspect. Let's hope he has a reliable alibi."

Stella had opened one pane of the sliding glass doors and called to Rupert. He arrived with a full glass of wine, but when Stella told him the news, he put it down on a coffee table and pulled his phone from his pocket. After a brief conversation, he told them both that the police were treating it as a murder investigation and Jonas was indeed a person of interest.

"That was quick," Hollie said. "Could it really have be Jonas? A crime of passion?"

Rupert nodded but added a few words of caution.

"We should not speculate on such matters. There's nothing we can do today, but they will want to interview us as our connection to the Comtesse is known to them. I suggest, for the time being, that we put this to one side and discover if any of those beef burgers are ready yet."

Hollie didn't say anything. Rupert's response had been world-weary and resigned, rather than surprised and shocked. She followed Rupert and Stella back out into the garden, wondering how they could think about food when one of their clients had just been murdered. A waft of fried onions told her how.

She touched Stella's elbow to hold her back a moment.

"Do I still have a job?" she whispered. "I mean this was the only case I was going to be working on."

She had an image of going back to Gordon, tail between her legs, and getting all the worst classes for the next couple of years.

"Of course you do. We'll talk about it later. But don't mention this to anyone else, Rupert won't want the firm to be the source of any gossip."

The afternoon proceeded as if nothing unusual had happened. Stella fetched bowls of salad and warm, sliced ciabatta. Wine flowed, as well as elderflower pressé for those who were driving. As the sun dropped in the sky, Hollie, Stella, and Rupert found themselves on a swing seat, out of earshot from everyone else.

Rupert asked when the firm had last met with the Comtesse. Stella mentioned Hollie's interview and the ongoing surveillance of Jonas. He nodded slowly. You could almost see him thinking, or it was a ploy to convince those around him that he was in control. He spoke suddenly, standing up as he did so.

"We need to reconvene tomorrow, ten o'clock, both of you please in the conference room."

Hollie wasn't sure what there was to discuss, but at least she was expected to be at the office so presumed she still had a job. Quite what that would now entail was unclear. Jeremy was still fussing over the barbecue with Oliver as they both surveyed the display of charcoaled food. She heard Rupert asking cheerfully as he approached them.

"How are those sausages doing? Any of them ready to be interred in a bun yet?"

CHAPTER 7

Oliver had left for work on Monday morning whilst Hollie was still in the shower. The hot water relaxed her shoulders while she kept repeating, 'you can do this', until she almost believed she might be capable of carrying off her new role. Clothes still littered the bedroom, over the bed, on hangers, draped on a chair. Oliver had been no help at all in selecting her first day outfit.

"Just wear whatever you would if it was a parents' night at school."

His advice was no help at all. She never knew what to wear on those occasions either. But the present problem was even worse. She had no frame of reference, unless everyone dressed like Stella, in which case she was doomed. Her gumshoes would be totally inappropriate in an office setting, and they would draw far too much attention. At the other end of the scale, she had no chance of competing with Stella's easy elegance and glamour.

Growling at her own prevarication, Hollie grabbed a two-piece outfit she had last worn to Oliver's aunt's funeral. Slate grey slacks, tailored jacket, and a scalloped neck, cream blouse. She put on one flat shoe and one with a low heel. Too secretarial on one foot, too accounts department on the other. Hollie screamed and clenched her teeth. The flats were comfortable, and as she couldn't compete with Stella's height, an extra inch and a half of heel was inconsequential.

Her hair was rarely a problem nowadays; she kept it fairly short and relatively manageable. In her teens, she had tried growing it out, processing the waves out of it, and even lightening it. She had used so many products that at times her mother had complained their bathroom smelled like a chemical laboratory. Her hair was her main inheritance from her father, if you discounted brown eyes and a full mouth, neither of which bore any resemblance to her mother.

If her co-workers took one look and labelled her as a radical feminist, there was nothing she could do about it. They would just have to get to know her and adjust their opinions – or not.

Almost as an afterthought, when they had been about to leave the barbecue, Stella had handed her a lanyard with a laminated ID card attached and a key fob for the office car park.

"This will get you into our carpark and into the lift," she said. "Third floor, ten o'clock, or a bit earlier to give me a chance to introduce you to everyone."

Hollie hung the lanyard round her neck. Looking at the ID card more closely, she realised Stella had used a picture of her from a shared weekend in Cornwall a couple of years ago. She checked herself in the mirror, looked at her watch, wondered what 'a bit earlier' meant. Should that be half an hour or more like fifteen minutes.

She closed her eyes, counted to ten, turned and bumped into the bed, cursing both the bed and her own stupidity. Now her shin hurt, which at least took her mind off the challenge ahead for a few brief seconds.

The barrier swung up at the entrance to the car park when she pressed her key fob against a shiny black panel. Driving forward slowly, she saw that some of the parking spaces had names. She noticed Stella's name and then her own on the space next to it. The job became real at that point; this was so different to working in a school. There it had always been a lottery as to how close you could get to the entrance on a rainy day. Here, she was part of the establishment and hadn't even set foot in the building yet.

Hollie checked her makeup in the rear-view mirror, ruffled her hair with both hands, making no difference to the random curls. She delved into her bag for a brush and tugged her always-ready-to-create-mischief hair into a semblance of order. She made a mental note to get it cut again, as soon as possible, and threw the brush onto the back seat of her car – it was of little help.

There was no receptionist at the desk on the ground floor. Hollie punched the 'up' button for the lift and waited. The walls in the lift were mirrored. She checked her reflection and would have happily changed almost everything about her appearance, from height to shoe choice.

When she pressed the third-floor button, the doors closed, and the lift started with a jerk. Hollie's stomach did a somersault, only settling when the doors pinged open again. She knew she would be scrutinised by everyone she met.

A young woman was standing with her back to the wall, immediately opposite the lift. She smiled as soon as Hollie appeared from behind the doors.

"You must be Hollie. Hi, I'm Sharon. Stella told me to take you straight to Meeting Room One. Would you like a coffee, tea?"

"No thank you. I'm fine."

The surprise of being greeted so quickly prompted her to refuse. A coffee would have been welcome, her nerves needed caffeine to settle them. Sharon showed her into an elegant room, panelled in pale wood. In the centre was a large round table with eight chairs equally spaced around it. There was a screen at the far end of the room, a floral arrangement on a side table and, at each place setting, a notepad and glass. A large pitcher of iced water stood in the centre of the table.

Left alone, Sharon had remained outside when she closed the boardroom doors, Hollie chose a chair two places away from the one in front of the screen. There was no indication there was a head chair which she would naturally have avoided. She put her bag on the seat, turned, and looked out the window. Surrounded by railings was a private, leafy square, directly opposite the main entrance. She turned quickly when she heard the door open again. It was Stella.

"Hi, sweetie. Has Sharon sorted you out with coffee yet?"

"I don't think I should have one right now. I'm so nervous I'm not sure I could swallow anything."

"Don't be so silly. Everyone here is a pussycat, apart from me, of course."

"What am I doing here? I'm not an investigator, I've got no experience of this, especially now someone's been murdered."

"Stop worrying, you'll be fine. Rupert will be along any minute. He'll explain everything."

When Rupert entered the room, he barely acknowledged Stella or Hollie, just dropped a slim folder on the table, poured himself a glass of water and drank half of it before he spoke.

"We have a complication."

Hollie followed Stella's lead, sitting at the table almost opposite Rupert. He looked at them both in turn.

"Not unexpectedly, Jonas Moon was taken to the police station last night in connection with the murder of the Comtesse du Colbert."

He took a short pause before continuing.

"A duty solicitor was appointed who has since contacted us and Jonas has asked us to represent him. Hopefully, he will be released without charge. He is, at this moment, only helping the police with their enquiries, but we don't know whether that situation will remain the same."

Hollie was about to ask how they thought she might help, but was not sure it was the right time to pose such a question. Stella put a hand on her arm, maybe sensing her temptation to interrupt. Hollie poured herself a glass of water. Her hand shook and a few drops spilt onto the polished tabletop. She pulled a tissue from her bag to mop them up. Stella spoke once she had put the tissue away

"As we represent the Colby Group, and Jonas Moon will inherit the Comtesse's estate. He will therefore become the main shareholder, so we are, I presume, obliged to represent him?"

"Precisely Stella," Rupert nodded. "And as such our contract would include covering any legal requirements, including defence in criminal matters."

Hollie was confused as she thought they were working for the Comtesse.

"But don't you, I mean we, represent the Comtesse."

"Sadly, she is no longer a client. Our contract was not with her personally. In the case of her murder, the Crown will represent her. Our responsibility is vested in the Colby Group and therefore Jonas Moon. He is, or will be, in due process, the majority shareholder."

Rupert said that he would like to have Hollie on his team as she was probably more familiar with the Comtesse than he was. He made the point that she was the last person in the firm to have met with her. He asked whether anything the Comtesse had said might be relevant to the present situation.

"He may have a second phone," Hollie said, glancing at Stella to make sure she wasn't speaking out of line. "Jonas, I mean. The Comtesse had a message from a number she didn't recognise. But she suspected it might have been from her husband."

"What did the message say?"

Hollie kicked herself for not having written down the precise wording. Any experienced investigator would have made a note of it.

"It suggested their marriage was not real, and it referred to the Comtesse as the Condom Queen."

"And do you have a note of the number it came from?"

Hollie scrambled for her own phone, buried in her bag, and opened her notes app. She turned it to face Rupert who made no attempt to read it or take the phone from her. In fact, he leaned away from her and spoke quietly and carefully.

"The police will no doubt want to interview you at some time. Whilst we cannot conceal evidence, we do not necessarily have to present everything to them gift wrapped. I presume you are familiar with the term plausible deniability?"

Hollie nodded, sliding her phone back over the table and slipping it into her bag. She realised that Rupert Patterson did not want any details which did not support Jonas's defence.

"Good," Rupert said. "Now, even if we had the means to trace that number and determine the sender's identity, it would not be legally permitted, prudent or proper to do so. I suggest you discretely mislay that piece of information – for the time being."

Hollie nodded again, her ability to speak appeared to have deserted her. She almost wished she was back to complaining about lesson planning for the next academic year. It may have been tedious but there was much less subterfuge involved.

"So, we are now representing Jonas?" She wanted to double check her understanding of their position.

Rupert nodded once, checked his watch, grimaced, picked up the folder in front of him and said he was sorry to rush, but he had another meeting. Before either of them could say anything else, he had taken two silent steps on the thick pile carpet and had his fingers wrapped around the door handle.

He turned back to Stella and Hollie before he opened the door.

"That telephone number, before you accidentally mislay it, would you let Stella have it. I believe she has access to some resourceful people – about whom I would prefer not to know."

He paused again, half-way out the door.

"Oh, Hollie, I forgot to say, welcome to Patterson Wilkins. I'm sure we'll be seeing a lot of each other over the next few months. I only wish it was a less dramatic start for you."

The ability of Rupert and Stella to switch allegiance so fluently was difficult for Hollie to grasp. Stella explained again that the firm is employed by the Colby Group, not the individual. Jonas would now be the majority shareholder as the Comtesse had no children. Stella paused for a moment.

"Now I think about it, she does have a half-brother. He might be tempted to contest her will, but I doubt he could successfully argue for more than the minority shareholding he is due to inherit. I'm reasonably confident he'll have no legitimate grounds to contest it."

Stella paused, frowned, and made a quick phone call.

"Tony, hi. Can you put an original copy of the Comtesse du Colbert's will on my desk, please... Yes, the paper copy... Thanks Tony."

She drummed her fingers on the table, was about to say something, checked herself, and turned to Hollie.

"There is an outside possibility that Benedict Colby could have a claim. I advised Juliette not to mention him in her will. The fact that he is listed in the beneficiaries gives him a possible opening."

Hollie knew nothing about wills. "On what grounds could he make an objection?"

"Undue influence from Jonas, or a previous commitment that isn't honoured in the current will. There are often loopholes in the law, how else would we make a living from it? But I am reasonably sure we didn't leave any grounds for a challenge in this instance."

Hollie's brain was imitating a washing machine, lots of swishing and no discernible items in view. Stella seemed to have forgotten about Jonas being arrested and had moved on to who benefitted from the death of the Comtesse. But, of course, that was exactly what she should also be working on.

"They had only been married for, what, ten or eleven months? Could that be relevant?"

Stella patted her on the arm while Hollie counted out the months on her fingers.

"Of course, I knew we needed you on board. The court might

be willing to hear any challenge as the marriage was less than a year old. And if Jonas is found guilty the whole landscape changes. We must be cautious."

Stella stood up.

"I think you have your first task. And I will have to double check that will."

"You want me to look into the half-brother?"

Stella told her that Juliette and her brother were not the best of friends, according to the Comtesse, but she did not know much about their past.

"It wouldn't hurt to know a little more about his current situation, relationships and his precise location – especially on the day in question."

"So, you want me to follow up on that?"

"We should have his address on record somewhere. Social media will probably give you a starting point, but I think it's time those pink gumshoes of yours got a bit of wear and tear on their soles."

Hollie let her shoulders drop and her body relax, but her mouth was dry, and her tongue felt like leather. She reached for the glass and took another sip of water.

"So, I still have a job?"

"Of course. Your presence and skills are even more important than before."

"And we are assuming that Jonas is innocent?"

"Until proven guilty. Now, where is that telephone number, before you lose it?"

CHAPTER 8

Sharon was waiting outside the room when they both emerged. Stella said she would leave Hollie in her capable hands and check in with her later. In a stage whisper, she said it was Sharon who was the true fount of all knowledge in the firm.

"Anything you need to know, I mean absolutely anything, just ask the redoubtable Sharon."

Sharon giggled, and her cheeks turned slightly pinker than they already were. Stella winked at Hollie as she left them alone.

Hollie wasn't sure if the wink implied something special. She felt herself beginning to blush too, on behalf of Sharon. Stella had been romantically involved with many different partners before she settled down with Jeremy, not all had been men. Hollie wondered if she had witnessed some sort of playful exchange between Stella and Sharon, something a little more than friendship. If so, surely it would be out of place in a work setting; there were boundaries these days. Hollie shook her head to clear it of any such errant impressions; she must have misinterpreted the situation.

"Are you okay?" Sharon asked. "Rupert, Mr Patterson, said I should show you to your new office. And is it okay to call you Hollie? I should have checked."

"It's fine," Hollie replied. "I got the impression that everyone here is on first name terms."

"Well, most of us are, but Mr Wilkins is a little more old-fashioned. And if there are clients around, they prefer that I refer to everyone more formally.

"That sounds complicated for you."

"It's fine, I'm used to it. Now, let's get you settled in."

Sharon led the way down a flight of stairs to an open plan area, then along a short corridor to a small office that had Hollie's name on the door. A single window took up almost the whole of one wall of her room. Sharon explained that the Firm occupied all four floors of the building. The ground floor housed the main reception and small meeting rooms, a kitchen, and other facilities, the first floor was admin, the second floor for services and the top floor was partners offices and the main meeting rooms. Hollie already felt lost.

"I'm on the ground floor, of course – just in case you need me for anything. But I'll get you set up here before I go back to reception."

Sharon was wearing a headset, positioned over one ear. Hollie had been wondering why she was had it. Sharon must have seen her looking and explained that it was a Bluetooth device linked to reception so she would know if anyone arrived.

"Now, the first time you log into your computer you will have to set a password. And you'll find that some of the server areas are locked, for confidentiality reasons."

She went on to explain that if Hollie needed access to any of them, she should check with Stella.

"Your work mobile will connect to your computer so that all calls go through the firm's secure system. Oh, and IT services are in the main office. You just passed him, he's called Taylor, he's lovely, if you can understand what he's talking about. He loses me in seconds. Switch it off, switch it on again is about my tech limit."

Sharon went on to explain about the coffee and tea facilities, the pass security system, which café most of them frequented for lunch, where the nearest sandwich bar was and what Mr Wilkins looked like, so that she'd recognise him.

"You'd expect him to be in a suit, like the rest of them, but he looks more like someone from a period drama, all tweedy and brogues. He's a darling if you stay on the right side of him. Never mention vegetarians. You're not one, are you? Not that there's anything wrong with them, of course."

Sharon hardly ever took a breath, and by the time Hollie was alone in her office, she needed a strong coffee and a few minutes to recover from the onslaught of information.

The view from the window was over a park. She could see the end of a lake where joggers were making steady progress across a dam. A woman, about her own age, was sitting under a tree, reading a book. Hollie wondered if she had made the right choice. She could be sitting, reading a book, instead of being trapped on the second floor of an expensively furnished, but ultimately soulless building.

She stared at the computer and entered a password, twice; the same one she had used since college. The screen opened, and Hollie clicked on a search engine icon.

Thirty minutes later, she had established that there was no relevant Benedict Colby on any of the regular social media sites, and she wondered if he used an alias. She had used her childhood pet's name, combined with a random number ever since she had graduated and started teaching. It was something she had been advised to do to avoid being stalked or pestered by pupils.

Hollie typed his name in again, this time enclosing it within quotation marks. She even tried different search engines. Eventually she found one article about an art student called Benedict Colby, but it was seven years out of date. She sighed, leaned back in her chair and spoke to herself out loud.

"I'm useless at this. Stella was wrong about me."

There was a knock on her already half-open door. It was Sharon again.

"I was just wondering if you wanted a sandwich or something. We usually have a delivery just before lunch and I could add something for you."

Sharon slid a printed-out menu onto her desk.

"How's it going? I mean I know you've only been here a couple of hours, but I just wondered... you know... how you were settling in, if there was anything you needed?"

Hollie breathed out and decided to unburden her fears onto Sharon.

"I think I'm going to be useless at this to be honest. I've been trying to track down a name since you left me here, and I'm getting nowhere."

Sharon asked what the name was, and when Hollie told her, she broke into a smile.

"I know a Benedict Colby. He's one of the teachers at my little brother's school. I don't suppose it's him you're looking for, is it?"

Hollie wanted to hug Sharon but held back in case the gesture was misinterpreted, and it would have been awkward to do from where she was sitting. But she wasn't sure what to do with this snippet of information. It might be a different Benedict Colby.

"How old is he?"

"Fourteen."

"Sorry, no, not your brother. I meant the teacher."

"Oh. I've no idea. I've never met him."

Sharon shared what information she had, which wasn't very much other than identifying the school and her brother's opinion that Benedict Colby was 'rad'. Hollie knew the school by reputation, and she thought Peter, from her old school, might even knew a couple of the teachers there. There had been a joint project between the two schools, and he had been involved, although she couldn't recall any of the details.

"You are a genius, Sharon. Thank you."

"Did you want any lunch?"

"No, I'm okay. I think I'll try that café you mentioned.

After a visit to the café, as much for a change of scenery as anything to eat, Hollie opened the St Edmund's College website. Without a staff login, there was no mention of the elusive Benedict Colby. Her own school had tightened its data security, even in the last few years, so she was not surprised to find yet another dead end.

It wasn't until later that afternoon, and a lot more fruitless searching on the internet, that Stella made an appearance. She had a brown manilla envelope with her, which landed on Hollie's desk with a gentle swoosh and slid across the polished surface towards her.

"I hope you've eaten, and that you're not feeling squeamish?"

"Why?"

Stella raised her eyebrows and Hollie opened the flap of the envelope. A few colour photographs slid out, along with a single page of notes, written in capital letters. The pictures looked like they had been copied, but the graphic nature of them was not diminished. They were crime scene photographs of the Comtesse's murder.

"Where did you get these?"

"I have an inside source. Best not to ask too many questions, it's a informal arrangement."

Fortunately, Hollie wasn't squeamish, or her bacon and avocado sandwich may have made a reappearance. There was nothing glamorous about the pictures. They recorded the murder scene in every detail, some of which Hollie thought she might never forget.

The handwritten sheet of paper confirmed that Jonas Moon's fingerprints had been identified on the shoes. It also noted that rigor mortis indicated a time of death within a four-hour window, placing the event between 6am and 10am on Sunday morning. The cleaner had not been in that room until she discovered the body. She had entered by the back door and assumed the Comtesse was busy in her study.

"Four hours?" Hollie said quietly, more to herself than to Stella. "That seems quite vague."

"Don't believe what you see on television. They may settle on a more precise time after the post-mortem is completed."

"What about Jonas? I presume he would have been in the house at that time?"

"Unfortunately, he doesn't have an alibi that will stand up in court. He claims to have been walking in Mulberry Park, reading through lines of a script. That's the park you can see from your window."

Stella was sat in the spare chair, opposite Hollie. She glanced round the room as if unfamiliar with it.

"Have you had any luck locating the brother, Benedict Colby?"

Hollie explained that luck, and Sharon, had played a major part in her search, but she still had to confirm that the one she had found was indeed the one they were looking for.

"How many can there be? It's not that common a name."

They both thought that it probably was the right one, and Hollie promised she would try to get a bit more information from a mutual acquaintance. She asked Stella what they needed to know about him?"

Stella said it was a matter of getting a sense of who he was, what he might want, if he was capable of premeditated murder, was he happily married, anything that could help with the bigger picture. She confessed that he had not made much of an impression on her, during the few occasions they had met, but those meetings were only to countersign some legal documents, so she hadn't taken much notice of him.

"Assuming that Jonas is innocent, which we must take as our default position, there would have to be another person out there who is guilty."

"To be honest, with that message he sent the Comtesse, and his fingerprints on the shoe, he does seem the most likely suspect."

Stella agreed that was heart of the problem. The inspector in charge of the case had a reputation of being at bit 'old school'. He was the type who wouldn't look too far if he had a suitable culprit in front of him, especially if he had some scraps of evidence to back it up.

"Fingerprints are hardly a scrap of evidence. Jonas may actually have done it."

"He claims he didn't, and I am inclined to believe him. I've met Jonas on a number of occasions. And, unless he is a very good actor," Stella put a hand up to prevent Hollie from pointing out the obvious, "he simply doesn't seem the type to me."

Stella described Jonas as quite gentle, more interested in acting than money. He had made no objection to any of the clauses they had written into the prenup, and he had signed it without even wanting an independent lawyer to read it first.

"We had to encourage him to get representation. I think he was genuinely in love with Juliette. I simply can't see him murdering her."

"So, why was he cheating on her? Could it be a crime of passion."

"We don't know that he was. Juliette was not the most trusting of souls. She could be suspicious over the toss of a coin. She would probably demand to inspect the piece before the event, just in case it had two heads, or two tails."

They both relapsed into silence for a while. Stella stood up and wandered around Hollie's office, inspecting the bookcase and a reproduction of a film poster on the wall. She stopped at the window, staring out at the park, and made a small 'hmm' sound, as though she had spotted something of interest or had a bright idea. Hollie got up to stand beside her, following her gaze. There were different joggers lapping the lake, the woman with the book had gone, but she had been replaced by a group of teenagers, the term over, enjoying their six weeks of freedom, something she could have been doing herself.

"You have a more pleasant view than I do from my office," Stella said.

"I presume the police have not found the phone yet? The one

that sent that message."

"No, not that we've heard. I believe they've searched Jonas's car and the house. But if it's ever switched on again, they'll find it. They have the number."

Hollie said she would make some phone calls that evening and try to find out a little more about Benedict Colby, assuming the one she had found was the right one.

"How long do we have, before Jonas is charged, and the case goes to court?"

"Well, depending on the evidence and the Crown Prosecution Service, he may or may not be charged. From what we know so far, the evidence does appear to be somewhat damming. As far as a trial goes, if he is charged, that could be months away, even a year."

Hollie nodded, trying to take it all in. Watching crime dramas on television was one thing, being in the middle of one was quite different. She wasn't even sure how she could help and whether she would be trying to set a guilty man free.

"There is one thing to bear in mind," Stella said, a serious tone in her voice. "If Jonas is innocent, the longer the police focus on him, the more likely it is the true killer will get away. Evidence will go cold or might disappear completely. And by the time DI Gilroy gets around to discovering anything, it might be too late."

Hollie was aware of more pressure in one morning as an investigator, than she usually experienced in a year as a teacher. Stress was an everyday occurrence in school, but lives were rarely at risk when analysing works of literature, marking essays, or controlling unruly children.

"I like your office," Stella said. "When you're not here, I might use it as a bolt-hole – assuming you have no objections?"

Hollie said that would be no problem, and asked about office hours and what she should do about signing in and out.

"Oh, for heaven's sake Hollie, we don't run the firm like that. It's not a factory. Your office is here when you need it.

Providing we can get hold of you, you can work from home, from a café, roam the streets, hide in dark doorways. Just ensure you're contactable and try to ferret out any information we need when we need it. In fact, it's already four o'clock, quite enough work for your first day, and you've got phone calls to make. So, go and commune with that lovely husband of yours and give him a kiss from me."

Hollie wanted to ask about her and Sharon but decided that was best left to another time.

CHAPTER 9

Hollie was home long before Oliver returned from work. She made herself a mug of peppermint tea and retreated to the garden to enjoy the late afternoon sun. Armed with her phone, and a newly purchased moleskin notebook, she made herself comfy in Oliver's director's chair. Hollie had also purchased a disposable fountain pen. She thought it might give her the kind of cachet that Oliver commanded, but without the risk of leakage.

Determined that she wouldn't repeat the error of not taking notes again, Hollie had purchased the small black notebook because it looked both professional and apt for an investigator. Safely stowed in an integral pocket on the inside back cover was her new company credit card. She rang Peter, willing him to answer, remembering that he had been involved in some joint art and science project last year which involved Benedict Colby's school. She hoped he might be able to confirm she had the correct Benedict and give her some clues as to his nature.

"Hey Peter. I want to pick your brains, but it must remain just between the two of us. Can you live with that?"

"Gosh, clandestine stuff already. So much more exciting than decorating the bathroom. Let me put my brush down and then ask away."

When she explained the dead end her search had hit, Peter wasn't surprised.

"How many teachers can you name who would expose themselves online, on social media? Oh dear," he added quickly, "don't answer that. The music teacher who comes to my mind in that context was, thankfully, an exception."

Hollie remembered the fallout following a scandal involving a teacher at another school. She shuddered at the recollected details.

"At least he's locked up now."

"So, what do you need to know about this mystery teacher of yours? And, more interestingly, why do you need to know?"

Hollie impressed on Peter she was only after general background information, nothing scandalous or private. You've heard about the murder of Juliette du Colbert I suppose? Well, Benedict Colby is her half-brother. And I just want to find out what he's like, does he have a partner, what does he do outside of teaching, that sort of stuff.

"Ben? Well, I already knew that he was the Condom Queen's brother, everyone does, but he's also a fitness freak, a committed runner in fact. He tried to sign up Marcus and myself to Parkrun last year. Is he a suspect in the murder?"

"No, no way. Tell me, do you know where that run thing takes place?"

"Mulberry Park, every Saturday morning, I think. All the details will be online."

Hollie asked whether Marcus had been tempted to take up the offer of running with Benedict. She was thinking that she could use the two of them as some sort of smoke screen if she wanted to get close to him.

"Marcus liked the idea of buying a new set of kit, but he claimed that running was only for people who were late for something. So, I took that as a no. But you can count me in if you're joining. I already miss your company."

Hollie thanked him, told him he was sweet, but liked the idea of both of them being with her, the larger her group, the less she would be noticed.

"What's the chance you could change Marcus's mind and the three of us give it a go?"

Peter said he would ask, but she shouldn't hold her breath.

They chatted about school for a few minutes, but Peter said Marcus had supper simmering on the stove, so he had to go, or face the consequences.

"Okay. Give me a ring when you've spoken to him. Tell him he can be my sidekick."

"Is there anything else I can do? Your life already sounds so much more exciting than mine, and I have a whole summer of decorating ahead of me."

She said that the job she had been hired to do had changed more than just a little. When she explained all the circumstances, Peter said he knew who Benedict's sister was, but he hadn't made the connection when he heard about the murder.

"I expect it will be all over tonight's news. Please don't mention that I have anything to do with it. I think it would be best if I kept a low profile."

"You sound more like a secret agent with every word you say. Marcus is going to be so excited about this when I tell him. He may even be persuaded to take up running."

"If you feel you must tell him all the details, please emphasise that this is all highly confidential. I only want to find out a bit more about Benedict Colby because he's the Comtesse's half-brother. It's nothing more than a background check."

Peter agreed to keep it hush-hush. He also thought he might be able to locate a picture of Benedict from the inter-school project. He promised to email it to her.

"By the way, he usually goes by the name of Ben, not Benedict. Not sure if that's helpful."

After she had hung up, Hollie texted Stella to tell her that she may have found a way of getting close to Benedict Colby without raising his suspicions. She thought about it for a moment and sent another text. She asked Stella if she could put some running clothes and shoes on her account, explaining that she might have to go under-cover as a jogger. Stella's reply was several different laughing emojis followed by a thumb's up.

Hollie sipped her tea, which was already cool, closed her eyes and tipped her head back towards the sun. Being a private investigator was more fun than teaching, even though, in this instance, it had involved someone dying in a grizzly manner.

Oliver returned home from work an hour later to find Hollie dressed in a bikini and dozing on a sun bed in the back garden. An empty wine glass lay on its side on the grass, a paperback book beside it, splayed open with the pages face down. She didn't hear him approach and was startled when he spoke from very close to her ear.

"Tough first day, was it?" he asked.

Hollie cursed and hit him on the shoulder.

"You scared the life out of me."

Although the sun had lost some of its power, her shoulders were stinging and pink, even viewed through her sunglasses. She scrambled for a blouse and wrapped it round her.

"Anyway, I haven't been home that long."

"So, what was it like, your first day as a gumshoe?"

"All a bit serious, to be honest, and a bit complicated. I never expected the job to involve a murder investigation."

She explained what had happened. Even that a half-brother was mentioned in the Comtesse's will, and she had to track him down.

"I'm going to have a snoop around to see what he's like. Oh, yes, and I'm joining Parkrun next Saturday."

Oliver had brought a glass of wine out into the garden with him, but he hadn't taken a sip at the point Hollie mentioned running. If he had, he might have choked.

"You've never jogged in your life. What on earth has brought this on?"

"Well, I suppose there's a time for everything. And it wouldn't hurt if I lost a pound or two in the process and got a bit fitter."

"But you have a perfect body. I like cuddly."

She told him that the word 'cuddly' was not exactly a compliment, but that the real purpose of the exercise was to stalk the Comtesse's half-brother. I just need to jog the same route as he does and try to get a casual introduction.

"He's not a potential murderer, is he?"

"No. No way." Hollie hesitated for a moment. "Well, I don't think so. Anyway, he's not a serial killer."

"Even serial killers have to start somewhere."

"Shut up. You're not being helpful."

He wasn't being helpful, but he was being sensible. Benedict Colby might well be dangerous if he was his half-sister's killer, especially if he thought someone was on to him. She knew she had to be cautious. Oliver went back indoors, but reappeared a few minutes later in shorts and carrying a bottle of wine.

"You might be right, Oliver. I'll be careful. Hopefully, I'll have Marcus and Peter with me."

"Marcus? I mean, Marcus, running? Are there going to be paramedics on stand-by."

"Don't be cruel. And I thought you liked cuddly."

"I'm not being cruel. I'm showing concern, and Marcus is way beyond cuddly. I've always thought he's punching way above his weight with Peter." Oliver made a small guttural moan. "Oh, bloody hell. Now I've got an image of Marcus in my head, in skin-tight running gear."

Oliver pulled an exaggerated grimace. Hollie punched him on the arm again and he winced, pretending to be hurt. Her phone rang with an excerpt of 'School's out for Summer.' It was Peter. He had already contacted Ben, who had said he would be at Parkrun on Saturday, and he confirmed with Hollie that he and Marcus would both be joining her.

"That was quick work."

"Also," Peter added, "there's a group of teachers who have decided to get fit during the summer instead of sitting in the garden drinking wine. They're meeting on Wednesday mornings, the same park, if you want to have a bit of a practice. Ben should be there, with his partner, Kendra. And there'll be fewer distractions if you want to get to meet him."

"I can't imagine who would want to spend their summer holidays doing that."

"To which option are you referring, the running or the wine drinking?"

"Guess."

"Cheers."

She heard the clink of a glass and Marcus's voice in the background, joining in.

Peter had thought it unlikely he could encourage Marcus to join anything that involved organised physical exercise. But told her Marcus had shown surprising enthusiasm when he realised it was an opportunity to buy a whole new outfit and become part of Hollie's 'crew'.

"I don't have a crew."

"Well, you do now apparently."

Hollie left for work at around the same time as Oliver the next morning. But she had already messaged Stella to say she would be in a little late as she was going to get kitted out with an appropriate jogging ensemble.

Oliver had asked what was wrong with the gumshoes he had bought her. Hollie explained they might be a bit too distinctive when she wanted to blend in with the crowd and not be noticed. She wasn't even sure they would stand up to jogging, and being made from recycled chewing gum, they might decide to bond with the tarmac path again.

It was almost noon when Hollie finally arrived at the office. Sharon told her that Stella was tied up with a client all day. Hollie resisted a risqué reply to the double entendre.

"I'm sorry, but you've missed the deadline for a lunch order too," Sharon said.

"No problem. I think I need to cut out some of the carbs anyway."

In the lift, she thought Sharon might have been a bit more supportive, said something about her not needing to lose any weight. The mirrors on three walls of the lift created a strange illusion. At the right angle, she could see an infinite number of reflections of herself disappearing into the distance. None of them quite the shape she would like to be.

Signing up for Parkrun was simple enough. Hollie decided to use her personal email address as she thought she might continue with it if she enjoyed the experience. With nothing else to do, she took the folder of crime scene photos from her locked desk drawer and spread them out in front of her. Worried that someone might come in who should not see them, she got up and closed her office door.

Hollie could feel her face tighten into a grimace as she once again studied the close-up photos of the crime scene. It was difficult to believe the victim was a woman with whom she had only recently drunk tea. And difficult also to see past the horrific details of her demise.

Hollie began to wonder why the murderer had chosen such a strange weapon. They would have had to wrestle the shoe from the Comtesse before employing it. If the murder been premeditated, they would surely have chosen something more appropriate, something that would have done the job more efficiently, like a kitchen knife.

A knock on the door interrupted Hollie's thoughts. She pushed the photos and note back in her drawer, then dithered over saying 'come in', or getting up to open the door. She chose the latter. It was Sharon.

"Sorry, I hope I'm not disturbing you?"

Hollie asked her in, leaving the door open.

"You have such a nice view," Sharon said, standing in front of the window.

"Is there something specific you wanted?"

"Oh, sorry, yes, almost forgot. Stella rang in to say she wouldn't be back this afternoon, and her phone would be off most of the day, but she would give you a ring this evening."

Sharon nodded as she spoke, a bit like one of those toy

animals you once saw in the rear windows of cars. She wondered what had become of them. Had their owners all died, or simply got too old to drive?

"Did you find Benedict Colby?" Sharon asked, breaking Hollie's daydream. "I spoke to my brother about him, but all he said was that he was cool, not like most of the teachers. He has him for art, I think. My brother likes art, he's quite good at it."

"Yes, I did find him, thank you. It turns out we have a mutual friend. But your information was really helpful, I wouldn't have known where to look otherwise."

Sharon giggled and blushed. Hollie wondered why she had trekked up from reception.

"Why didn't you just ring me? I assume my phone and computer system are all linked up now?"

"Ah, yes, sort of, but the internal system won't update until tonight. It had a little wrinkle in it according to Taylor. That's why I couldn't put Stella through to you. So, I came up personally."

"Does that mean reception is unattended right now? You don't have your headset on."

Sharon put a hand to her head, and gasped, as though she hadn't realised until Hollie mentioned it.

"Oops, I'd better get back down there."

She edged out the door as though retreating from royalty, giggled, gave a little wave, and disappeared. Hollie wondered what on earth was going on in her head. Sharon could veer from efficient to dizzy in a matter of moments.

Hollie walked over to her window, having been reminded of the view by Sharon. There were still one or two people jogging round the lake; tomorrow she would be doing that too. There was another problem though. When and where was she going to change into her jogging kit.

CHAPTER 10

Before she left work on Tuesday, Hollie had asked Sharon whether there was anywhere she might be able to change. To her surprise, on the ground floor there were not only changing rooms, but showers and lockers too.

"There are several people who cycle to work," she said. "So, the firm put them in a couple of years ago, before my time. I get the bus, but I have used them occasionally if I'm going somewhere straight from work."

She had given Hollie a locker key, from a small box kept behind reception, and entered her name and number on the computer records.

The changing rooms had no windows, but a ventilation fan maintained a steady drone and kept the air fresh. Hollie changed into her new jogging outfit. She had tried it on the previous evening and Oliver had remarked how sporty she looked. She felt far from sporty, more like when she had been required to turn out for hockey at school, out of place and uncomfortably 'on-show'. She didn't want anyone at work to see her like that, nothing about the outfit was flattering.

Thoughtfully, Sharon had also directed her to a second staircase, leading down to the car park. That way she didn't have to risk running into anyone by leaving through the main entrance. There was a keypad on the exterior door for which Sharon had also supplied the code.

"It changes on a frequent basis, for security of course, so best to check with me before you go out that way in case it's just been reset."

Hollie had stowed her work pass, notebook and a few odds and ends in a pocket in a small, lightweight, backpack also purchased at the sports shop which had fitted her out. She was acutely aware that everything she wore was brand new and that people would know she was a beginner.

She skulked along the side of the underground car park, cringing, and almost hiding, at the sound of every car. After jogging gingerly up the exit ramp to the side of the building and along a quiet side street, Hollie headed for a pedestrian gate which afforded entry to Mulberry Park. The lake was not far away. She had memorised a map of the park but was kicking herself for not having reconnoitred the location in person. It would have been easy to do so the day before.

There were a group of half a dozen runners near the dam end of the lake. As far as she could see, Benedict Colby did not appear to be amongst them.

Hollie had not given enough thought as to how she could infiltrate a group of teachers from a neighbouring school. She decided a straightforward approach was her best option.

"Hi," she said as she got close to them. "Are you the teachers from St Edmund's who have started a running group?"

She thought she had judged her approach incorrectly when an older man replied rather tersely.

"We are, but you're not a member of our staff, are you? Unless you're about to join us. I know there always seems to be a vacancy being filled somewhere nowadays."

"No, I'm at Pirton Lane." Not entirely a lie as she was technically still under contract. "It was just that I heard from Peter Evans you were starting this group, and hoped it was okay for me to join. Peter's an old friend of mine, he knows Benedict Colby, and mentioned you were meeting today – my friend that is, not Benedict."

"Okay, that's fine by me. The more the merrier I reckon. I'm John, History."

"Hollie, English. Nice to meet you."

"If you were hoping to meet Ben today, you're out of luck I'm afraid. He has something else on."

"No, not especially."

Hollie was introduced to everyone. The pressure of pretending to still be a teacher, a friend-of-a-friend of Benedict Colby, and a runner, meant she forgot nearly every name as soon as she heard the next one.

During some stretching exercises, before they set off, Hollie could feel the tightness in her calf and thigh muscles, muscles. They were unused to being tested so thoroughly, or so early in the morning, or at any time of the day. come to that.

One of the younger teachers took charge. Maybe in the absence of Benedict she was the most experienced. She said they were going to do four laps of the lake and, if anyone got tired, to drop down to a walking pace until they felt able to resume jogging.

"I'll stay with the back marker. And this isn't a race."

The group set off. Always, when someone emphasises it's not a race, there will be a couple of people who take the opportunity to demonstrate their fitness. On this occasion, two men were out of sight around a bend within the first half a minute. Trees soon obscured them from view. The remaining runners stayed in a straggly group.

The woman, who had taken charge, was running next to Hollie; they were doing little more than a gentle jog.

"I think we've met before?" she said.

Hollie glanced at her, and although there something familiar about her face, she couldn't place where or when that might have been.

"I think you got the first post I went for. We interviewed on the same day."

It came back to Hollie in a flash. It had been so many years ago. The slender, toned woman, jogging next to her, must be the formerly plump and nervous woman she had been up against for the job she had just resigned from. Now the positions felt like they were reversed, at least physically.

"I'm so sorry. I didn't recognise you," Hollie said.

"It's been a few years. And I'll take that as a compliment. You were my inspiration to start running and get fitter."

"I was?"

"I was so out of breath that day, totally in a flap, and you were all cool calm and collected."

From Hollie's recollection that was nowhere near an accurate description of her first job interview. Panicked and sweaty would have been closer to the truth, as she remembered it.

Her running companion's name was Kendra, and she was Benedict's partner. Hollie cursed that her research abilities had let her down again. She could easily have asked Peter for details like that and been better prepared.

They jogged the first lap-and-a-half of the lake. It wasn't quite as strenuous as Hollie had feared. One woman, Jean, if Hollie remembered correctly, slowed to a walk. Kendra dropped back beside her, but Hollie pressed on, jogging alone, enjoying the experience and gathering her thoughts. How much information could she get from Kendra. And where was Benedict? Just after the start of lap two, Kendra caught up with her.

"Jean has pulled out. She's had enough for her first day. How are you doing?"

Hollie was doing better than she expected. But it struck her that a short period at the back of the field would grant her Kendra's company a little longer.

"I think I could do with a breather."

They both slowed to a walk.

"You said you have a friend who knows Ben?"

"Yes, Peter Evans. He teaches at Pirton Lane, like me, did I mention that already? He's Science."

"Oh, yes, Peter, I think I might have met him. There was a crossover project last year. Were you involved in that?"

Hollie tried to steer the subject back to Benedict, and why he was not able to be there that day. Kendra volunteered that he was seeing a solicitor about the recent death of his half-sister.

"You've probably heard of her," Kendra added. "The Condom Queen, or Juliette du Colbert to her friends."

Hollie played ignorant, claiming she had heard of her but didn't really know why she was called that. Kendra said she knew – and launched into a detailed explanation.

"It's a bit cruel really, a nickname like that. Ben never uses it. And he hates me or anyone else referring to her as that."

"I suppose they got on well, Benedict and Juliette, being siblings? And it must be hard to lose your sister."

Kendra revealed they hardly saw each other. They hadn't grown up together because of the age gap, and he was a product of his father's short-lived second marriage. Juliette was their dad's favourite, that's what Ben says. But I don't think parents have favourites, do you?"

Hollie explained she wasn't a parent, and was an only child, so had no way to judge such things. Kendra said she had an older brother who was, without doubt, her parents' favourite.

"First born and all that. Difficult to get excited a second time round, I suppose. Not that it's ever worried me. It kept me under their radar as a teenager. I was a complete tearaway and could get away with murder."

Hollie wondered whether she meant that literally, and how far she could question Kendra before her suspicions were aroused. She seemed happy to talk about anything and everything, so Hollie pushed a little further.

"Does he stand to inherit millions? I mean, his sister must have been wealthy from the little I've read."

"Ben doesn't care about money. It can be quite frustrating sometimes. He has the materialistic bones of an amoeba. Anyway, his father left him enough that he doesn't need to care, doesn't really need to teach, but he still does."

"Sorry if it sounded like I was suggesting he was a gold digger or something."

"It's okay. It's a bit of a sore point with us. I was never that keen on the woman but didn't wish her dead. And I come from a family who counted every penny – it's a difficult habit to break."

Hollie added Kendra to her list of people who needed an alibi, and she wondered if the police would get to her at some time. There was no way she could ask her where she was between the hours of 6am and 10am on Sunday morning, not directly anyway.

"Do you run often?"

"Four or five times a week. We always do Parkrun on Saturdays. Why don't you join us?"

Hollie thanked her, and said she was seriously thinking about it and had already registered.

"Great, hopefully we'll meet again there. It's not supposed to be competitive, but everyone is trying to improve their times, so there's not so much chance to chat during the event."

They had just got back to the start point. Jean was sitting on a bench smoking a cigarette. An unusual sight nowadays and one that did not quite go with the ethos of getting fit.

"I think I might sit out the last lap," Hollie said, thinking that if she asked many more questions Kendra might become suspicious.

She sat next to Jean. Both watched as Kendra picked up the pace again and disappeared round the first bend of the path.

"Crazy fit, isn't she?" Jean said, taking a long draw on her cigarette. "You want one?"

She pushed an open packet of cigarettes along the bench in Hollie's direction. Hollie had never been much of a smoker, but was tempted to try one, just to calm her nerves. Detective work was not without stress.

"I don't," she said, summoning her resolve and wondering what Oliver would say if he smelled cigarette smoke on her. "But thank you."

"Very wise. I don't normally, but when we break up for the

summer I just want to smoke, drink, eat and have sex. Well, maybe not so much of the last one. I haven't got the energy for it nowadays."

Hollie knew what she meant about indulging in bad habits. That normal switching off process, sleep-ins, afternoon wine, lunches out, none of them were options this year. She wondered again whether she had made the right choice. Six weeks of doing practically nothing rather appealed at that moment.

"Do you know Kendra and Benedict very well?" Hollie asked.

"Bloody well hope so. I am their head teacher after all."

Hollie had heard of the legend of St Edmund's but had pictured someone taller, more stern, more authoritative, and probably a little more conservative. The image she had formed had not been someone dressed in an old track suit, slumped on a park bench, pulling on a cigarette, and coughing occasionally.

It was not often Hollie was completely lost for words, but stating the obvious was the only thing that came into her head.

"You're Jean Carpenter, head of St Edmund's?"

"The very one. Guilty as charged"

"I've heard about you, of course, but we've never met. It's nice to finally put a face to the name."

"Not quite the face you expected I suppose. I know I have a reputation, but I'm no Jean Brodie. Not as young as she was, not as slim, and not as well spoken. Part of that is why I'm here. Not to improve my elocution, no curing that now, but bloody hell, this jogging business is a killer."

Hollie sat quietly, slightly intimidated.

"You teach at Pirton Lane? English, I hear?"

"Yes."

Hollie wondered what was coming next. An invitation to collaborate between departments? Too late for that.

"I heard you resigned."

"Yes, sort of."

"Fancied a change, I suppose?"

"Something like that."

Jean fished in her pocket, pulled out a card and handed it to Hollie.

"I can usually find an opening for a good teacher. Give me a call if you change your mind about quitting. Any time will do."

Jean stubbed her cigarette out on the ground. Put the butt back in the packet, picked up her bag and stood up.

"Unlikely you'll see me here again but remember what I said. I meant it."

She walked away with a slight limp and a few strong and quite audible swear words between throaty bouts of coughing.

CHAPTER 11

Later, after she had taken a shower at work and was back at her desk, Hollie started scribbling a short list of names on the back of the receipt for her running shoes. It didn't feel right to commit her thoughts about potential suspects to a computer file which might be accessed by anybody in the firm.

Jonas was top of the list; his fingerprints on the murder weapon couldn't be ignored. Just beneath his name was Benedict Colby, then Kendra and, after her, a question mark. Hollie felt there was something or someone she was missing but couldn't put a name to that sensation. She leaned back in her chair and rattled the end of her pen between her teeth. The noise helped her concentrate.

A tentative rap of knuckles on her partly open door made Hollie jump. The chair tipped back beyond the point of stability, and she grabbed at the edge of her desk. The chair continued to topple, and Hollie was left in a sort of half crouching position, her pen gripped between her teeth, the desk gripped between her fingers.

"Oh, sorry, did I startle you?"

It was Sharon again. Hollie wondered if she looked for any excuse to escape the reception desk and the monotony which must accompany that role.

"It's okay," Hollie said, the pen slipping from her mouth and clattering onto the top of the desk. "No damage done."

"It just that Stella asked me to tell you that Mr Colby is coming in tomorrow morning, and she thought it might be helpful if you sat in on the interview."

Hollie asked if the internal system was updated and working. Sharon confirmed that it was.

"You're linked in now."

She hesitated in the doorway, examining one fingernail with intense care.

"I came up to see you because I wanted to ask you something. I never know what's being recorded through the telephones, probably everything, even though I can't imagine anyone would want to listen to me rambling away. Anyway, if it's okay, and because I know you and Stella are old friends," she hesitated, bit her lip, and glanced behind her, as though to check nobody was listening. "You are, aren't you, old friends I mean?"

Hollie had a horrible premonition that Sharon was going to ask her something very personal as she didn't want to risk it being on record. It sounded like it would be a question Hollie might not want to hear, never mind answer.

"It's just, I wondered." Sharon closed her eyes and dropped her head.

If there were many more hesitations Hollie decided she would scream. Sharon closed the door, it clicked into place, and she leaned back against it.

"Do you think she fancies me? Stella. Like as a girlfriend? I mean, I have a boyfriend, we're practically engaged, but he hasn't got around to buying me a ring yet. So, I'm not a lesbian, or bi or anything, not that there's anything wrong with being a lesbian. I don't want to offend her. And she's married. And, I mean, I like her." Sharon looked at Hollie, a pained and uncomfortable expression on her face. "But, you know, not in that way."

Sharon had turned a brighter pink than her nail varnish, which Hollie wouldn't have thought possible.

"Leave it with me. I'll talk to her when I get a chance. I'm sure it's simply a misunderstanding or crossed wires or something like that."

Hollie had no idea what she could say to Stella. It was

bordering on sexual harassment if Sharon was reading the situation correctly. Surely Stella would know better than to act in that way. A seed of doubt crept into Hollie's head. Stella had always been impetuous, unpredictable, and she often took risks. Coming from a privileged background meant she would often act as though she was above the rules everyone else had to follow. The more Hollie thought about it, the more she thought there was likely to be some foundation in Sharon's reading of the situation.

Sharon thanked her and made a hasty exit. The interruption had broken Hollie's train of thought. She picked up her chair and pushed it back into place. Leaning on the back of it, she stared at the pen on her desk. Navigating the stormy waters of murder was one thing, but this business with Sharon and Stella was a potential minefield. She walked over to the window, looked out at the park, and sighed. Suspects, motives, hidden agendas, social politics, unrequited love, none of it was that different to dealing with the hormonal tsunamis of teenagers at school. But, in this job, she couldn't give anyone a detention or confiscate their phone. And Stella was her employer now, not just a friend she could take to one side to broach a difficult conversation.

Hollie looked at the clock. It was only half past three. Stella had said that she could work from wherever she wanted, but if she left the office now, she knew she would only end up in the garden again, with a book and a glass of wine. She vowed not to have a drink before six in the evening, knowing that the promise was as likely to be kept as her New Year resolution to give up biscuits. She shook her head and tried to concentrate.

"Come on, Hollie, you're good at puzzles," she said out loud, trying to convince herself. "That was precisely why Stella offered you this job."

She decided that all she had to do was treat this like any other puzzle. She dug in her bag for her little black notebook and, on a blank page, wrote Juliette's full name and the date and approximate time of her murder. On the next page, she wrote SUSPECTS in capital letters. She paused and added a list of names, everyone she could think of, with possible motives next to them.

Jonas Moon - Money, affair, escape from marriage?
Jonas's lover - Jealousy, greed.
Ben Colby - Money, historic grudge, sibling rivalry?
Kendra - General dislike of Comtesse, history?
Jean Carpenter – Definitely tough enough, but why?
Cleaner - Envy. Was anything stolen? Abusive employer?
Neighbour - Some secret Juliette had discovered.
Jonas's agent – Publicity. Control. Envy.
Someone in the Colby Group – Who? Why?
Previous lover – Check if there was anyone prominent.

It was all very well writing a list, but there were no clues which narrowed down the suspects. She added on the next page:

To do list:
Jonas's phone - check with Stella.
Anything stolen – check with Maryam.
Alibis - for everyone.
The Comtesse's social history - from newspapers?

Hollie screwed up the receipt on which she had previously scribbled her list and looked around for a wastepaper basket. There wasn't one. She dropped the crumpled paper in her bag and made a mental note to check with Sharon if there was supposed to be a bin. She wondered whether this was the ultimate paperless office and didn't even need one. Maybe she should start collecting them as antique curiosities of the future.

On a fresh page, Hollie added a list of things she needed to check.

Details of the Comtesse's will - might be something.
The history of Jonas's career.
His personal earnings.
Past enemies in show business.
The Comtesse's enemies in business.
Exact wording of that phone message to Juliette.

The more Hollie thought about the crime scene, the more likely it seemed to have been a crime of passion. If it was, then Jonas would still have to remain on the top of the list. She could see why DI Gilroy wasn't looking further afield.

The clock on the computer had crept towards ten past four. If she popped down to see Sharon, it might be approaching five before an inevitably long explanation regarding wastepaper bins would draw to a natural conclusion.

Hollie looked at her list again. Not everyone involved with the Comtesse was on it. Even Stella's name could be added, but surely that would be stretching probability to its limits. Her pen hovered over the page for a few anxious seconds before she closed the cover. Stella's name was not added to her list – for the time being.

Sharon wasn't at her desk when Hollie got to reception, so she made her way down to the car park, still wondering whether she should have added the name of her old friend to her list of potential murderers.

On the drive home, she couldn't get it out of her head that the perfect way to cover a crime would be to employ an inept and inexperienced investigator who would be sure to miss vital clues and connections. Had Stella been involved with the Comtesse at some time and could that history be threatening her career in some way?

When Oliver got home that evening, Hollie was stretched out on the sofa, a cold flannel covering her eyes and forehead.

"A hangover?" were Oliver's first words on seeing her. "At this time of day?"

"Very funny. I have a migraine if you're really concerned."

Oliver sat on the edge of the sofa and asked, more sympathetically, if there was anything he could get her. He had never had a headache in his life, let alone a migraine, so he could sympathise but not empathise.

"Maybe a different job," she said quietly. "It is possible I shouldn't have jumped ship quite so eagerly. Teaching wasn't that bad."

"I thought you made a considered decision. And didn't Gordon say he'd take you back? Anyway, need I remind you that teaching was stressful. Remember that evening with the currant stuck to your face."

"I know." Hollie breathed out a long sigh. "Can I ask you something, and don't laugh, even if it sounds stupid?"

"When have I ever laughed at you – maybe don't answer that."

Hollie had lifted the edge of the flannel so that she could see Oliver's face, she now adjusted it so that it covered her eyes completely. She didn't want to see his reaction when she asked her question.

"Is it in any way possible that Stella might have murdered the Comtesse?"

There was a long pause before Oliver responded.

"Where on earth did that come from?"

Hollie explained how it would be a perfect plan to hire a friend to be the investigator in a murder case, rather than someone who knows what they are doing.

"But she didn't know the Comtesse was going to be murdered."

"But she would have known if she was planning to do it."

"I suspect you may be overthinking this. I mean, what motive do you imagined Stella might have had?"

Hollie groaned and reached for Oliver's hand, groping his

thigh in the process.

"I'm clutching at straws."

"Are you sure it's straws you're looking for?'

"Shut up, you idiot. I already told you I have a headache."

"Worth checking though."

Oliver said he'd organise supper. He had all their favourite food outlets on speed dial, claiming it was more efficient than learning to cook as he could conjure up all sorts of meals at a moment's notice – and without any of the necessary ingredients. He asked her if she fancied any specific cuisine.

Hollie ruled out Chinese and Indian as either might contain MSG and aggravate her migraine. They settled for fish and chips. Oliver phoned through their order, cod for him, scampi for Hollie and, once he had hung up, peeled the flannel back from Hollie's eyes.

"Maybe there's no great puzzle to solve. Maybe Jonas murdered his wife."

"Spoilsport."

"I'm just saying, the obvious is sometimes the answer."

Oliver let the flannel drop back into place and said he was going to change out of his suit.

Hollie tried to think of something other than her list of potential murderers. It was growing by the minute and now included Stella's husband, and any of the Comtesse's extended family – of whom she knew nothing.

"I need edge pieces." She said when Oliver returned in shorts and a t-shirt.

"What do you mean?"

"It's like when you do a jigsaw puzzle. It's easiest to get all the edge pieces and then you can see the shape of the puzzle."

"This seems more like a 'Where's Wally' puzzle to me."

"Yes. If only someone was wearing a stripy shirt that said 'murderer' on it."

Hollie's headache had subsided a little by the time Oliver returned with their fish and chips. She had also opened a bottle of white wine.

"Good to see you're feeling better," he said, trying to keep a note of sarcasm out of his voice.

Oliver had put plates in the warming oven before going to collect their supper. While he organised their food, Hollie leaned on the work surface, nursing her glass.

"There is something else that's a bit of a problem."

"What's that?" Oliver asked without turning towards her.

"Stella might be hitting on our receptionist Sharon. She told me about it today, Sharon that is. She wants me to talk to Stella."

Oliver sighed the sigh of a manager who had walked this precarious employee tightrope before.

"Is that really your department? Shouldn't Sharon go to HR to sort it out?"

"She doesn't want to make a fuss. And I'm not sure Patterson Wilkins has an HR department. She asked me if I could speak to Stella about it on the quiet."

"Well, if you do, I am going to predict you will be back teaching before you know what's happened to you, and you'll have lost an old friend."

"There must be a way of broaching it tactfully?"

"Tread very carefully. That's my advice. And could you grab the ketchup please?"

CHAPTER 12

That night Hollie woke several times. She was either too hot or too cool but was always thinking about how she could approach her best friend on the delicate matter of Sharon.

Stella's love life, before she married, had been a complex affair. A subject only broached with care and a glass of wine. Once she had started to climb the ladder, which she hoped led to partnership, Stella's taste in lovers became more selective and conservative – at least, outwardly so.

The matter was still on Hollie's mind when she was driving to work. As she pulled into her parking place, she couldn't remember any part of her journey, any corners, or any junctions. It was a complete blank. She avoided Sharon by taking the stairs. Once at her desk, a series of messages and emails popped up on her computer screen. There was an apology from Sharon about bothering her, telling her to ignore their conversation, without making any reference to the subject matter. An email from Peter, she had given him her work contact details, included a few pictures of Benedict Colby. Another message was from Stella, which simply read – Meeting room three, nine-thirty, interview with JC.

Hollie glanced at the clock. She had five minutes to find the room and prepare any questions she wanted to ask – assuming the JC in question was Jonas Colbert, aka Jonas Moon, and not a second coming, which would have demanded a different set of questions. She assumed he had kept the name 'Moon' for professional engagements but that the Comtesse had ensured her father's name would continue if they had children.

She called Sharon who must have picked up on the urgency in her request for directions because, for once, she responded quickly and succinctly. Hollie said she hadn't forgotten their chat and promised to deal with it as soon as she could. Sharon tried to protest, but Hollie told her it had to be done. Sharon whispered a thank you.

Deciding that lifts, especially those with mirrored walls, were for people who had lots of time to spare, she ran up the stairs, jumped the last two steps, almost stumbling, and arrived, slightly flustered, outside meeting room three. Taking a deep breath, and exhaling slowly, Hollie tried to relax her shoulders and knocked twice on the door before opening it. The room was empty. She took a step back, checked the number on the door, and looked down the corridor, wondering if she had misread Stella's message. But Stella emerged from another door, a little further along, and smiled at her.

"Ah, brilliant, we have..." Stella glanced at her watch, "fifteen minutes to catch up before Benedict arrives."

"I thought you said nine-thirty?"

"Did I? Sorry. But he's not due until ten. Anyway, Rupert will be here soon to brief us, so it's just as well you're early."

Hollie pushed the door open again, walked in ahead of Stella and asked if there was any coffee available. She tried not to sound grumpy about being given the wrong time but wasn't sure she managed it very well.

"Sharon will be bringing refreshments shortly. But tell me, how are you settling in? Has Sharon been helpful?"

Fifteen minutes should be plenty of time to drop Stella a few hints, and with other people arriving soon, it would prevent any conversation becoming an extended and awkward discussion.

"She's actually been very helpful, but there is something I wanted to ask you."

Hollie wished she had rehearsed exactly what she was going to say. She waited until Stella had settled into her chair. The room was almost square in its dimensions, the table round, there was no head seat, no right or wrong place to sit.

Choosing the chair next to Stella, Hollie arranged her notebook and pen next to a pad of yellow, lined paper. Each place at the table had been provided with a new pad, probably a tradition dating back decades.

"Actually, Sharon and I had quite a long chat about her boyfriend yesterday." Hollie tried to achieve a throwaway tone to her voice.

"She has a boyfriend. I thought she was..." Stella left the sentence hanging.

"Sharon is practically engaged. She's expecting a ring to appear any day now."

Hollie wondered if she might be enjoying this almost too much. She rarely had the upper hand with Stella and could sense her friend's discomfort.

Stella didn't respond immediately. She had opened her laptop and was focussed on the screen, pretending to read. Hollie could see she was only pretending because all that was on the screen was a list of files.

"Looking for something special?" Hollie asked, leaning towards her. "You thought Sharon was a lesbian, didn't you?"

Stella closed her laptop slowly and turned to Hollie. She spoke in a stage whisper, even though there was nobody there to overhear them.

"She has been coming on to me for months. I swear, I've not been imagining it. She must be bi."

Stella was biting a fingernail. Hollie hadn't seen her do that since they were teenagers.

"Please tell me I wasn't imagining it. She's not straight, is she?"

"She is as straight as I am."

Stella raised an eyebrow. Hollie chose to ignore the reference to their single kiss after a lot of wine at some ungodly hour of the morning and in the kitchen of a party house.

"But she practically propositioned me last Christmas. I've

been trying to play it cool whilst still trying to remain friendly."

Hollie asked what Sharon had said at the Christmas party, but Stella couldn't remember.

"I'd had a couple of glasses of wine, maybe three, it's not easy to recall a conversation from over six months ago."

"Just treat her like you do me. I'm sure everything will be fine."

"You mean look down on her and drop hints to her boyfriend that I'm available if he wants a fling?"

"You don't do that, do you? I mean you don't do either of those things."

"No, of course not. Well, not both and not often."

"Which one of those do you not do often?"

"Well, Oliver is a very good-looking man."

Stella avoided eye contact by flipping her laptop open again just as Jonas Colby, née Moon, was ushered into the room by Rupert.

"Jonas. You know Stella of course. And this is Hollie, our in-house investigator."

Jonas nodded in Hollie's direction. Surprisingly, he did not offer a handshake. She assumed all actors would be touchy-feely people. But maybe the circumstances were unusual. She would forgive him this time.

"Let's get straight to it, if we may," Rupert said. He pulled a chair out to indicate to Jonas where he should sit.

"Now." Rupert already had his pen poised over a blank sheet of paper. "We would like you to tell us, in your own words, exactly what your movements were on the morning in question."

"Why?" Jonas asked.

"I know you've been through all this with the police, but we don't have their notes, not yet, and we won't unless they charge you. We need to be prepared for all eventualities."

Jonas sighed and went through his movements that morning in as much detail as he could remember. He claimed to have got up early, around six. He told them he had a lot on his mind, particularly regarding an offer his agent had informed him of the previous day, a new series for which he was preparing.

"She gave me the scripts for the first two episodes of a promising detective series. It looks very good, I think. Of course, I'm not allowed to say anything about it yet. All very hush-hush. So, you'll have to trust me on that one."

There was nothing in his voice or demeanour to suggest he was at all concerned with the possibility of being charged with his wife's murder.

"I went for a walk, in Mulberry Park, to read some of the pages out loud. It helps me get a feel for the character. I assume somebody must have seen me there. I am quite well known, and people do tend to recognise me.

Hollie interrupted, collecting a frown from Rupert. "Who is your agent please?"

"Erica Whitely. She runs First Person Management. But why is that relevant? I didn't see her that morning. I mean, I was scheduled to have a meeting with her, but she had to cancel at the last minute."

"What time was your meeting?"

"Nine-thirty. But, as I said, I didn't see her."

Hollie added the name to her list. Erica Whitely could be another edge piece in her puzzle.

"And how long has she been your agent?"

Jonas crossed his legs and turned slightly away from Hollie.

"Ever since I left drama school. But what does this have to do with whoever killed my wife?"

Stella and Rupert were both looking at Hollie. She wasn't sure if the expressions on their faces were those of interest, bewilderment, intrigue, or impatience.

"I thought it might be significant in terms of your alibi - if they manage to fix the time of death more precisely, which I presume they will be able to do."

Hollie looked left and right at her colleagues, hoping her

explanation would satisfy everyone. Stella was nodding slowly, but not very convincingly. Rupert cleared his throat and turned back towards Jonas.

He pitched into the formalities of what Patterson Wilkins would be doing for Jonas, and the circumstances under which a barrister would be required. Rupert sounded both confident and competent, and told Jonas that they would keep him informed of any information the police released or any other developments that occurred. Most of it seemed quite inconsequential to Hollie as, unless Jonas was formally charged, she suspected the police were not obliged to disclose anything regarding their investigation. Of course, her knowledge of police procedure was based entirely on television dramas, so maybe not entirely accurate.

Jonas insisted that he had nothing to do with Juliette's death and sniffed loudly, before digging in his pocket for a huge tartan handkerchief which covered most of his face. After a few snuffles and dabbing at his eyes with the corner of the miniature tablecloth, Jonas proclaimed his innocence once again and said he would never have hurt Juliette and that he loved her dearly.

"The police said my fingerprints were on her shoes, but they couldn't be. We had separate dressing rooms, and I never handled her shoes or clothes, except to help her with a coat or smooth a wrinkle in her dress. It's all an awful mistake. I'm sure it will be put right soon."

"I think we might keep that information about the dressing rooms between us, just for the moment," Rupert said. "No need to hand the police any details they haven't requested."

"I still can't really believe it's happened. I worshiped her. I know those vultures in the press kept on about it being a marriage of convenience, but Juliette was a truly beautiful person. You only needed to spend an evening with her to realise what a wonderful soul she had."

Hollie hadn't formed quite the same impression from her own brief meeting with the Comtesse, but Jonas did sound as if he were genuine in his claims. The meeting drifted on for another twenty minutes. Hollie only interrupted to try to establish more precise timings for Jonas's movements, but he was unable to fill in very much detail. His morning had consisted of wandering around the lake, sitting on a bench for a while, and then setting off for a stroll through the trees.

"I don't stare at my watch when I'm trying to get inside the persona of a character. I can only tell you that the police approached me when I was on a bench by the lake. That must have been almost noon. I'm sure they will have a note of the precise time."

Hollie jotted down her impression of Jonas in the same way she and Stella had done with boys at university. They had done the same with girls too, but with much more contrasting results. It consisted of trying to think of a two-word description based on first impressions. They would then compare notes and decide whose choice of words was the most accurate. Hollie had written 'self-centred' and 'loyal'. She hesitated with her pen, wondering whether she was allowed hyphenated words and still count them as a single unit.

After Rupert and Jonas left, Stella asked her where 'loyal' had come from.

"Were you reading my notes?"

"Of course."

Stella's frankness and honesty sometimes disarmed Hollie.

"He loved Juliette. At least that's the impression I got. I had assumed it was just a celebrity marriage, short term, doomed to failure, but I now suspect I was mistaken."

Stella agreed. She said it had always appeared as though they were both in love with each other.

"I think that's why Juliette was being so cautious. She has always been worried about being betrayed. I suppose it's the penalty of growing up with extreme wealth. Never knowing who you can trust. Beneath that tough façade I think she really wanted us to prove Jonas was faithful."

Hollie wondered what it must be like to have so much money you could simply pay someone to track down your every suspicion. If she were that wealthy, would she have to get someone to check on Stella and Oliver - even though she was sure Stella had only been teasing her earlier about approaching him. Thinking about Stella, reminded Hollie that she had those connections within the police, namely whoever had supplied the photographs.

"Who is your inside man, or woman? The one who sent you those photos. It can't be a reporter. It must be someone in the police or the forensics team."

"Ah, now, I am afraid that is something I can't reveal. But why do you need to know?"

"I don't have a specific reason. It just seems to me that we might do better if we pooled our thoughts and resources at some stage."

Stella made a steeple of her fingers and focussed her eyes on them. "I'll talk to her. That's all I can promise."

"Thank you."

It was more than Hollie had hoped for, even if it was only a maybe. She decided to push her luck while Stella was in a helpful mood.

"And that confusion over Sharon?"

"Oh god," Stella sighed. "Can you sort it out with her? Tell her I never intended for her to get that impression — off the record of course. I need this to go away, or I may as well apply for a position in a convent as hope to get a partnership here. I'm sure you will find the right words to say. I'll even apologise directly to Sharon if it would help."

Stella blushed, a rare sight, made her excuses and left the room. Hollie tried to imagine her becoming a nun, and the terrible knock-on effect that might have on the other sisters. They would need a larger cellar in which to store the communion wine, and probably more regular visits from the priest.

CHAPTER 13

Once back in her own office, Hollie sat and stared at her computer screen. There was just the one file on her desktop, and she knew it only held a list of maybes, nothing more. She also had another list in her head, questions she should have asked Jonas. One thought which kept wriggling around in there, like a tiny piece of gravel caught between a sock and a shoe, was the full story behind Jonas's first wife and her untimely death.

His wiki page only contained a small note about her. It said she died in a traffic accident but gave no details. His profile, in various professional biographies, on movie websites and fan sites, gave no mention of her and therefore no further clues. After nearly an hour of trawling through numerous sources in search of something tangible, she rang Sharon.

"Do we have a local records office near here?"

"There's one at the library. What are you looking for?"

"Local newspapers, from a few years ago." She checked her notes. "Four years ago, to be precise, local or national, I'm not sure which would be best, probably both."

"I can give you online links for the nationals. We have a login for those archives. But I think you'll have to go to the library if you want to look through old copies of local newspapers."

Hollie spent the rest of the afternoon online, researching Jonas's first wife and, after no success there, at the library where they kept microfiche copies. Access was simple to obtain, but even after what seemed like hours of reading, she still arrived home before five o'clock.

When Oliver breezed through the front door, a little earlier than usual, he found Hollie with small pieces of cardboard, cut from a cereal packet, spread across the kitchen table.

"Ah," he said, draping his jacket over the back of a chair. "These have to be your jigsaw puzzle edge pieces?"

"They are. And I've found something weird. It probably doesn't mean anything, but it's like life repeating itself. It's either a strange coincidence or it demonstrates unbelievably bad luck on Jonas's part."

She showed him a printout from a local paper which she had retrieved from the library records. It was a report about his first wife, Mei Ling, and how she was killed in a hit-and-run accident. It said she was on a bicycle and the article speculated that it must have damaged the vehicle which hit her, but all the local garages were contacted, and no car had been reported with significant damage, not even scratched paintwork.

"Now, I'm not saying it was murder, or is it manslaughter when it's an accident, but they never found the driver because they never found the car. There was only one witness, who described the vehicle as small, maybe pale blue, or green, and they didn't take a note of the number plate. I suppose it could have been someone visiting the area. The witness was not named in the report."

"But you think it was murder?"

Hollie admitted her imagination might be heading in the wrong direction altogether.

"I know there's no similarity in the method, but it's a bit strange and a bit of a coincidence if you have two wives, both dying in suspicious circumstances, before you reach your thirtieth birthday."

Oliver asked if his first wife had also been wealthy. Hollie shook her head.

"She was here on a student visa, I think. No family is mentioned in any of the reports. And it doesn't look as though Jonas gained anything from her death. Just as well I suppose, or it wouldn't look good for him."

Oliver rescued an open bottle of wine from the fridge. He poured two glasses, took a sip, and emptied the remaining few drops from the bottle into his own glass. He took another bottle from the rack in the kitchen and slid it into the fridge on its side.

"If it wasn't just a normal accident between a car and a cyclist, and God knows they're common enough," Oliver said, sitting down opposite Hollie, "and if she was deliberately targeted, who would have had a motive? Not Jonas by the sound of it."

Hollie knew that Jonas could easily look guilty. It was possible he wanted to get out of the marriage, maybe he had been tricked into it in the first place. But the police would surely have looked at those possibilities. If he'd owned a car anything like the vague description the police had, they would have followed that up. She shrugged. Her assignment was getting more complicated every day.

"So, do you know who was leading the investigation? In the case of the first wife's death."

"I don't think any of the reports mentioned anyone by name."

Hollie knew she was going to have to go back and check. She had noticed the accident was in the same general area as where she now worked, a street just to the west of Mulberry Park. There was a strong likelihood that it would be the same police officers; as it was only four years ago. She was biting a dry patch of skin on her finger, a habit she thought she had broken several years ago.

A small red weal appeared on the edge of her index finger. Hollie cursed quietly and got up to find a plaster to cover the wound. While she tended to her self-inflicted injury, Oliver fetched the only slightly cooler bottle of wine from the bottom shelf of the fridge and put a couple of ice cubes in each of their glasses to chill it.

"If it's the same detective, they might be trying to make up for something they think had been missed regarding that accident. Maybe they thought Jonas was involved but couldn't find the proof."

If Oliver was right about the detective, and the detective was right in his suspicions, that would make Jonas potentially guilty of two murders, a serial wife killer. Hollie accepted she had no experience with murder or murderers, but Jonas simply didn't seem devious enough to have mown his first wife down with a stolen car, disposed of it, and then killed his second wife with one of her own shoes, driven into her neck. But she had to admit, if only to herself, it was a gruesome possibility. They could both have been crimes of passion.

"I'm going to mow the lawn," Oliver announced.

"It's not Saturday. And you don't actually do the mowing now."

"Someone has to supervise Mo.'

"Has it decided on its gender yet?"

"Mo is gender fluid. They are exploring their options."

Hollie looked at all the pieces of cardboard on the table and sighed. Her life had changed from a pile of paper which she at least understood, to a collection of notes which made no coherent sense. She picked up her phone and messaged Stella.

'Did you contact your source? Any chance she might talk to me directly?'

There was no immediate reply, so Hollie took her glass into the garden to join Oliver. He had placed two chairs facing the sun with a small folding table between them. Mo head-butted a shrub, re-orientated themself, and set off wandering across the lawn, following a seemingly random route. They both watched it in silence, fascinated.

Hollie wasn't sure how a robotic lawnmower could look contented and cheerful, but it did.

They sat, heads tilted back, eyes closed. When Hollie's phone pinged, she was almost dozing off. She grabbed it, knocking over an almost empty wine glass in the process and swore. There was no message. She wasn't used to having two phones and reached for her other one, which had fallen on the grass. The remains of her wine spilled on her blouse. She swore again.

"The detective will attend to your call in a minute, just as soon as her assistant has topped up her wine glass and mopped up her shirt," drawled Oliver, barely opening his eyes and using a terrible faux American accent. "

"Shut up."

"Certainly, ma'am."

The message was from Stella. Her contact had agreed to talk to Hollie, but only in the strictest confidence and only by phone in the first instance. Hollie stared at the screen, frowning.

"So, anything interesting?"

"Possibly. Probably. It's Stella's inside source. They have agreed to talk to me."

"Inside where?"

"I don't know for sure, but inside the police, I'm guessing."

There was no indication of when they might call, but Hollie didn't have to wait long. She had just taken a sip from her replenished glass, and asked Oliver what he wanted to make her for supper, when her work phone rang.

The caller's number was withheld. Hollie answered cautiously, only saying hello, and not giving her name.

"Who is this?" It was a female voice with a slight accent which Hollie couldn't place.

"Hollie Parker. And who you are?

The caller would only identify themselves as Maryam. No surname was offered, no hint as to their work or position.

"What did you want to ask me?"

"Are you with the police?"

There was a long silence, followed by an audible sigh. Maryam said it was safe to assume that she might be.

Their conversation continued in the same cautious, defensive manner. Hollie eventually managed to elicit that Maryam was familiar with the death of Mei Ling, and that she too believed it might not have been an accident. But she also didn't think Jonas was guilty or directly involved in her death. Maryam refused to be drawn further on her own suspicions.

"So, you do have a theory about that accident?"

"Just my intuition, for what that's worth," she continued. "My DI didn't agree with me."

There was a silence. Maryam obviously realised she had not only confirmed she was in the police force, but possibly indicated her rank, being somewhere close to, but below, a detective inspector.

"I won't reveal your name to anyone." Hollie assured her. "Stella said this had to be kept confidential.

"I'd appreciate that. My career would be over if you did. She told me you are old friends, and totally trustworthy."

"What's he like? Your DI."

"I think I've said quite enough on that topic for now."

"Okay. So, can we meet?"

Hollie was certain she could find out more if she could get face to face with Maryam.

"Maybe. I'll call you."

The line when dead. Oliver had been listening, but only to one side of the conversation.

"That sounded both curious and interesting."

"Yes, very."

Hollie didn't want to say too much. She didn't want to keep secrets from Oliver, but she also needed to respect Maryam's anonymity.

"Nothing definite, but maybe help with another edge piece."

Hollie went back indoors to fetch her notebook and a pen. She flicked back through the few jottings she had made, including her reconstruction of the strange message the Comtesse had received from an unknown number.

A call to Stella went straight to voice mail. Hollie, concerned that someone might overhear the conversation, left a vague message regarding a mystery number and whether anyone had had any success in tracing it.

She didn't expect a quick response and looked over at Oliver who was leaning back in his chair, fingers lightly holding the stem of his wine glass. Mo was still trundling around the lawn, unaware that their overlord had his eyes closed. Mo was, apparently, not one for shirking work.

Oliver never brought his work home with him. He had a shoulder bag, a birthday present from Hollie, and a laptop. Both accompanied him on his commute, but they were rarely disturbed from their overnight sojourn in the hall.

"Have you ever thought about working remotely? From home I mean," she asked.

Oliver turned his head towards her and opened one eye. "Why on earth would I want to do that?"

"Lots of people do. Even I can now."

He made a small harrumphing noise deep in his throat, a sometimes-annoying habit. After a pause, either for consideration or effect, Oliver replied.

"I don't want to work from home. I like leaving work behind when I leave the office. Clean break, two worlds, no cross contamination."

"So, why do you bring that laptop home every night?"

He closed his eyes again, orientated his face back towards the sun and sighed.

"Am I under interrogation?"

"Don't be stupid. And stop answering one question with another one. You're turning into a politician."

Oliver didn't reply for so long that Hollie was sure he was avoiding the subject. Was her new job already having a knock-on effect. She had never questioned Oliver before about his habit of carrying a laptop around.

"It looks good. It looks like I'm diligent. And it's a habit I suppose. A hangover from when I started work and wanted people to think I was putting in those extra hours."

Hollie wondered how she had never known that before, never asked. She was supposed to be both observant and intelligent. She looked at Oliver. His eyes were closed, his fingers trapping the foot of his wine glass against the arm rest of his chair.

Mo trundled across the lawn towards her docking station. The mower had to be female Hollie had decided. If it were male, it would simply have stopped and waited for someone to pick it up and plug it in.

Her phone pinged. She hoped it was a message from Stella, which it was, but not a very helpful one. According to her, the number had traced back to a burner phone. There was no way of knowing whether the police had the same information, or if they had recovered the phone. But it wasn't turned on.

Her phone pinged again while she was reading Stella's message. It had to be from Maryam.

"Café. Church Street. Ten tomorrow. Please keep this private. M."

Hollie half muttered, half hissed, a 'yes'. Her exclamation of success was loud enough that it made Oliver jump. He knocked his wine glass off its resting place, tried to catch it, and fell off his chair. He remained on the lawn, on his back, eyes closed once more.

"I presume that was good news," he said.

"Excellent news. Stella's inside source has agreed to meet."

"Is that like an edge piece, or part of the main picture."

"Not sure. But it's good either way."

"Would you like to pour me another glass? It would save me from getting up and I'm quite comfortable down here."

"Just don't let Mo see you laying down. She might get amorous once she's fully charged."

CHAPTER 14

On Thursday morning, Hollie left for work only a few minutes after Oliver. She went straight to the local library and arrived before it had opened for the day.

Sitting on a bench just outside the entrance, she watched as people scurried across the concrete concourse on their way to work. None of them could have guessed that the shortish, pale brown woman, in bright pink trainers, was trying to uncover a link behind two deaths. One, without doubt a murder, the other, at best, a suspicious accident.

A squeaking noise behind her, signalled to Hollie that it must be nine o'clock and the library doors had opened. She stayed seated for a minute while a few people waiting by the entrance had filed in, then followed them. She took the stairs to the second floor two at a time and showed her pass for the records office.

Once settled, Hollie scoured the reports in the local papers again, this time searching for names, and found the police officer in charge of the investigation. It was a DI Gilroy. She was reasonably sure she had heard him mentioned previously. But once again her notetaking had proved to be a little sketchy. Maryam had been cautious during their brief conversation and hadn't mentioned anyone she worked with by name. Hollie opened a new page in her notebook and wrote his name, in capital letters, right at the top. She continued reading, but there were only a few articles about the accident, and none of them revealed any fresh information.

Saying thank you to the woman on the desk, she checked the

time. The café, where she was to meet Maryam, was only a short walk away and she was early as usual. The sun was out, the day warm already, and Hollie walked without haste. The meeting, she hoped, would start to connect some of the edge pieces she had now collected or, at least, reveal some part of the picture.

She strolled the length of Church Street, relieved to find there was only one café, Sarah's Pantry. It had lace curtains covering the lower half of the windows, red and white check tablecloths, and a design style that suggested it had remained unaltered for decades. It couldn't have looked less like a venue frequented by police officers, on or off duty, but that was probably why Maryam had chosen it.

Pushing open the door, Hollie realised that she had no idea what Maryam looked like, other than the unreliable clue suggested by her name. A tall woman, in a dark blue hoodie, was looking directly at her. The woman nodded to her and then tilted her head towards the seat opposite. Hollie approached the table, resting one hand on the back of a vacant chair before sitting down.

"Maryam, I presume?"

A curt nod confirmed she had found the right person. The detective glanced at the door just as a waitress materialised at their table.

"Coffee for me please. A skinny latte," Hollie said.

The girl didn't attempt a smile. If she had, the number and variety of piercings adorning her face might have linked together and required an engineer to free her.

"The usual for me, I suppose," Maryam said to the waitress, who half smiled, half smirked.

"Are you expecting someone else?" Hollie asked the detective. Maryam had barely taken her eyes off the door for more than a second or two.

"I hope not. That's why I chose this place. It's not quite to my colleagues' taste."

Hollie's coffee arrived, accompanied by a small biscuit in its own individual wrapper. She took it off the saucer and pushed it to the edge of the table.

"Dieting?" Maryam asked.

"Sort of."

"Peer pressure?"

"Not really. Trying to show some restraint, I suppose. But trying to live up to society's expectations is probably part of it."

"In my case, it's my mother." Maryam paused and sighed. "Not to mention my aunts, my cousins, my father and my uncles. Pretty much everyone I know, including my boss."

Hollie was not quite sure how to respond. It was a lot to share when they had only just met, and she hadn't even had a sip of her coffee yet. She noticed an empty biscuit wrapper on Maryam's side of the table. If she bonded with Maryam through confession of personal history, it might make her more willing to share information.

"I didn't have any relatives to speak of, not even a father when I was growing up."

Both fell silent. It was not the kind of start Hollie had expected, but it did give her the opening she needed.

"Your boss sounds like a bit of a Neanderthal. Surely, he can't get away with personal comments about you. Not nowadays."

"Welcome to the modern police force. I could complain, but that would be on my record, and I would then have a reputation as a troublemaker, probably as a radical feminist. It would be the end of my career prospects."

"I presume he's your DI. The same one who is overseeing the investigation into the Comtesse's murder?"

"He is." She sighed again. "His name is DI Colin Gilroy, or Boss. He much prefers to be called Boss."

Hollie said she'd come across his name when she was reading about another death, a traffic accident a few years ago. Maryam knew instantly what she was referring to.

"You have been doing your research, I'll grant you that. Gilroy was convinced that was premeditated murder, not any sort of accident. He had Jonas Moon in the frame for it, but he couldn't make it stick. Too many factors which didn't fit the crime, if it was a crime."

Maryam caught the eye of the waitress and reminded her about her own coffee. She also requested a slice of caramel shortbread. Hollie asked for a piece too.

"It's on me," Hollie said. "I have an expense account apparently."

"Are you trying to bribe a police officer?"

"Is a coffee and a piece of shortbread sufficient for the purpose?"

"On a day like today, it's ample."

Maryam explained that DI Gilroy was determined to nail Jonas Moon for this murder. In part, she said, it was because he was still convinced that he had missed something when Mei Ling had been knocked off her bicycle.

"Why did he think Jonas was responsible for it?"

"His alibi was almost too neat. Gilroy thought something about it smelled wrong. He called it his *copper's nose*. I never felt Jonas was guilty, but still had that sense that someone was not telling the truth about something. But I was stuck with Gilroy's theories."

Maryam went on to explain that Jonas had been with his agent all that afternoon. Corroborated by her, of course, but their statements didn't match on what the meeting was about.

"That's why my boss is determined to make it stick this time. He was certain Jonas Moon slipped from his grasp four years ago."

"So, why hasn't he already charged Jonas with murder?"

"He wants it all neatly packaged, put in a box and tied up with ribbons and bows for the prosecution service."

Hollie went to take another sip of coffee, but found her cup was empty. She was no closer to solving the murder of the Comtesse but was happy that Maryam appeared to trust her enough for her to share confidences.

"Did you interview his agent, the one that provided his alibi?"

Hollie hadn't taken out her notebook, fearing that Maryam wouldn't want her taking a verbatim record. But she had set her phone to record their conversation. Whether it would successfully pick up their voices from inside her bag was yet to be tested.

"She was a cool customer, his agent. I couldn't read her at all. But I suppose she's used to negotiating deals, so not that surprising. And she almost provided his alibi this time too, or would have, if their meeting hadn't been postponed at the last minute. We're still looking into that early morning walk in the park. There's no CCTV in that area, but it's possible that someone spotted Jonas."

The agent was going to be underlined in Hollie's list although how she could engineer a meeting with her was not clear. Maryam checked her watch and pushed her coffee mug away. It had hardly been touched.

"I've ought to get going. Duty calls. Literally. My shift starts in half an hour."

"Do you have her address? I mean Jonas's agent."

Maryam bit her bottom lip and looked straight at Hollie.

"She should be easy enough for you to find, so I suppose I'm not giving away confidential information if I tell you. She goes by the name of Erica Whitely. But her real surname is Black, Erica Black. Easy enough to find if you look up First Person Management. That's her company name."

Hollie risked getting her notebook out and scribbled the details on a fresh page. As she did so, Maryann stood, hesitated, put both hands palms down on the table and leaned in close to Hollie.

"Look, you seem okay, and Stella said you could be trusted, but if this is going to work it has to be a two-way thing. If you discover anything significant, anything at all, I need to hear about it."

Hollie nodded her agreement but couldn't imagine she would

be uncovering evidence the police wouldn't already have. She promised to keep Maryam abreast of anything that came to light. When Maryam had left, the part-metal, part-human waitress returned to clear the table.

"You're paying for the copper too, I suppose?"

"Yes, I suppose I am." Hollie slid her new credit card out of the inside pocket of her notebook.

"What makes you think she's with the police?"

"Same way I know you're a reporter. You both stick out like a pimple on a beauty queen's forehead."

Hollie nodded, confirming the waitress's theory.

Being mistaken for a reporter could be a useful cover, so Hollie was not about to correct the girl. And she didn't know how she would describe herself anyway, claiming to be a private investigator would sound ridiculous, even though she was wearing her gumshoes.

The waitress had a problem with making eye contact; she was always looking vaguely at the table or down at her feet. Hollie had met many girls like her while teaching. Some were brighter than they appeared to be – or, at least, not nearly so dumb as they pretended to be.

"You have some seriously weird trainers," she said. "Where did you get them?"

"A friend brought them back from Holland for me. If you want a pair, I could ask him."

"Not really my style."

The girl smiled, or maybe sneered, it was difficult to tell with all that metal. She was still holding the tray loaded with their cups, not making any move to get the bill."

"I could tell you stories about that Jonas Moon," she said. "He comes in here sometimes with a woman. They always sit in the corner, over there."

The girl nodded towards a table at the back of the café. She must have been listening to their conversation. Hollie didn't push her, all information could be useful, but this girl was likely to be relaying gossip from social media. Neither reliable nor helpful.

"I'll get your bill." She hesitated, lowering her already quiet voice even further. "Service isn't included, if you know what I mean, and if you put it on a card, I won't see much of it."

Hollie told the waitress that she didn't have any cash on her. It was a lie, she knew she had some notes in her purse, but that was her own money, and far too much for a tip. She wasn't even convinced that the waitress would have any information relevant to the Comtesse's murder or Mei Ling's accident.

"I work here every day but Sundays. Maybe come back for another coffee when you've got some cash and I'll see what I can remember."

The waitress drifted away and returned a couple of minutes later with a bill and a card machine. Hollie paid, adding a generous tip. Even if it didn't all make its way to the girl, hopefully a decent proportion might. The waitress smiled, risking the potential linking of several rings and studs, and retreated behind the counter.

Outside, the air was fresh. It felt charged with oxygen after the stale warm of the café. Her meeting with Maryam had added to the questions in Hollie's head, rather than answered any of them. And she couldn't think what she had been hoping to achieve or discover when Maryam agreed to meet.

Amongst other things, Hollie was wondering how this special relationship between Stella and Maryam had come about. There was no wedding ring on Maryam's finger, but maybe police officers didn't wear jewellery whilst on duty. But there wasn't any mark where one might have been.

Hollie was aware that she was now looking for intrigue and complexity where there might be nothing to find. The coincidence of Jonas's agent providing his alibi, on both occasions, might be nothing more than happenstance. If it was an intentional cover story, their meeting at the time of the Comtesse's death would not have been postponed, or they would have lied about it.

And then there was the waitress, and the mystery woman Jonas met in a secretive corner of a nondescript café. Was he indeed having an affair, as the Comtesse had suspected? Hollie wondered if she could make a case for a petty-cash bribery fund, just in case those meetings were pertinent, and she could get more out of that waitress.

The jigsaw puzzle now had more edge pieces than were useful, especially with the sparsity of centre pieces, and no picture on a box lid to follow. Hollie looked at her watch. It wasn't even close to lunchtime, and she had eaten that shortbread which she shouldn't have – and something was now stuck to the bottom of her gumshoe.

She leaned one hand against the wall and lifted her leg backwards, to identify the problem. It was a lump of chewing gum, trying to bond with its ancestors no doubt.

The waitress came out of the café holding a steaming hot, wet cloth by its corner.

"You look like you need a hand. I hate that stuff. It gets stuck to my boots all the time."

Hollie took the cloth, thanked her, and managed to detach the lump of glutinous gum before it became part of her shoe. Carefully folding the cloth up, she offered it back to the waitress.

"Nah, chuck it, there's a bin at the end of the street. And thanks for the tip, I get paid rubbish here. That woman Jonas meets, her name's Black, if it helps. I've seen it on her credit card."

CHAPTER 15

Her office didn't feel like the right place to be, not after the meeting with Maryam. Hollie needed space and time to think and restructure her approach. Three walls, a computer screen, and a large window, even though it offered a very nice view of the park, wouldn't allow her the freedom to reflect on the situation. A clear blue sky and a gentle breeze also encouraged her to stay outdoors for a while longer.

Retracing her steps, Hollie found herself back at the library, sitting on the same bench, now in full sunshine. The day was already heating up, perfect for lazing by a pool or reading in the shade of a tree, but not ideal for loitering in the centre of a concrete concourse. Her clothes were beginning to cling to her body, and she had no clear plan for the day and no idea what to do next.

To escape the heat, Hollie wandered through the double glass doors of the library. She climbed a single flight of stairs to the study area and reference book section. She had no plan for what she was going to do until her eyes fell upon tables bearing ranks of unattended computers.

Her library membership gave her free access, and as a screen sprung into life in front of her, she knew exactly what her first task should be.

Erica Whitely's website was easy enough to find, but there was no physical address shown there, just an enquiry form that would ping off to an unknown destination. In fact, the website was quite sparsely populated and didn't look like it had been updated recently. Taylor might be able to tell her more about it with his expertise. Erica Whitely obviously wasn't looking for more clients through that particular portal. A more general search proved equally futile in finding an address for her.

After repeatedly tapping her pen on the table and drawing disapproving glances from a staff member on the enquiries desk, Hollie tried another tack. She entered 'Erica Black' in the search box and hit the return key.

The resulting links were not particularly helpful, unless Jonas's agent was also a dog groomer, an illustrator, or had a side line in therapeutic massage. A few more attempts, with various extra search terms, proved equally fruitless.

Hollie checked her watch. Somehow lunchtime had drifted past without her noticing. For an investigator, she was proving useless at the basic task of discovering the address of someone who wasn't even hiding.

Retreating to the furthest corner of the library, Hollie hid her head in a gap in the bookshelf, amid titles on art techniques and craft materials. Glancing around, to make sure nobody was close enough to hear, she rang her new best friend and source of arcane knowledge.

"Hi, Sharon, I have a question for you."

"You're very quiet. Is that you, Hollie? I can only just hear you."

After telling Sharon where she was, and why she had to whisper, Hollie explained her problem. Sharon laughed and told her she was in the right place. But she probably needed the next floor up.

"They'll have a copy of the electoral register there, but you'll have to ask the librarian nicely. They can be quite picky about what they'll let you see and even for how long. And if that doesn't work, we have a login for a database that's virtually the same info. I'll zap all the details over to your phone."

After thanking Sharon, and while she was waiting for the text message to arrive, Hollie wondered whether Stella should have offered the job to Sharon, rather than to her. She seemed to be in possession of such a wide range of information.

Tracing the address for Erica Black proved relatively simple after following Sharon's advice. The street where she lived sounded familiar and, when Hollie checked the location, she discovered it was walking distance from her office, on the other side of Mulberry Park.

A late lunch came from a small sandwich shop and consisted of a coronation chicken sandwich which she consumed by the lake in the park. Hollie needed a plan. She couldn't just walk up to his agent's front door and enquire politely as to whether she was helping Jonas Moon cover up a crime, or possibly two crimes. She had also found a phone number for First Person Management, her agency, while searching for her address, and found herself tapping the number into her phone before she had thought what to say. Her call went straight to an answering service.

"Hi." Hollie thought quickly. "Someone suggested to me that you would be the right person to talk to about..." she could hear herself floundering. She should have thought through what she was going to say before calling. "Well, actually, it's for a magazine piece on successful talent agents." Flattery might work. "I wanted to write about the trials and tribulations of representing people in the Creative Arts. I'm planning to interview writers, artists, musicians, and actors. Or, more specifically, their agents."

If I was Erica Whitely, Hollie thought, I would delete this message without a moment's hesitation.

"Anyway, Ms Whitely. I'd love to talk to you, especially as you represent Jonas Moon. So, could you give me a call, or text me, it would be so helpful. I'll look forward to hearing from you."

She hit the red button and swore several times under her breath. She had used her own phone, so at least the firm wasn't compromised by her amateurish attempt at subterfuge. But what if Erica Whitely did agree to an interview and asked for her ID as a journalist.

Hollie slumped on the bench, staring at the ducks which had gathered in front of her. There were a few crumbs left in her plastic sandwich carton, so she tossed them towards the shallow water on the edge of the lake. She pulled her feet back as a mad flapping of wings showered feathers in her direction. The ducks fought and argued over her meagre offering. It was all over in seconds, but two ducks turned back and approached her. Their waddling, aggressive attitude made her nervous.

Hollie stood and retreated, pushing her empty sandwich wrapper into a nearby bin. Without any specific plan in mind, she wandered along the tarmac track, following it round the edge of the lake. She had previously run the same route, but this time she branched off when a narrow side path gave her an idea. It led up a grassy rise to a stand of trees. The map had shown Erica's address to be on the north side of the park, and Hollie presumed there would be an exit somewhere near it. She reasoned that the path had to lead somewhere. Her guess proved right. A gate opened onto a side road, which led to Clarendon Avenue, the address she was looking for.

There were elegant houses lining the street, but only those on one side had the benefit of uninterrupted views over the park. They were tall houses, three storeys, and in their day would probably have been considered desirable residences. Now, many had been divided into apartments. Stone steps led to generous front doors. To the side of many of the entrances were arrays of buttons with handwritten names of the residents next to each.

Hollie counted the numbers down as she walked along the street, soon arriving at number twelve. She stood, looking up at the building, which was no better maintained than any of the others. There were only two cream buttons on the brick wall to the side of a wide, dark green, panelled door. Above and to each side of the door were stained glass sidelights with abstract plant designs in rich greens and yellows. A beautiful entrance, but possibly a promise of grandeur which the interior might fail to deliver.

One of the labels read 'Erica Whitely', the other 'FPM'. It was a surprisingly low-key location for a talent agent, especially one who represented a rising star such as Jonas Moon.

The First Person Management website had not revealed any names of its clients, not even Jonas. At the time, Hollie had assumed that was for security or confidentiality reasons. It now looked as though there might not be many names to list. A woman spoke from behind her, making her jump. Hollie couldn't have felt more guilty if she had been casing the house for a burglary.

"Can I help you? I live here. In number ten."

"I was looking for..." Hollie remembered a name from the list on the previous door, "Mr Farrow."

Her luck held when the woman told her that John was on holiday, camping in France. But also, she had the wrong house, he lived the other side of her, number eight.

"He only left this morning. Can I give him a message when he gets back? If it's urgent I do have his mobile number. But I'm not sure I should give it out to a stranger, or maybe you know him. Are you a teacher too?"

The tsunami of information and questions gave Hollie enough time to construct an answer.

"Yes, I am, but no, don't go to any trouble, I forgot he was going away. I don't need to get a message to him that urgently. It can wait."

Hollie had descended the steps and was back on the narrow pavement, ready to make her retreat before she was asked a question she couldn't answer. The woman stared at Hollie, smiling, as if she was thinking about something else. Then another voice made her jump.

"May I come past, dear. You are rather blocking the pavement."

An older woman with a small dog had appeared from nowhere. Hollie apologised. She started to move back onto the first step to allow the woman sufficient room to get by. The dog snuffled its way to one side of her, the woman took the other side. It made Hollie's escape more complicated. An extendable dog lead stretched across her shins like a trip wire.

"Don't worry about Monty, he doesn't bite. Although he does seem to have been getting very excited about people's feet recently."

Hollie side-stepped into the road and circled past the woman, not wanting to either trip over Monty or for her bright pink trainers to become the object of his desires. Once safely free, she lifted a hand to say goodbye to the woman from number ten who was still staring at her. Hollie set off in the direction of Mulberry Park.

The walk back to her office took less than fifteen minutes, even though Hollie took a small diversion to view the location where Jonas's first wife had met her fate. It was, according to Hollie's notes, the junction where Clarendon Avenue met the main road. It couldn't have been more than half a mile from Erica Whitely's apartment.

When she arrived at work, Hollie was still thinking about the accident site's proximity to the park, and to Erica Whitely's house. Sharon greeted her with a cheerful smile and, after leaning over her desk and checking nobody else was in earshot, spoke to her in an urgent, breathy voice. It was the kind of stage whisper which would attract the attention of anyone who might otherwise have ignored them.

"Stella gave me a box of chocolates."

Hollie sighed inwardly, fearing the chat with her best friend had somehow backfired. Sharon must have seen the concern in her expression because she immediately assuaged any fears Hollie had.

"No, it's okay, it's a selection box with dark and milk chocolates, and a bottle of champagne, the real stuff, that Bolly-thingy."

Hollie was none the wiser. Her blank look must have

communicated her lack of understanding.

"I can't eat dark chocolate. Stella knows that it gives me a migraine and she said they're for both Graham and me. She suggested if I get him in the right mood, he might pop the question. That's what the champagne is for, but I'm not sure he drinks any sort of fizzy wine."

"Ah, that's good. Can I assume that everything's okay now on the Stella front?"

"It's fine. It was probably just me being silly. Misreading messages that weren't there in the first place."

"Well, I'll get back to my office then, and good luck with Graham." Hollie pointed at the lifts as if to explain her plan.

"By the way," Sharon called after her. "Did you find what you wanted? I mean that address for Erica Whitely?"

"I did, thank you. And I suspect you might be better equipped for this job than I am."

Sharon giggled and rearranged herself behind the reception desk, smoothing her skirt under her as she sat. The lift pinged, announcing its arrival, and when the doors closed on Hollie, she also closed her eyes. She spoke to the empty chamber in which she was temporarily confined.

"What in Hell's name am I doing? I'm not cut out for this job."

The doors pinged again, opened, and pitched her back into the real world. Hollie pushed herself off the mirrored wall, having decided she didn't want to be confronted by multiple images of herself every day. Maybe taking the stairs would be better, and healthier. She opened her eyes to see Stella standing in front of her.

"Ah," Stella said. "Just the person I was looking for. Can we have a quick chat in your office?"

CHAPTER 16

Stella led the way into Hollie's office, but stood silently, looking out of the window. Hollie couldn't see her face and had no clue as to why she wanted to talk. The first words Stella spoke, after a long interval, were to ask if Hollie was all right.

"What do you mean?" Hollie replied.

"Well, the job isn't exactly the one you signed up for or expected is i?

It was true that Hollie had envisaged something closer to a role of making observations, maybe sneaking photos of Jonas in secret liaisons at cafés, or in restaurants. She might even have anticipated lurking in the shadows outside hotels or private houses taking notes about who arrived or left and at what time. Investigating a murder, however obliquely, had not been part of the job description.

"I was more concerned," Hollie said with a sigh, "that I wasn't really doing a good enough job. You are paying me rather a lot to simply follow hunches and join a running group."

In effect, Hollie was still being paid as a teacher, so felt doubly guilty that she wasn't contributing adequately to the challenge or planning lessons for her replacement.

"Don't worry about the money," Stella said. "Everything gets billed forward. In this case it's the Colby Group who are picking up the tab. And if you manage to establish Jonas's innocence, I'm sure he won't begrudge a penny of your time."

"But what if Jonas is guilty? I mean, he might be. It certainly looks that way," Hollie said quietly. "I'm not convinced he is, but he might be."

"Just in case he is, and I tend to agree with your assumption of his innocence, we do need to tread carefully. Neither Rupert nor Stephen will be happy if our reputation sustains any collateral damage. And there probably would be an impact on our relationship with the Colby Group and whoever takes over."

She turned to face Hollie. With her back to the window, and sunlight streaming past her making a halo of her hair, it was still difficult to determine Stella's mood.

"Aren't lawyers supposed to defend people accused of crimes?" Hollie asked. "I thought that was what you did."

"You're right. In general terms. It's not usually within my remit of course, more Rupert's side of things, and he would have to appoint a barrister if it went to court as a murder trial. But, as the victim was our client, we wouldn't want anyone thinking we let her down in some way. It is a tricky one."

"But you said the company was our client, not the Comtesse personally."

"That was before Jonas was likely to be charged. I had hoped he was not going to be implicated in any significant way."

"So, is he about to be charged?"

"Our mutual friend intimated as much."

"I never asked, how is it that you and Maryam have this special arrangement?"

"It's ancient history. We were both studying law when we met. She wasn't really in my circle of friends, or you would probably have met her."

"So, did she join the police after graduation?"

"Not exactly. She flunked out in her second year. Some family problem distracted her. But we sort of kept in touch."

"Were you two in a relationship?"

It was not that wild a guess by Hollie. Stella had a problem drawing boundaries between friendship and intimacy. She admitted that they had been quite close friends, but Maryam's family situation made such life choices very difficult for her.

Stella looked down, examining her fingernails.

"I suppose I was a sort of support group of one for her, or a sounding board. We met for coffee occasionally, nothing more than that, well, not much more. Then, a few years later, our paths crossed professionally. There was an alleged assault in a divorce case. We happened to agree on the evidence. That particular nine-out-of-ten ended up with a restraining order, and considerably less personal wealth after his wife appointed Patterson Wilkins."

"And have you cooperated with Maryam in other cases too?"

"Not significantly. But we've kept in touch. Life in the police force has not been straightforward for someone like Maryam. Promoted on merit, but always those rumours that she was benefitting from a quota policy. This is only the third case which has drawn us together. Talking of which, what do you really think of Jonas? Gloves off. Forget he's now the majority shareholder of the Colby Group. Is he the murdering type?"

Hollie had to admit that everything pointed towards Jonas's guilt, especially as his agent had failed to provide him with an alibi.

"What about the Comtesse's brother," Hollie suggested. "He stands to inherit a substantial sum, doesn't he? And we only have his partner's word that he's not interested in the money."

Stella nodded thoughtfully. It must have crossed her mind too.

"And what about that phone message?" Hollie asked. "Did your tech friend manage to find out anything about the origin of that?"

Stella said the number wasn't registered to anyone, and that the phone, if the card was still in it, was switched off.

"They will continue to monitor it, but I think, for now, we should consider that a dead end. It's probably at the bottom of a river, or maybe a lake in a park."

Both fell silent. Stella sat on the deep windowsill, her ankles crossed, head dropped in thought, hands supporting her weight to the extent that her neck appeared to have sunk into her shoulders.

Hollie opened her notebook. She flipped through a few pages to a note about Jonas being the majority shareholder in the Colby Group.

"What happens," she asked Stella, "if Jonas did do it, and if he is found guilty? Does he still own the company? And does he have to run it from inside a prison cell?"

She could almost see Stella thinking. Tension released in her shoulders, her head lifted, and she smiled at Hollie.

"No, that wouldn't be the case. There is a law called the Forfeiture Act, 1982. A perpetrator can't benefit from a crime they have committed. So, if Jonas murdered Juliette..."

Hollie interrupted her, immediately understanding the implication and asking who would inherit Juliette's share if Jonas was found guilty of murdering the Comtesse. Stella's grin widened further.

"Benedict. Her brother would have a strong case. And I have always thought he was a bit too good to be true. I mean, who wouldn't be interested in becoming obscenely wealthy?"

"So," Hollie said, "we just have to follow the money."

"You see, I knew you would be a perfect fit for this job. And I suspect you might be right in this case."

Hollie had only heard the phrase on television but thought it sounded good.

"He has never appeared to envy his sister. And he does get a fair share from the profits already," Stella said, still smiling, "but I know what you mean. We do have to consider Benedict Colby. Could he have framed Jonas somehow?"

Hollie quickly ran through everything she knew about Benedict, and realised it mostly came from just the one source, Kendra, his partner. She wasn't even sure if they were married but had formed the impression that they were.

"He should be at the Parkrun on Saturday."

Stella said she might have to get a pair of binoculars, after

Hollie told her that Peter and Marcus were also joining in the event. Stella tried in vain to stifle a bubble of laughter.

"Marcus? Isn't he the one that Oliver referred to as…"

"Please, don't say it." Jeremy had plied Oliver with too much whiskey that evening. "And you promised you would never repeat that nickname. It's cruel."

Stella apologised and promised that Oliver's indiscrete soubriquet for Marcus would never be voiced again.

"Tell me, are there going to be paramedics in attendance?" Stella asked, eyebrows raised in mock concern.

"That's not even funny."

"Oh, come on, it is."

They both retreated into a safe silence for a few moments. Hollie thought about her earlier meeting with DS Chandra, and the ridiculous message she had left for Jonas's agent.

"There is something else I wanted to mention. I accidentally claimed to be a journalist earlier today. I was going to ask if you think Natalie might be able to wrangle me a press pass?"

"What on earth for? Are you planning on becoming a junior reporter as a side-line? Are we not keeping you busy enough?"

"I tried to blag an interview with Jonas's agent. I thought it would raise fewer alarm bells that way. Especially if she does turn out to be involved in all this. I might have told her I had been commissioned to write an article about talent agents."

Hollie explained why she had made her flimsy excuse, and that she thought it would be worth getting a face-to-face meeting with the elusive Erica Whitely, if only to get another perspective on Jonas.

"Leave it with me. I'll call her. I have no idea how that sort of thing works. But there is another matter we need to confront."

Stella reminded her that Jonas might be charged very soon, and that the evidence they have is not simply circumstantial.

"Is that information from the same trusted source?"

"Do you think I have a whole raft of special friends inside the police and justice system?"

It wouldn't have surprised Hollie in the least. But Stella ignored the implication.

"She told me DI Gilroy considers the fingerprints on Juliette's shoes as something akin to a signed confession. And he is confident the CPS will see it the same way."

Hollie hesitated, not sure she ought to voice the thought that was rattling round in her head.

"Should I assume that you and Maryam are, or are not, an occasional item? I don't want to put my foot in it."

"Goodness, whatever made you think that. It would probably end her career if a rumour like that started to circulate."

Hollie knew her friend too well to ignore the possibility, and Stella had not specifically denied it. Stella never directly lied about her relationships, and rarely kept them a secret, not even from Jeremy. But there were exceptions to every rule, and any relationship she had with Maryam would be a sensitive matter.

Stella pushed herself off the windowsill. She walked to the door, ready to leave the office, but paused, turning back to face Hollie.

"So, it's just that press card you need?" she asked, raising her eyebrows as if to challenge Hollie to repeat her question.

Hollie nodded. She couldn't think of anything else to add.

"I'll see you Saturday then, in your running gear, and Marcus of course." Stella pulled a face, winked at Hollie, and left.

The computer screen flickered, also appearing to snigger at Hollie. Both she, and it, knew there was only the one relevant file stored on the drive, the one she had created a couple of days before. Her kitchen table, however, was covered in many more pieces of paper with her scribbled notes. That was where she knew she needed to be.

Hollie turned off the computer, telling it to mind its own business, and stuffed her notebook in her bag. She closed the office door on her way out and took the stairs to the car park, partly to avoid those mirrored walls but also to avoid Sharon, whose cheerful demeanour might have made her scream at that point.

On her route home, Hollie made a diversion to a large office supplies store. She used her company credit card without a single pang of guilt and loaded her purchases onto the back seat of her car.

Once in the privacy of her own home, Hollie draped her bag on the back of a kitchen chair, checked there was water in the kettle, and flipped the switch to make herself a cup of tea. The situation demanded wine, but it was mid-afternoon. She would get some work done first.

On a normal school day, at that time, she would have been winding down, possibly having a coffee with colleagues, complaining about the students, the repetitive routine, the state of the building, politics, parents, or partners. But now she was on her own and on a mission.

She was soon ensconced in their small home office. The tea had been drunk and replaced by a glass, and a bottle of red wine. By the time Oliver arrived home, the bottle was half empty. Hollie heard the door open and close, and called out to him.

"I'm in here. And you might want to bring a glass in with you."

There was only one chair in the large closet the estate agents had described as a fourth bedroom. A desk had been squeezed in, and a set of bookshelves. It was probably the smallest space that could have reasonably been designated a bedroom, unless one's guest was willing to sleep in a standing position.

The top of the desk had been cleared of all non-essential items. Remaining were a tape dispenser, a box of drawing pins, a set of marker pens and a roll of ribbon, which had been borrowed from the present wrapping kit in her wardrobe. They were all that Hollie required.

She had printed photographs of both Juliette and Jonas, downloaded from the internet. The printer was now under the desk, by her feet. The pictures were pinned top and centre of the board, other images were scattered on the display with ribbons joining them and scribbled notes pinned under them. When Oliver came into the room, Hollie took his glass and poured him a drink while he studied her work of art.

"You might have been watching too many crime dramas on television," he said. "Do they really still do it this way?"

He took a sip from his glass, without taking his eyes off the board, pulling a range of facial expressions, from grinning wildly to frowning in confusion.

"Okay, so I recognise those two." He moved his glass in the direction of Jonas and Juliette. "But what is Kanga doing there? You don't suspect Winnie the Pooh of being involved in this murder, do you?"

"That's Kendra, Benedict's partner. Wrong gender but nearly the right name."

"In that case, I presume Charlie Brown is Benedict?"

Hollie congratulated him, and before he asked, she explained that Cruella de Vil was Jonas's agent.

"Not that I have any evidence she's ever abducted or murdered any puppies. And I have no idea what her hair style is either."

A map, featuring Mulberry Park, was pinned on the bottom right of the board, alongside a newspaper report of Mei Ling's accident. A ribbon connected it to a point on the map, very close to a circle on a nearby road.

"So, who lives there?" Oliver said, tapping a finger on the map. "Or is that where the treasure is buried?"

"That is Cruella de Vil's residence. Somewhat less impressive than I expected it to be, but it probably has a good view of the park which Jonas frequents."

"Is she your prime suspect?"

"No. But she did conveniently supply Jonas with an alibi on the occasion of his first wife's accident, and she nearly did this time too."

"Ah, you suspect Cruella of protecting her investment in her client."

"Maybe, but I still don't see Jonas as a murderer."

Hollie sighed and leaned against Oliver, both for physical and emotional support. The wine was making her feel depressed, creating doubts in her reasoning. She asked him if she had made a mistake in leaving teaching so impetuously.

CHAPTER 17

Hollie woke aware of Oliver breathing directly into her ear. He had managed to roll half-way onto her pillow. It wasn't the first time. She ran a fingernail gently down his arm. He mumbled and turned over onto his other side. Peace returned, but she couldn't get back to sleep. It was summer, and the sun rose far earlier than it needed to on a Saturday.

It would be her first Parkrun that morning. She hadn't exercised formally since she was at university, even then it had only been a half-hearted attempt at playing netball. It was a game she had enjoyed at primary school, but her team mates and opponents kept growing taller as she advanced through the school system.

The short run she had done a few days ago hadn't felt too bad. Hollie was sure she could manage five kilometres if she paced herself. It couldn't be much more than two miles. She checked on her phone and, while her head tried to tell her three miles wasn't that much more, her body teased her with a spasm of cramp in her right calf muscle. Scrambling out of bed, she pressed her foot down hard, stretching the complaining muscle until it relaxed.

"Are you okay?" Oliver mumbled.

Hollie didn't bother to answer, suspecting that he wasn't fully awake. As she was now up, with little chance of going back to sleep, she decided to make herself a mug of tea. It was only just gone six o'clock, but there was too much on her mind for her to doze off again.

With a mug cradled in her hands, Hollie sat in their study

staring at the board she had populated with suspects. Along the bottom were small notes detailing people who might have murdered the Comtesse but were not prime candidates. Most of those on the list had come from Maryam's scribbled note, which had accompanied the crime scene photos. The cleaner who found her, the neighbour and the neighbour's lover, and of course the gardener, who must have left the mower on the lawn. If it hadn't been a casual remark by Stella, with Maryam's notes as the source, she probably wouldn't even have thought about the lawn mower.

Hollie knew that, in fiction, such seemingly insignificant clues always turned out to be the ones which led to the identity of the killer. She unpinned the piece of paper with 'gardener' written on it and positioned it higher on her board.

"The kettle is still hot,t I presume?"

Oliver had surfaced and was stood in the open doorway, leaning languidly against the frame. Hollie sighed.

"I suppose you want me to make you a mug and bring it up to you in bed?"

Her slightly sarcastic tone was not lost on Oliver, and he melted back into the hall. Hollie heard him fill the kettle and trip the switch to turn it on.

"I could drink another one," she called out.

There was no response, but she did hear a second mug hit the work surface a little more forcefully than the first.

"Thank you," she called. There was no reply.

A newspaper rattled through the letterbox at the same time as Oliver delivered her second mug of the day.

"I'm taking the papers back upstairs. Are you coming back to bed?"

Hollie said she was going to have a shower and get dressed.

"I want to be at the park early. I don't want to miss any opportunity to chat to Benedict."

Oliver was still in bed when Hollie set off. She opted to leave her car at the office. The park was only a short stroll from there.

As soon as she approached the entrance to Mulberry Park, Hollie realised the event was far more popular than she had expected. People were arriving from every direction. A couple of open tents had been set up to offer the organisers some shade, a large sign marked the start, and two lines of rope delineated what was probably the finishing lane. It wasn't going to be easy to find Benedict amongst those hundreds of runners.

Her phone pinged. It was Peter telling her that thy were waiting near the start point, and asking where she was. Hollie replied that she would be with them in two minutes.

While she made her way towards Peter and Marcus, Hollie scanned the crowd for anyone she recognised from her practice run. A small plume of smoke caught her eye. There was only one person she knew who might possess the audacity to smoke at a health-orientated event. It was most probably Jean Carpenter.

As she neared the head teacher, Hollie spotted Kendra, standing just to one side of her. Kendra had tied her soot-black hair into two large bunches, neatly perched on top of her head like oversized mouse ears. The man standing next to her was most likely Benedict. He was not easy to recognise from the photos she had seen, partly because he was wearing a baseball cap and sunglasses.

She messaged Peter. 'I've found Benedict. He's by the ice cream van'.

A minute later, Peter crept up behind her, not difficult to do given the noise created by all the people around them. He whispered in her ear, making her jump.

"Yep, that's Ben."

She turned, wanted to hit him for startling her. She was already at an event that wasn't exactly suited to her nature and her nerves were jangling. Marcus mouthed 'sorry', often more sensitive than Peter to other people's feelings. Peter asked if she wanted to be introduced to Benedict, or just observe from afar. But, before she could decide, Jean Carpenter spotted her, and beckoned all three of them over.

Peter introduced everyone to Marcus and Hollie. There were suppressed smiles at Marcus's lime green shorts and orange top. The colours did nothing to disguise or detract from his physique, but he didn't appear to care.

"I wasn't sure what the dress code was," he said in an extraordinarily camp voice. "I didn't realise that today's theme was monochrome."

Hollie hadn't noticed but, when she glanced around, there was a marked predominance of black, white, and grey outfits.

"Well, I think you look amazing," Kendra said to him." Is this your first time out?"

"Don't be silly, my dear. I've been out since I was fifteen."

Laughter dispersed any awkwardness, and Kendra offered to run alongside Marcus and help pace him. Benedict was already checking his watch and doing some rather painful looking stretching exercises.

"You go ahead, Ben," Kendra said. "We all know you like to be at the front of the field. We can meet up afterwards for proper introductions when you're not preoccupied with your performance."

A whistle blew, announcing the start was imminent. A small group to one side, who had been going through a beginners warm up routine, cheered and moved closer to the start line. Once the run began, any thought of keeping up with Benedict was out of the question, he was obviously a serious runner. He was far too fast for Hollie, and it had sounded like he wouldn't want to chat while he was running anyway.

Hollie enjoyed the event more than she expected, and even forgot the reason she was there, just for a while. She noticed Marcus drop out after the first lap. When she passed him again, he was eating an ice cream, while at the same time encouraging everyone else quite vocally and not always politely.

It was only when they had all finished that Hollie got to meet Benedict properly. He was pleased with his time, and more approachable than he had seemed before the run. When she found a suitable moment, she took the chance to offer her condolences.

"I'm sorry about your sister, Benedict. Someone told me what happened, and of course it's been all over the news."

"Half-sister to be accurate, and barely that to be honest. We shared a father, but she got the larger slice of him. And please, it's Ben, not Benedict."

"So you weren't close, you and Juliette?"

"Nobody was very close to Julie, except maybe her accountant and that toy-boy actor she married."

Hollie wasn't sure what to say. It was a surprise to encounter such a frosty attitude from Ben regarding his half-sister and her husband. She had wondered what he thought of the Comtesse's marriage to Jonas, and now she knew. She wondered if he saw the marriage as some sort of threat to his share of the company.

"Oh, come on," Kendra intervened." You two got on all right, you just had different interests in life. And Jonas is harmless."

Kendra was either a natural peace maker, or suspected the police might be looking at Ben, so wanted to put a little gloss on a lacklustre sibling relationship. And she probably wouldn't know about Jonas's fingerprints on the murder weapon.

Jean Carpenter leaned in towards Hollie and, in a quiet voice, told her that she had been serious about her offer. Kendra overheard the comment and grinned broadly.

"Are you thinking of joining us at Pirton Lane?" she asked, having guessed the nature of the reminder.

Hollie said it was just a possibility, maybe for the future, but wondering, at the same time, why she hadn't ruled it out completely. Insecurity, she decided, or just common sense. It was never a good idea to barricade doors you might want to squeeze through at some time.

"Why don't you come round for supper?" Kendra asked. "Get to know us all properly. Or at least a few of us."

Hollie wasn't sure that was a good idea.

"I'd have to check with Oliver, my husband. His diary can get quite busy."

It was a lie. Oliver was very much a nine-to-five man, he wasn't a golfer and simply pottered most weekends. But would socialising with Kendra and Ben be sensible. Getting too close to them could make things awkward, or on the other hand, it could be quite informative.

"Well, let's swap numbers and see if we can't find a free evening," Kendra said. Is Oliver in teaching too? If he isn't, tell him we'll promise not to talk shop all night."

Ben had been chatting with Peter and Marcus, overheard Kendra's suggestion and included them in the invitation. A provisional date for the following Saturday was made. If nothing else, Hollie now had Ben's address, but wasn't sure how that might be useful. She suspected that any details might be important, particularly the bruises and small crescent shaped wounds she had noticed on Kendra's arm. They could have been made by fingernails, maybe wounds from the Comtesse resisting her attacker. She ought to ask Maryam if DNA had been found under the Comtesse's fingernails, but would Maryam divulge that sort of detail to her.

As the crowd started to disperse, Marcus nudged Hollie.

"That Ben is a bit of all right. Peter never mentioned that when they were working together."

"And I suppose there aren't any attractive men in the fashion business?"

"My dear Hollie, you know I have always been attracted to straight men, or at least men who appear straight." He glanced at Peter and winked at Hollie. "And that's probably why you keep Oliver on such a tight leash when I'm around."

Hollie punched him on the arm playfully, and Marcus pretended to be hurt before giving up and giggling.

When Hollie got home, exhausted but feeling refreshed and alive, Oliver was tinkering with Mo on the kitchen table. He had, at least, had the sense to cover the table with newspaper.

"So, how did your first Parkrun go?"

"It was fun. More so than I expected."

"And did you manage to meet Benedict."

"I did, and his partner, Kendra. They have asked us to have supper with them next weekend. Peter and Marcus will be there too."

Oliver stopped what he was doing and looked up, frowning. "That could be interesting and possibly awkward."

He explained that he had met Benedict a few years ago. There had been some legal documents to sign, and he had been asked to be one of the witnesses.

"You never told me that. Is it a problem?"

"No, it shouldn't be." Oliver shook his head. "I doubt he'll even remember me. He hardly took his eyes off the Comtesse, and it was all over in a few minutes. I was very much part of the wallpaper."

Hollie asked him what the documents were, but Oliver reasserted that he was only there to witness the signatures.

"And, even if I did know, I couldn't tell you. Client confidentiality and all that. I believe it still applies, even though she is dead."

"Were they hostile towards each other, Ben and Juliette?"

"All I can say," Oliver sighed, "is that there were no hugs or kisses being shared, before or after the signing."

Hollie knew she wouldn't get any more from him, but at least she had confirmation that everything between Ben and Juliette was not quite as warm as Kendra had suggested.

"What's wrong with Mo?'

"Mo has a loose wheel. I'm just seeing if I can mend her rather than take her back to the store."

"Be gentle with her. You're the only owner she's known."

Oliver tapped the wheel with a small screwdriver. It was his default method of diagnosing, and hopefully mending, anything mechanical. Before going for her second shower of the day,

Hollie went into their home office and pinned Kanga a bit higher on her board. She scribbled 'bruised forearm, defence wounds?' under her name, and sat down, staring at the board, hoping for a revelation. Nothing came.

She sighed, dropped her marker pen back on the desk and headed for the bathroom.

Later that afternoon, Hollie received two emails. The first was her Parkrun time, just over thirty-one minutes. She wasn't sure if that was good or bad. A quick check of her position on the Parkrun website, and an online search for the average times for beginners, put a smile on her face. She would do better next time; she had a target to aim at now.

The second email was from Stella. It was headed with the words 'couldn't resist'. There were several photographs attached. One or two of her, and several of Kendra and Ben. There were also a few particularly unflattering snaps of an exhausted Marcus before he'd recovered enough to find the ice cream van.

Hollie printed out a couple of the pictures to put on her incident board. She only needed one more, and Cruella de Vil could retire from her temporary substitute duty.

CHAPTER 18

Clouds gathered on the horizon over the weekend, threatening a thunderstorm. It broke late on Saturday afternoon, confining both Hollie and Oliver to the house. The showers lingered into Sunday morning, which led Oliver to suggest a pub lunch.

Hollie couldn't get the murder out of her head, even though she had no idea what to do next. Remembering her diversion from Clarendon Avenue back to Mulberry Park, she suggested trying a new place she had found. It was a pub on the crossroads where Jonas's first wife had met her fate.

As it turned out the food was bland, the wine sour, and a window overlooking the crossroads showed only an intermittent traffic on the crossing. At no time did it look dangerous. And Mei Ling's accident had occurred just before three in the afternoon, on a Sunday. The traffic couldn't have been very different that day. Hollie hadn't checked the weather conditions, maybe a sudden thunderstorm had been a factor. But that would have been mentioned in the newspaper reports.

They made their way home mid-afternoon, and Oliver found a rom-com on television that they hadn't seen before. It proved just as uninspiring as their lunch.

Monday morning found Hollie sat at her desk, still with no idea how to proceed. She messaged Stella and asked if it would be okay to talk to Jonas and get his memories of the day of Mei Ling's accident. The reply came back almost instantly.

'Don't do anything yet. Bit busy. Meet at ten, Room three.'

Hollie sighed and walked over to the window. She stared out

of it, without any real interest, at Mulberry Park. Trees shimmered as a gentle breeze moved through them. A newspaper skittered across the grass, finally caught by the man chasing it who folded it as best he could and returned to the bench where a woman was laughing at his antics. Life was simpler when you weren't involved in solving a murder.

She pictured Jonas, walking those paths at the same moment a stiletto heel was being forcibly driven into the Comtesse's neck. Hollie wondered just how much strength it would take. She pressed a finger to her own neck, felt the soft, pliable flesh, the chords of muscle and sinew that the heel must have slid between. Could you do that by pushing with your hand, or would it take more force, maybe stamping on someone while you were wearing the shoe. There had been an injury to the back of her head, Maryam had mentioned it, but no weapon had been identified with which that blow had been struck. Not as far as she knew.

Hollie returned to her desk, opened her notebook, and jotted down her thoughts. Check Jonas's shoe size and ask Maryam if the pathologist had said anything about the force required for the heel of a shoe to fatally pierce a neck. Ask about the head wound. She looked at the crime scene photos again. The shoe had been distorted during the attack; the heel breaking and ending up still attached, but at an angle to the sole.

It was almost time to meet Stella. She made her way to Room three, where she poured herself a glass of water and waited, trying to think how the police would present their case and what evidence they might have other than Jonas's fingerprints. They were on the murder weapon, which had to be damming, but that could also be easily explained. Aside from that, Hollie couldn't see how they could link him to the actual crime, but even then, he may still be guilty.

Stella breezed into the room with an armful of old-fashioned folders. They landed on the table with a thud. She had arrived with a smile on her face which suggested she was about to ask a big favour. Hollie had seen that same look many times. Sometimes for Hollie to cover her absence when one of her boyfriends turned up, but occasionally to simply lie about where she had been and who she had been with.

"Darling, do you think you could fit a little bit of light stalking into your schedule?"

Hollie wasn't sure if she was being sarcastic; it was often difficult to tell with Stella. As to her 'schedule', she had virtually run out of ideas. A spot of following someone around, the kind of task she had been expecting in the job description, might prove a welcome break.

"It's not connected to Jonas's problem," Stella added. "But he might be in attendance on the night."

"What do you mean? And who am I stalking?"

"It's an award's ceremony. Nothing fancy. It's not the Oscars, so there won't be any television coverage, or not much, only marginal I expect. It's just one of those industry things where they all pat each other on the back and pretend it's important."

Stella explained that a client would like her husband watched, and Hollie's cover would be as one of the catering staff.

"How do I get the job. Do I have to apply or something?"

"All taken care of. An old friend of mine owns the catering company. You'll only have to pour some wine to keep the guests glasses topped up and observe our man at the same time. Perfect cover. It's all arranged."

A more extensive briefing followed from Stella, aided by printouts of emails their client had intercepted. On reading through them, Hollie understood that the man was suspected of having a fling with one of the other writers on a daytime show. Both he, and the woman in question, would be in attendance. Hollie's role was simply to observe and report back. None of the emails incriminated the man directly, and Hollie thought it sounded like an over-suspicious wife with too much money and too much time on her hands. There was one problem though.

"If Jonas is there, won't he recognise me? He might say something and blow my cover."

Hollie heard her own words and thought she was beginning to sound ridiculous.

"Buy a wig. Buy two. They will probably come in handy on other occasions."

"When is this awards ceremony?"

"Don't panic, it's not until this Saturday. You've got plenty of time to get into character. And get a decent wig, not one of those nylon Halloween monstrosities. Now, what was it you wanted to see me about?"

Hollie explained that she was hoping to talk to Jonas about what he did that Sunday, hoping he had remembered some more details. She told Stella she was also curious about what he could remember on the day of his first wife's death.

"Oh, and I was going to ask if the Comtesse had a gardener. There was a mower abandoned on the lawn."

Stella said that, as far as she knew, Jonas was in a studio this week, filming something, and not to be disturbed. But she would ask Maryam about the gardener.

"As for talking to Jonas, I can't see a problem with that, but it would have to be left until after he returned on Saturday.

Having a company credit card was a novelty and Hollie hesitated over the purchase of a single wig, let alone buying two. She even messaged Stella with the surprisingly high cost of them, getting a simple thumb's up in response.

Once at home, she scraped her hair back, which took little effort, and slipped the first wig into position. To complete the disguise, she had also acquired a pair of wire framed glasses with plain lenses.

Oliver came home to find an empty wine glass on the kitchen table, with a note saying, 'please ring for service'. There was a small bell weighing down the note. Intrigued, he picked it up and rang it.

Hollie had heard him coming and hidden in the lounge with a bottle of wine. On the sound of the bell being rung, she appeared in the kitchen doorway. Not only was she wearing her new blonde wig and glasses but was dressed in a short black skirt and white cotton blouse.

"You rang, sir? Would you like a glass of wine?"

Oliver sat down slowly at the kitchen table, pushing his chair back, and stretching his legs. He nudged a glass, which she had left on the table, towards Hollie.

"Who on earth are you? And What have you done with my wife?"

Managing not to smile, Hollie held the bottle in front of her so Oliver could read the label. He nodded, she poured him a glass of wine, and took a pace back. Oliver took a sip before speaking again.

"Long hair suits you, and I do rather like the blonde look."

"I'm going undercover. So don't get used to this kind of service, I'm just practising. And I am never bleaching my hair. Dark and short is my signature look."

Hollie explained what she was doing on Saturday evening. It didn't feel like the information was particularly confidential.

"Will you still have that wig on when you get home, and that outfit?"

Oliver started to get up, and Hollie backed away, giggling. She put the bottle on the end of the kitchen counter and kept retreating until she was in the hall.

When she got to the stairs, she turned and climbed them slowly, looking back over her shoulder at Oliver.

"I'm sorry, sir," she said in a husky voice, "but customers are not allowed upstairs."

She giggled again and ran up the last few steps. Oliver caught up with her in their bedroom. Hollie was laughing so hard that she had lost all her strength.

The next morning, Hollie was still in bed when Oliver left for work. She came downstairs barefoot, dressed only in cotton shorts and a T-shirt, and with half a mug of cold tea. Slumping on the chair in their small home office, she stared at the board she had created. The jigsaw puzzle she first imagined solving, had turned into some sort of human tangram - a set of pieces which you could rearrange to reveal almost any solution you wanted.

She took a sip of her cold tea, grimaced, and wandered into the kitchen to make a fresh mug. The room was spotless. Oliver had disposed of the empty pizza boxes, ordered after she had finally taken off her wig. He had cleaned everything, put the plates in the dishwasher and set it going. She wondered how many times that blonde look could be employed before the novelty wore off.

Her phone pinged. It was Stella. The message said Hollie's press accreditation card had arrived at the office by special courier. She was surprised it had come through that quickly, but presumed Natalie must have some serious connections - that would be how it had been expedited so quickly. The kettle made a half-hearted attempt at a whistle and turned itself off. With a fresh mug of tea, Hollie made her way upstairs to get changed for work.

The moment she set foot in reception; Sharon beckoned her over. There was a new sparkling adornment on her ring finger, so ostentatious that it looked like it had come out of a Christmas cracker rather than a jeweller's window - a thought that Hollie dismissed as ridiculous. It wasn't even Christmas.

"It's not real," Sharon said, still grinning broadly. "We were at that theme park, you must know it, Colne Castle."

Hollie had heard of it, but the idea of speeding along a vertiginous track, in something that looked no more robust than a dodgem car, was not her idea of a fun day out.

"Anyway, apparently Graham had this idea of proposing to me, at that place on the roller-coaster, the one where they take a picture of you before the big drop."

She showed Hollie a picture on her phone of herself screaming and a man beside her, bent forward like he was about to be sick. He was wearing a baseball cap, so it was difficult to see his face.

"It was amazing," Sharon said, after a long sigh. "He bought a ring in the souvenir shop. It was all done on an impulse, but now we're officially engaged."

Hollie politely examined the ring while Sharon was holding her hand out. She hoped the relationship would last longer than the glass and plastic monstrosity on her finger. Although, as far as she could remember from some posters in school, plastic could take half a million years to biodegrade.

"He said he'd get a proper ring as soon as possible. But I'll keep this one forever, because it's the actual one, isn't it. The one I got engaged with."

Hollie nodded politely. "Have you set a date?"

"Oh, we can't actually get married until his divorce is finalised."

Hollie was lost for words by the admission that Sharon knew he was still married while he was proposing to her. She made her escape after complimenting Sharon on her engagement once again. On the way to her office, her route took her past Taylor, the IT specialist. She stopped at his desk.

"Taylor, you know Sharon on the front desk?"

He made a sort of half shrug in acknowledgement, and Hollie noticed a blush creep up his neck.

"Do you know her boyfriend, or fiancé I should now say."

"Why would I? He doesn't work here."

"I just thought you might have come across him somewhere."

Taylor was focussed intently on a printout laying on his desk when he replied.

"Are you asking if I've stalked him online?"

"Well, have you?"

There was a pause before Taylor replied, in an almost

whispered mumble.

"He's thirty-four, married, and he's bald. I mean, bald like an old man; he's got a comb-over."

"He's told Sharon he is getting divorced."

"That's what he's told her? That sounds about as likely as me walking on the moon."

Taylor explained that, not only did Graham's wife have all the money, but they had already booked a winter skiing holiday in Canada.

"Not exactly what people do when they are splitting up."

Taylor thought Sharon was too nice to get played like that, and Hollie agreed. She asked him if he could send the information he had to her work email address. She promised to see if she could do something, but knew that if Taylor was right, confirmation would likely break Sharon's heart.

As soon as she reached her office, she sat down and woke up her computer. A file arrived from Taylor. It was very detailed, to the point of being quite disturbing. If she ever needed anyone stalked online, she knew who she could rely on in the future.

CHAPTER 19

Hollie went to make herself a coffee in the firm's kitchen and, while making it, thought more about Sharon and her dubious paramour. By the time she returned to her office, Stella was sitting at her desk, reading the file Taylor had compiled on Graham.

"Assuming Taylor's research is correct, we can't let this situation continue," Stella said. "The man sounds like an absolute toad. Am I right in assuming that it was Taylor who compiled all this information?"

After Hollie had updated Stella about Sharon's engagement revelation, they agreed that something had to be done. With Stella in possession of her chair, Hollie stood by the window, resting her bottom against the sill. She took a sip from her coffee mug. It was a bit too hot to drink yet.

Stella grimaced, wrinkling her nose in the process. "It doesn't sound like he's about to leave his wife, does it? He's off on a skiing holiday. I hope he breaks a leg."

Hollie nodded in agreement; her lips pursed. That possibility had crossed her mind too – assuming Taylor was right.

Stella sighed. "It will be a bumpy landing for Sharon, once she finds out what he's really like."

"But we can't say anything to her yet. We need to be certain. And, anyway, I doubt she would believe us; she's completely besotted. From the way she talks about him, you would think he was some sort of cross between Casanova and an angel."

"That means Graham is going to have to do the decent thing and end the relationship himself." Stella looked up at the ceiling, deep in thought. "Someone needs to persuade him towards the right course of action. Or maybe his wife might find out about the affair, accidentally of course."

After further discussion, they agreed that approaching Graham's wife would only complicate matters. She might already be aware of the situation and be looking for any evidence so she could throw him out. Sharon could end up with both the emotional and financial consequences of that. Stella leaned forward with her elbows on the desk. She steepled her fingers and looked unblinkingly at Hollie.

"How do you feel about having a quiet word with this Graham? You must have quite a bit of experience in dealing with lying little toe rags after all those years of teaching."

"Some, but none of those students were conducting extra-marital affairs with a law firm's receptionist – not that I knew of."

Stella persuaded Hollie to arrange a meeting with Graham, if only to get a sense of what he was really planning. She sighed deeply.

"Of course, we only have Taylor's take on this," Stella mused, "and he may be wrong. But you could also subtly remind Graham that his fiancée works for some very astute divorce lawyers. The kind of people who care deeply for the welfare of their employees."

Hollie agreed to giving it a go but wasn't sure how to engineer a meeting. Stella suggested keeping it simple.

"Send him a text message. We have his number from Taylor's research. Give him a version of the truth, but don't complicate it, that should work."

Hollie wasn't sure what Stella meant, but between them, they composed a message. It claimed that Hollie was a friend of Sharon's and would like to talk to him confidentially. She suggested meeting over a coffee, and that a weekday lunchtime might be the best option. Stella leaned over and pressed 'send' on Hollie's phone before she could change her mind.

"There you go," Stella said. "All sorted."

There was another matter which had been nagging in Hollie's head. As Stella was there, she decided to run it past her.

"Do you think Jonas will be there on Saturday night, at that awards ceremony. I mean, it's less than two weeks since the Comtesse was murdered, so the press will be all over him. And if they know I work for you, and therefore for him, they might get a bit inquisitive."

Stella reminded her that Jonas was not her primary focus on Saturday night, and she would be in disguise, so it didn't really matter if he was there or not. But she did accept that it was going to be a difficult decision for Jonas to make. On balance, they both assumed he would have to attend. He was probably contracted to appear at any major publicity event.

At last, Stella vacated her seat behind the desk. But Hollie remained by the window, otherwise it might have looked like they were playing musical chairs. She was also worried about what she was going to say to Graham when they met.

After Stella left the office, Hollie remembered her other question, the presence of the lawnmower on the day of the murder. She went out into the corridor, hoping to catch her, but Stella had already disappeared. Opening her phone, Hollie found the number for Maryam, but hesitated a moment before texting her. There was surely no harm in asking, and it could be something nobody else had thought about.

She pressed send, could see the message had been read almost immediately, but there was no instant reply.

Before Hollie could reclaim her seat and her desk, her phone had buzzed twice. The first message was from Graham. He said he was busy for the next couple of days but could meet on Thursday.

He suggested a Starbucks in the centre of town, at noon, if that was convenient for her. The second message was also from him, asking how he would recognise her when they met. Hollie replied, saying she would be wearing the brightest pink trainers he had ever seen, and that she had shoulder length blonde hair, styled in a bob. That wig might as well get a public trial before Saturday.

While she was working out exactly what she could say to Graham, her phone buzzed again. It was a text message from Maryam.

"Lawnmower left out by gardener on Friday. Wife pregnant. She'd gone into labour. It was a boy, 8lbs 4oz - but a good spot by you."

Thinking she had found a significant clue, for it only to be dismissed, Hollie slumped in her chair. The news that the lawnmower, and the gardener, were both innocent bystanders was probably not that big a surprise, nor was the fact that the police had already thought about it. She sat for a few minutes, wondering what she could do. Her press card was laying on the desk in front of her, so she rang Jonas's elusive agent, but an answerphone cut in almost immediately. Hollie repeated her request for an interview, but suspected Erica Whitely was not about to agree to one.

The only other thing she had to arrange, was an interview with Jonas. But as she wasn't even sure what she was going to ask him, that arrangement could probably wait until after the weekend, once he was back from the studios.

Hollie sighed, walked back over to the window, and stared at Mulberry Park. She decided to go for a walk, through the park and up to the street where Erica Whitely's house was situated. She couldn't bring herself to think of Jonas's agent as Erica, much in the same way that thinking of the Comtesse as Juliette felt a little too familiar; they hadn't really been friends. Erica Whitely's house must command a good view over the park, and Hollie wondered just how much she would be able to see from her rear windows, and whether she might even have seen Jonas on that Sunday morning.

She passed by Taylor's desk on the way out and stopped to have a word with him. The outcome of her meeting with

Graham might cause ripples and she thought he should know. He had appeared to be quite concerned on Sharon's behalf.

"Hi, Taylor, I was just wondering how long you have known Sharon?"

He continued to stare at his computer screen, his head nodding slightly, and Hollie wondered if he had heard her question. She was just about to repeat it when he finally spoke.

"Eight years, nine months and, I think, fourteen days. I'm not sure if you should count the first time you meet someone as day zero or day one."

She assumed they must have met at school as they were roughly the same age when she thought about it.

"Have you always liked her and looked out for her?"

"It was the other way round to be honest. She looked out for me – even though she was in the year below me. I was..." he hesitated, looking down at his knees. "I was bullied a bit. Actually, a lot."

"I'm sorry to hear that. So, that's what you're doing, returning a favour? There's nothing more to it than that?

She saw a smile creep across Taylor's face, like there was some kind of in-joke that she wasn't privy to.

"I think you might have been misinformed, or not informed in the first place. I'm gay. I have a boyfriend. We're engaged."

Hollie felt her neck flush. It would only be a few seconds before her face produced bright red cheeks worthy of a circus clown. She was about to apologise and realised that might sound wrong too.

"It's okay," Taylor said. "I don't suppose anyone thought to mention it."

She apologised for jumping to conclusions about his relationship with Sharon. Hollie couldn't understand how she could make such a stupid assumption. She had always been so careful about such things at school, but only weeks into a new job, she had managed to be unthinking, clumsy and have demonstrated unconscious bias.

"It's no problem," Taylor smiled. "I'll take it as a compliment. Sharon is a very pretty girl."

Once out in the fresh air, the tingling heat gradually dissipated from her cheeks, and she took a couple of minutes on a bench to regain her composure.

There were so many loose ends, and she doubted the police were doing any better. If they were, they would have arrested and charged Jonas by now. The strange message from the untraceable phone was one mystery. Who owned it, and why had that message been sent to the Comtesse? And Jonas's fingerprints shouldn't have been on her shoes, not if his description of their wardrobe arrangements was true. And why would he invent it if it were not true; it would only serve to incriminate him further.

Hollie wandered aimlessly into Mulberry Park. She had no particular purpose in mind but found herself following the route which led to Erica Whitely's house. Armed with her press card gripped firmly in her hand, she pressed the button for First Person Management and heard a faint buzz, somewhere inside the building. But the door didn't click open, no crackling voice came from the intercom panel, no footsteps echoed from a staircase to announce the imminent arrival of the resident.

Retreating down the steps to the pavement, Hollie stood, staring up at the windows, hoping that some insight might descend on her. The front door of the adjoining house opened. A woman came out, but only as far as the top step. Hollie glanced in her direction, fearing a challenge regarding her reappearance.

"I thought I recognised you the other day but couldn't place you. You're Mrs Parker, aren't you?"

Hollie recognised the woman from their previous doorstep encounter but had no idea where else she might know her from.

"I'm Tony Mordant's mum. God knows how, but you got him through his English exams, two years ago now. We met on a couple of parents' evenings, but I suppose you meet hundreds of parents, all thinking their kid is the most important."

A memory surfaced from somewhere, deep in the catalogue of students and parents she could happily forget. It was as much of a mystery to Hollie as to how Anthony Mordant had scraped a pass mark. And his mother had been even less memorable than her son.

"What are you doing up here, Mrs Parker? Are you looking for First Person Management?"

Hollie had to think quickly. It was quite likely that Erica Whitely might be a friend of hers. They did live next door to each other. There was an 'under offer' sign on a house a couple of doors down.

"It's Hollie, please. And I was looking for a place for my mother. She wants to move closer to us. I thought being near the park would be nice for her. The agent sent me details for a property, but I missed my chance to see it. Then someone told me this house might be going on the market soon and I just thought I'd take a chance and call."

"Did you not get to view number 6 before it sold?"

Hollie said she hadn't, that the possible move had only recently been discussed. The woman, who introduced herself as Wendy, invited her in to see what the houses were like.

"The grape vine round here is notorious. I doubt that Erica Whitely is thinking of selling, but we might be moving soon. My husband's been offered a post abroad and we're not sure what to do. We might even be looking for a long-term tenant if that would interest you. Come in, have a peek around."

She showed Hollie into the lounge, it had been knocked through into what would have been the old dining room, making a now huge open-plan space. Tall windows at the rear overlooked the park, but the view was partially obscured by trees.

"I'll put the kettle on. Would you like a cuppa? Why don't you have a look upstairs while I get it sorted. The bedrooms at the back of the house benefit from a wonderful panorama of Mulberry Park. Oh goodness, listen to me, I'm beginning to sound like an estate agent already."

Hollie smiled and asked if she was sure that would be okay.

"Absolutely. I feel like I know you already. You're not exactly a stranger who wandered in uninvited."

The staircase was pine, but old, stripped to bare wood and polished to a lustrous sheen. The whole house had a sense of bygone times, high ceilings, ornate cornices, and original cast iron fireplaces. It was a house Hollie could imagine living in herself.

The back bedroom on the first floor gave a spectacular view of the park. There were still areas that were partly obscured by trees, but most of the lake, and the paths around it, were clearly visible. If you wanted to know if someone was in the park, you might well be able to confirm it from there.

CHAPTER 20

Hollie was looking out Wendy Mordant's back bedroom window, lost in her thoughts. She had momentarily forgotten that she was a guest in someone else's house. Wendy's voice startled her, and she jumped as though she had been caught in the act of evaluating the curtains before stealing them.

"It is a wonderful view, isn't it, and I'll miss it when we leave. I've made tea. It's downstairs."

Letting go of the curtain she was holding back, but unsure what to now do with her freed hand, Hollie touched her earring. She followed Wendy out the bedroom and back downstairs, but not before casting a final glance over the park.

In the lounge, there was a tray with cups, a pot of tea, milk, and a small plate of biscuits.

"Does your mother live alone?" Wendy asked.

Having already forgotten her hastily created cover story, it took Hollie a moment to recover her composure. She only just managed to stop herself from revealing that her mother was dead, and she had never known her father. The tightness she experienced in her chest was a consequence of using her mother as an excuse, and she silently apologised to her. It was over ten years since her mother had died, but the memories of that day could still leap out at her with the least provocation. The newspaper reports on Mei Ling's death had caused a similar reaction.

"No," Hollie said, after what seemed like an interminable interval. "She lives with my stepfather, Bernard."

She instantly regretted making her lie even more complicated and had no idea where that name had come from. Students always made that same error when inventing stories for why they hadn't finished their homework. Keeping it simple was the best way to lie successfully. Wendy must have sensed an unease in her voice but hopefully misinterpreted the reason. She busied herself in pouring two cups of tea and slid a bowl of sugar lumps across the table. Hollie wondered how many people would still use lump sugar in their home, never mind owning a pair of sugar tongs. Wendy noticed her looking at them.

"They were a gift from a neighbour, last Christmas. Seems a shame not to use them, they're antique and probably quite rare."

"Was that whoever owns First Person Management? I noticed the name by the door and wondered what sort of business it was."

Wendy confirmed that her neighbour was the source of the gift and told her that Erica knew lots of famous people in film and television. Her face was even more animated when talking about Erica and her clients than it had been talking about the view.

"I've seen that Jonas Moon pop in occasionally, but he's getting to be quite famous, so I suppose he'll be keeping a lower profile in the future."

Wendy had made quote marks in the air when she mentioned Jonas's name, a gesture which made Hollie want to scream, and always wanted to ask those people why they didn't make similar gestures for full stops, commas, and question marks. There was a secret pleasure in knowing that Wendy had no idea just how famous, or notorious, Jonas might become. She wondered what words the air quotes might stress if he turned out to be a convicted wife murderer, or even a serial killer.

Hollie picked up a chocolate biscuit and managed to bite half of it off without dropping any crumbs. Having her mouth occupied prevented her from divulging any details about the case and inventing any more lies about her mother.

"He's quite a looker, that Jonas Moon. He used to live in a

flat, just up the road here. Then he married that condom queen and became famous. Oh dear, I shouldn't really speak ill of the dead, should I."

Wendy's monologue continued, allowing Hollie to finish her biscuit and take a sip of tea, which was scalding hot and tasted of cheap perfume.

"I hope you like jasmine tea, it's all I keep usually, unless I have decorators in."

"You said that Jonas Moon used to live near here? Did you know him then?"

This was news to Hollie. She hadn't thought to research Jonas's whereabouts before he married Mei Ling. Living close to Erica Whitely might mean they knew each other before she became his agent.

"We didn't really know him then. He was just another drama student, you can imagine what they're like, not really our type of people. A few of the houses here have been converted for multiple occupancy, terrible shame, but they don't usually cause any significant trouble. I got the impression once, from Erica, that she and he were, well, how can I put it delicately, quite closely acquainted."

Hollie stayed for another twenty minutes, expressing her own admiration for Jonas, as an actor, and confessing that she had once met the Condom Queen. Even with that revelation, there was little more of use to be found out. Wendy was vague about when, or how often, Jonas visited Erica. She didn't really know much about how they met, claiming that it was mostly neighbourhood gossip, not to be trusted, and she should probably not have mentioned it in the first place.

"Anyway," Wendy said, in way of an excuse, "I volunteer for two different charities so I'm rarely around during the day, and I haven't really seen them together myself, not as such. In fact, that reminds me, I am due to attend a meeting this afternoon, so I really ought to be sorting a few things out. I'm so sorry if I'm hurrying you, but time seems to have sped by."

She put the teacups and sugar bowl onto the tray and was ready to take it back into the kitchen. It was obviously a heavy hint for Hollie to leave. Wendy turned back to face her when she reached the lounge door.

"Should we exchange phone numbers? Just so that I may contact you if we do decide to sell or lease our house."

Once again Hollie took a second to recall her cover story and didn't respond before Wendy took the opportunity to expand her argument.

"I do so dislike estate agents. That whole process of being examined and assessed like some sort of common commodity."

Within a couple of minutes, Hollie found herself back on the street, being seen off by Wendy from her front door. She realised she hadn't asked about Wendy's son. It seemed only polite to do so.

"By the way, what is Tony doing now?"

There was a long pause before Wendy answered. Hollie watched as she stood a little straighter, a little stiffer. Her face lost whatever humour it had previously shown.

"Given the weather, probably weeding the prison vegetable garden."

The door closed without a single extra word being spoken by either of them. Hollie walked back in the direction of Mulberry Park, wondering what series of events had resulted in a dull, but otherwise harmless, boy ending up behind bars. A modicum of responsibility could never be dismissed from her mind when a former pupil ended up in trouble. Between colleagues, they would blame the parents, peer pressure, society, government policy, underfunding of social services, but most felt they might have missed an opportunity to set someone on a better pathway. She decided to look up Tony's story, if only to assuage her own underlying sense of guilt.

No significant revelations had emerged concerning Jonas or his agent, except, possibly, the early and somewhat carnal beginnings of their social and professional relationship. But

Hollie was also curious about how easy it would be for a young actor to secure an agent. Maybe chance had thrown him close to Erica Whitely, and guile had guided his actions. He was, it had to be said, a very good-looking man. And Erica Whitely would have been a useful and powerful ally. Maybe his success was down to that age-old adage of who you knew and who you slept with.

Hollie thought she remembered Marcus having a friend who was an actor, so sent him a text while she was walking back through the park. He responded almost immediately, asking if it was to do with the Condom Queen's murder. Hollie told him it might be, and he said he would ask his friend and get back to her asap.

When Hollie arrived back in reception, a little warm and grateful for the comfort of an air-conditioned environment, Sharon had just transferred a call to Stella. She took off her headset and beckoned urgently for Hollie to come closer. She was grinning and almost bouncing up and down on her seat with excitement, clapping her hands like a child who has spotted the perfect birthday present. Even before Hollie reached the desk, Sharon blurted out her news. This time it didn't seem that she minded who might overhear.

"Graham is going to take me shopping this Friday afternoon and Stella's said I can have the day off. We're going to choose a ring. He said diamonds are traditional, but he thinks a sapphire would go better with my eyes. He's such a silly romantic."

It sounded like it should be good news, and Hollie might have accepted it as such, if she hadn't been in receipt of Taylor's research. Trying to be tactful, and honest at the same time, she chose her words carefully. Hollie said what an unexpected and extraordinary turn of events it was. Only when Sharon had settled back to a state of simple euphoria, did she try digging for a little more detail.

"I realised the other day, when you showed me that ring, that you never told me how you and Graham met in the first place. I wondered, have you known him a long time?"

The answer surprised Hollie. She had assumed Sharon was in her early twenties, but she claimed to have known Graham for almost seven years. Either she had estimated Sharon's age incorrectly, or Graham was a child snatcher.

"We met on a sort of holiday. Well, not really a holiday, it was a residential course, for creative writing. It turned out we were both completely useless and we sort of bonded over just how hopeless we were. We even got told off for giggling too often."

It was quite a lot of information to take in. From the little she knew of Graham, the image of him giggling just wouldn't come together in her head.

"I don't suppose you're able to set a date for the wedding as Graham is in the process of getting divorced?"

Sharon's cheeks flushed when she explained that they couldn't talk dates just yet, because of the loveless marriage in which Graham was trapped.

"He told his wife their marriage is over and asked her for a divorce. But he hasn't mentioned me because she gets terribly jealous and might refuse to cooperate, simply out of spite."

Hollie said it all sounded very complicated and messy.

"Graham is too caring, too much of a softy. He doesn't like causing waves and she's totally unreasonable. But it all works out in the end. That's what Professor Pangloss taught Candide."

Hollie was surprised by the reference to Voltaire, but she had said that she met Graham on a writing course, so maybe one shouldn't judge a receptionist by her nail varnish alone.

Sharon went on to explain that Graham's wife had booked a winter holiday without even asking him, when she knew of his dislike of cold weather, and he had to cancel it. Hollie foresaw a tricky meeting approaching on Thursday. Sharon was in full confessional flow, and it was difficult for Hollie to find a gap where she might make an excuse and escape to the sanctuary of her office.

"It's not like Graham even likes skiing. He'd much prefer to be reading a book or laying on a beach. He told me as much. We're very similar in so many ways."

Fortunately for Hollie, her phone pinged, and she was able to use it as an excuse to move away from the reception desk and Sharon. She pushed the button for the lift, praying it would come quickly. It must have been there already as the door opened immediately. The text was from Maryam, asking if they could meet. It said there were matters they needed to discuss. As she stepped inside the lift, she remembered the mirrored walls and closed her eyes.

She only opened them when she heard the doors swoosh and clunk, and stepped out with her eyes firmly fixed straight ahead. Hollie closed the door of her own office behind her and leaned back against it, the small simple room had become a safe and quiet space. She looked at the room properly, maybe for the first time. The view from the window was pleasant, but not spectacular. Stella had exaggerated its quality for some reason. The walls bore a few marks from where posters or maybe a calendar had been hung. The bookshelves were only sparsely populated with remnants from the room's previous occupier; they were not even books relating to law.

She pulled one randomly from a shelf. It was a self-help guide for making friends in the workplace. The rest of the bookshelf comprised of a few computer-related volumes, probably one of them for the model sitting on her desk, a couple of curious books on codes and cyphers, and one on programming languages. The bottom shelf was entirely populated with what looked like a complete set of well-thumbed Terry Pratchett hardbacks, a slightly incongruous sight given the technical nature of the other inhabitants. Hollie backed out of her office and walked straight to Taylor's desk.

"Have I stolen your office?"

"I didn't really like it," he replied, his eye's never leaving the screen. "I prefer it out here. I see more people."

Hollie wasn't sure whether he was being polite or honest.

"But is it okay if I leave my books in there for now? Stella said they'd look odd if clients saw them out here, and I like to read at lunchtime."

"No problem. As long as you're okay with me taking over your old office."

"I used to sit in there alone, all day sometimes. I never spoke to anyone unless they had a problem. I'm more in the swing of things here."

Hollie knew what he meant. The small office had some qualities of a prison cell, an enforced personal space. She had a sudden longing for the staff room at her school, even with the perpetual moaning about things that would never change. She decided to buy a pot plant to cheer the place up, a large one, maybe two or three, and a picture to cover the marks on the wall.

"You can read in there anytime you want, when I'm not there, which is most of the time."

Taylor smiled. He looked almost like one of her students when she'd given them an unexpected, good mark for an essay.

Hollie's phone pinged. It was Marcus. His friend had said that as a young actor, there were four ways to get an agent. Be related to one, blackmail one, sleep with one, or be born to the right parents.

Hollie smiled. Her money was on number three.

CHAPTER 21

Soon after arriving home that evening, another message announced itself on her phone with a cheerful ping. It was from Maryam this time. Hollie had just poured herself a glass of wine. Before reading it, with the glass in one hand and her phone in the other, Hollie carefully lowered herself onto a sun lounger in the back garden. Maryam wanted to meet at ten the next morning, in the same café as they had met before. It was intriguing, but that was tomorrow. She took a sip of her wine, put the glass and her phone on a small folding table beside her, and decided to take a break from everything. She lay back and closed her eyes.

The next morning, Hollie arrived at the café ten minutes early. The same waitress as before wiped her table down and asked quietly if she would be paying by cash or card today.

"I will be paying by cash. I haven't forgotten."

The waitress smiled. Hollie half expected a jingling sound to accompany the facial movement. She wondered if Maryam would be concerned that the waitress recognised her as a police officer. Maybe it had been a guess. It was probably best to mention it just in case Maryam wanted to change their meeting place or be more guarded about who might overhear them.

A bell hanging over the café door tinkled, an old-fashioned sound and one that reminded Hollie of her childhood. She glanced at her phone to check the time; the numbers flicked to a one and three zeros precisely as the door closed. Maryam appeared to be one of those people who were habitually punctual. She probably frowned on anyone with a more flexible approach to time keeping.

Once they were both settled with coffee, and the waitress was back behind the counter, Hollie took the opportunity to warn Maryam.

"I thought I should tell you; she knows you're with the police."

Hollie indicated who she meant by flicking her eyes back towards the waitress. The girl, and her silver armour, was still looking at them.

"You mean Grace? Of course she does. I have cautioned her on several occasions, but she always wriggles free."

"Really? What for?"

"Nothing that serious, not so far, petty theft, nothing violent – despite the way she looks. Her aunt owns this café. I'm not sure who else would employ her."

"Maybe a scrap metal dealer?"

Maryam tried to laugh whilst taking a sip of her coffee. It turned into a coughing fit and Grace brought over a couple of spare paper napkins. She dropped them on the table and retreated without saying a word.

"She thinks I'm a reporter," Hollie said. "For a newspaper, I suppose. I haven't corrected her."

Maryam recovered her voice and suggested it might be best to set the girl straight.

"Grace is someone you might find useful. Although if you quote me on that, I will deny I ever said anything of the sort."

When Hollie asked how she could possibly be useful, she learned that Grace was not just any thief, she was one of the best lock pickers Maryam had ever encountered.

"We've never been able to nail her for anything significant and believe me, we've tried. By the way, how does your coffee taste?"

Hollie frowned, took a sip, and said it tasted fine. Maryam smiled.

"She likes you."

"How do you know?"

"Because mine is usually made with yesterday's used grounds. At least, I hope that's why it tastes like it does."

When Hollie pressed her about why she would ever need the services of a thief, Maryam simply shrugged and changed the topic. She asked, almost offhandedly, whether Hollie was aware of any unusual messages that the Comtesse might have received prior to her death.

Hollie focussed on her coffee cup, turning it so the handle was positioned for her left hand. She stirred it again, buying time to think. Stella had said not to offer information which might incriminate Jonas, but not to lie if directly questioned. It was like walking a tightrope.

"The Comtesse did mention a strange text message, but she said she didn't recognise the number it came from. I don't think she was overly concerned about it."

Maryam pressed harder, and Hollie admitted that she had read the message, and taken a note of the number it had come from, but she hadn't copied the text so couldn't confirm exactly what it had said.

"We need to be honest with each other if this relationship is going to work." Maryam took a breath before continuing. "We have had a close look at Jonas's phone. We found a tracker app on it. Is that something you might know about?"

Hollie studied her coffee cup again before replying.

"I believe the Comtesse might have installed it on his phone. She was a very cautious person as I understand, wary of being deceived." Hollie looked up to meet Maryam's eyes. "I had access to the tracker, but there was nothing to see of importance. Nothing unusual in his activity, other than his phone was hardly used, not even turned on most of the time. I presumed he didn't want to be disturbed when working. That's why I never mentioned it. It didn't seem relevant."

Maryam's face didn't give anything away. She kept looking at

Hollie, waiting for her to add to her story. It was the same trick Hollie had used with students, when she would wait until they felt they had to break the silence. She knew the method, and it wasn't going to work between two equally stubborn women.

"Okay," Maryam said, taking in a long breath and leaning back in her chair. "If the phone that sent that message to the Comtesse is switched on again, we'll find it. We have an alert set up for it."

Hollie wasn't sure whether an element of trust had been established, or a barrier had come between them. An inside line to the police investigation was always going to be a valuable connection, in this or any future case.

"Juliette has a brother," Hollie said. "His wife, or partner, I'm not sure exactly what their relationship is, well, she has a bruise and some scratch marks on her arm. Her name's Kendra if that helps."

Maryam gave nothing away. Hollie couldn't tell whether she didn't react because she had pursued this already. Hollie tried to explain why it had struck her as significant.

"There's a lot of money involved with the Colby Group. Benedict Colby will inherit the majority of the Comtesse's estate. At least, I understand he will. I met him last weekend. Although he claims not to be interested in money, I don't know if the same is true of Kendra. And I only have Kendra's word for Benedict's lack of interest in the inheritance."

Hollie described the marks on Kendra's arms in detail. She said they looked like they had been caused by fingernails, gripping her tightly, maybe defensive wounds she suggested. Were all those police dramas she had watched, providing the right vocabulary, or was she sounding like an idiot.

Maryam leaned forward, her arms resting on the table. She spoke quietly, meaning Hollie had to lean forward to hear her.

"You didn't hear this from me, remember that?"

Hollie nodded, and Maryam told her that they had already spoken to both Benedict and Kendra Colby, and they were married. Not only did they claim to have been home, in bed, that Sunday morning, but Benedict had confessed to causing the bruises on Kendra's arm.

"Forensics photographed the bruises and are of the opinion that they don't match Benedict's hand size. She, however, claims they were acquired during her work with problem students, which does seem to pan out – she deals largely with society's rejects."

Maryam went on to admit that she was not totally convinced by either of their stories but, for the time being, her DI viewed those injuries as irrelevant.

She asked Hollie if there was anything else she could think of, something she hadn't shared, something that could be important. When Hollie shrugged, Maryam emphasised that she wouldn't want to be found withholding evidence from the police, Hollie felt a hot flush creeping up her neck.

"So, nothing else at all?" Maryam prompted.

"Honestly, no. Not that I can think of." As far as it went, Hollie's statement was accurate. She had lots of suspicions, but no facts she could share with Maryam. "If I do think of anything, I'll message you, straight away."

Hollie couldn't help but think about Stella, and how well Maryam must know her. A chill formed in her tummy, as though she had just swallowed an ice cube, or maybe a small iceberg.

Maryam nodded a couple of times but didn't say anything more. She pushed her cup towards the centre of the table, stood, looked at Hollie again for what felt like several minutes, exhaled loudly, as though disappointed, and walked out of the café. Ten minutes had gone by, and Maryam's coffee was left almost untouched.

Hollie closed her eyes and tried to focus her thoughts. She couldn't face going into the office. If she bumped into Stella, she wouldn't know whether to mention her meeting with Maryam. She would have to tell her that they had found the tracker app, the one that Stella didn't want to know existed. The chair opposite her screeched against the floor. Maryam must have returned to interrogate her again.

"I'm sorry," Hollie said. "There's nothing more I can add."

Hollie opened her eyes when there was no response. Grace had taken up position opposite her. She was leaning forward, sniffing Maryam's coffee cup.

"You're not actually a reporter, are you?" she said.

"And you're not just a waitress, are you?"

"Fair enough. I have talents other than serving coffee."

Grace asked if she was a snitch, a CI, a police informant. It took plain language for Hollie to understand her meaning.

"Oh God, no, nothing like that. I'm a private investigator.

It was the first time she had introduced herself as anything other than a teacher and it didn't feel convincing.

"I didn't know that was a real job. You, like, follow people for a living?"

Hollie thought for a second or two, not certain exactly what her job entailed. She hadn't followed anyone yet, but she had lingered around a few people.

"Not so much follow, as observe. Do you ever do jigsaw puzzles?"

Grace looked at her as though she'd asked if she ever murdered babies.

"You see, I'm employed to try to find little pieces of information and then put them together to reveal a bigger picture. Something we can then all recognise."

Hollie thought it sounded rather good when she put it like that. At the same time, a bizarre idea was forming in her mind.

"You steal things, don't you?"

Grace hesitated before answering.

"I might occasionally have been accused of being in possession of items which did not, strictly speaking, belong to me. I prefer to think of it as redistribution of wealth."

"Have you ever broken into a house?"

"I don't break anything. I don't need to."

Hollie asked Grace if she knew anyone who could be trusted to get into a house, search for a specific item, but then leave it where they found it.

"What would be the point of doing that?"

"I suppose they could redistribute a few other items, more valuable things. In fact, it might be a good idea if they did, but not too much."

"It sounds like you have a plan, crazy investigator woman."

It was half a plan, and Hollie wasn't yet ready to put it into action, but Grace might prove useful if she got to that point.

"You can call me Hollie. Tell me, how long have you known DS Chandra?"

"Long enough for us to appreciate each other's point of view."

Hollie smiled. She no longer thought Maryam had chosen this café because of its decor. Grace had skills which Maryam couldn't employ, but maybe she could. This meeting place had been chosen because Grace worked there.

They exchanged numbers, Hollie giving Grace her personal number. She wasn't confident that her new work phone didn't have additional software embedded in it, like a tracker app, and there was nobody she could safely ask to check.

After those two curious conversations, Hollie decided to take the rest of the day off. She had a difficult meeting with Graham fast approaching, and at the weekend, she was playing the role of both waitress and stalker.

When Oliver came home that evening, he found Hollie at the kitchen table, once again slumped, half asleep. Her head was resting on one arm, which in turn was covering printouts of newspaper articles, wiki pages and celebrity news websites. She lifted her head when he asked how she was.

"I think I might be a magnet for paperwork."

"You don't have to stick with this job if you're not enjoying it. Stella will understand, she'll have to."

Hollie sighed, picked up her glass of wine, and stared at the pieces of her jigsaw.

"But that's just it," she said. "I am loving every minute of it."

CHAPTER 22

Early the next morning, Hollie messaged Stella to say she wouldn't be in the office until later, reminding her of the lunch meeting she had with Sharon's boyfriend.

Stella didn't respond, so Hollie sent a further voicemail, suggesting they ought to have a chat about the outcome of her meeting and discuss any subsequent action they thought they should take. She asked if there was any chance Stella might be free later in the afternoon as news of the meeting might get back to Sharon.

By the time Hollie left home, she still hadn't heard from Stella, which was unusual but not of any great concern. Her morning, spent in her home office, had been consumed with endless searches for anything about Graham Dankworth. His name had struck Hollie as unusual when she first heard it, but there were far more results from an online search than she had expected. The newspaper archives, quite tedious to trawl through, had revealed nothing at all. The Graham Dankworth she was interested in didn't appear to have any social media presence, wasn't newsworthy and had nothing happening in his life that interested the cyber community. Just before she left home to meet him, she remembered that she had told Graham he would be able to recognise her by her hair style. She rushed upstairs for her new blonde wig and, not wishing her neighbours to see her wearing it, folded it carefully into a carrier bag and took it with her.

She had arranged to meet Graham in a branch of Pret-a-Manger, a suitably anonymous location where nobody would give them a second glance. She arrived twenty minutes early and went straight to the restroom to don her disguise. Checking her reflection in the mirror, she felt a tsunami of self-consciousness sweep over her. She believed everybody was going to know she was wearing a wig.

As she stood in the queue at the counter, Hollie could feel that familiar warmth creeping up her neck that forewarned of an embarrassing blush. She purchased a Danish pastry and a coffee and made her way to a corner table with a good view of the door. Her tummy was rumbling, either with nerves or hunger, so she broke off a piece of pastry and popped it in her mouth. The café was gradually filling up with its lunchtime crowd, mostly looking bored and impatient, but thankfully all uninterested in her.

She studied the men's faces, trying to spot Graham from the picture Sharon had shown her, and from Taylor's description. Piece by piece her Danish pastry disappeared, until there were only tell-tale flakes left on a serviette. She had eaten so quickly that she unexpectedly hiccupped. One woman turned to look at her, smiled, and returned to nurse her bowl of salad. How she was going to conduct a serious interview with hiccups and a red face was beyond her.

Hollies 12oz chai latte was still untouched when she spotted Graham loitering in the doorway. When she saw the dithering lone figure, there was no doubt in her mind. Two people had to squeeze past him before Hollie raised a hand to attract his attention. It still took him a couple of nervous scans of the room to notice her during which time he was jostled by several more impatient customers. Graham didn't notice them, simply allowing himself to be pushed one way then another.

Once he saw her waving, he broke into a surprisingly huge grin and waved back at her. In his eagerness to reach her table, Graham weaved between customers in an uncoordinated shuffle. He bumped into one woman, causing her to spill her coffee, apologised profusely and tried to mop the woman's hand with his handkerchief. But she quickly withdrew it, leaving Graham flapping his handkerchief in mid-air, as though surrendering.

When he finally arrived at Hollie's table, he was red in the face and started to sit down but had only managed a half-crouch before he began to stand up again.

"I ought to buy a drink or a meal or both I suppose. Can I get you anything?" He had frozen in a sort of half bowing position like a polite Japanese businessman. "You are Hollie, aren't you?'

She nodded and was immediately aware of his peppermint scented breath as a sigh of relief drifted across the table from him. She declined his offer, pointing to her almost untouched drink. Graham started to weave his way back towards the counter. The woman he had previously bumped into, saw him coming. She lifted her cup just before he reached her, and once more bumped against her table.

Hollie watched him at the counter, comparing him to the other male customers. He was dressed in an ill-fitting, slightly creased, brown suit and shock white trainers. And Graham was short, no more than 5' 5" she estimated. A taller, slimmer, younger man might have been able to carry off such a look, but on Graham it suggested unemployed status, a beggar maybe who had scraped enough pennies together to buy himself a treat. Sharon must be an inch or two taller than him, even without her habit of wearing four-inch heels. Graham's waistline also suggested an unhealthy familiarity with donuts. His hairline, as hinted at in the theme park photographs, was not so much receding, as in full retreat.

He represented a strange choice of partner for Sharon, and Hollie was intrigued as to where the magic lay, and how she had fallen so heavily for such an unusual looking man. Graham returned a few minutes later with a black tea, a bowl of fruit salad, and a granola bar, all balanced on a small tray. The woman at the next table saw him coming and executed a rapid change of seats. In the end, Graham made it back to Hollie without further mishap. Once he had unloaded his tray, he looked around for somewhere to put it. Finding nowhere, he put everything back on his tray and sat down. He obviously felt it necessary to offer an explanation for his choice of lunch.

"Sharon says I'm not overweight, that she loves me as I am, but I think I need to spruce myself up a little, and maybe lose a few pounds."

He patted his tummy in way of explanation. It responded with a jelly-like motion under his shirt. Hollie chose not to comment. She should have chosen fruit too, rather than several hundred calories of pastry, not to mention the chai latte. She was wondering how to start this conversation, or interrogation, when Graham beat her to it.

"You work for Patterson Wilkins, don't you? Sharon told me you've been really helpful, vis-a-vis the misunderstanding with Stella."

This wasn't how the meeting was supposed to start, but Hollie adjusted her approach.

"We like to see ourselves as an extended family, all looking out for each other. In fact, that's one of the reasons I wanted to have a little chat with you."

Graham nodded rigorously, which distracted Hollie because his hair attempted to restore itself to a more natural location. Graham, in a habitual gesture, smoothed a few long strands of hair back into place.

"You must be worried that I'm not a suitable match for Sharon, or that I'm leading her astray, being married and all that. Maybe you see me as some sort of lothario?"

That wasn't the word on Hollie's lips, although it had been in her head. Seeing Graham as some sort of Svengali or Casanova, even a father figure, was difficult to imagine.

"We do share a lot of interests you know, Sharon and me. We both love books, and creative writing, that's how we met in the first place. Has she told you that story?"

"She did mention it, yes, the writing course."

Graham went on to explain, in some detail, how he had always wanted to be a writer, a weaver of tales. After he met Sharon, he went on several more writing courses, hoping to impress her as his skills improved.

"It's all got rather complicated really. That's why I was so glad when you said you wanted to meet."

Hollie decided to say as little as possible, Graham was obviously quite capable of carrying on a conversation without much input from her.

"I have, sort of, become a bit of a success story, and I have never found the right time to tell Sharon. Also, I might need some legal help and I know you're a law firm, but I don't know if you do contract law. I'm not even sure if that's exactly what I need. It's all got a bit more complicated than I expected."

When Hollie asked him exactly what the problem was, he looked around at the other diners, leaned forward, and whispered as though they were spies exchanging top secret information.

"I want a divorce, so that Sharon and I can be together, properly, legally, married if she'll have me."

"Well," Hollie said, "I'm not a lawyer, but I'm sure the firm has someone who can handle that for you."

He explained his home situation in some detail before asking Hollie what her role was at Patterson Wilkins. Hollie still couldn't bring herself to use the word *investigator*. She said that she checked things for the firm, describing herself as a sort of researcher. He looked at her, his eyebrows raised a little, and asked if she had been researching him. When she didn't answer immediately, his face broke into a grin. He looked several years younger when he smiled and almost interesting.

"You didn't find much, did you, apart from Karen and the kids. But knowing my online identity might have helped. It's the Shargrays. Most people probably assume it's one person behind it, but it's really a couple, Sharon and me, but of course she doesn't know anything about it yet."

Hollie was no wiser. If anything, she was getting more confused the more he told her.

"I've just been made an offer, three to be precise, for a series of books. But although I have an agent, I don't have any legal representation yet. And I haven't written anything either, well, nothing suitable for a book, unless I can simply duplicate my online content. But apparently that doesn't matter. They can get a ghost writer to work with me."

Hollie was mentally connecting the pieces of an entirely new, and unexpected, jigsaw puzzle. One that couldn't possibly belong to the man in front of her, although he claimed it did.

Graham explained that he had started posting on social media about eighteen months ago, mainly about romantic fiction, but also posting on themes from teen fiction. He'd used his nickname from school because he felt it gave him more freedom to express his thoughts, or his and Sharon's thoughts.

"Nobody wants to read about romance from a near thirty-year-old, bald, nobody. You see, my full name is Graham Dankworth, a bit of a mouthful, so the other boys in my year just called me Gray, they said it suited me. I knew it wasn't a compliment, but what can you do? The nickname even followed me to university."

There was a lot for Hollie to unpack in the stream of information Graham was downloading. Apart from his nickname, his age had genuinely surprised her. His hair loss probably made him appear older than he claimed, and his choice of clothes did nothing to dispel that illusion. But she wondered what the Shargrays might be posting that a publisher would be interested in, and how it could have generated the kind of offers he was suggesting.

"The offers have come probably because I have close to five million followers."

That last piece of information, delivered with Graham leaning across the table, and proffered in a conspiratorial whisper, was the most surprising. To Hollie, it sounded like a large number, but as a teacher, she had avoided engaging in social media so didn't know how significant that figure might be, or how to respond.

"That sounds quite a large number of followers. It's impressive."

"I've had several meetings with my agent. She says she can get me a book deal, maybe a tv series, even a movie option. It's all happened very quickly."

Hollie asked how his wife felt about this potential success. Graham's whole demeanour changed. His face, previously soft and squidgy, set into a rigid stare. He said his wife didn't deserve to share in his success, that she had always made fun of his literary ambitions and that he had not even mentioned the Shargrays to her.

"Sharon believed in me. I want to share all this with her. But I need advice. Quite a lot of advice, I think."

Hollie said she would consult with Stella over the best way forward, if that was what Graham wanted. He asked her not to say anything to Sharon yet, that he was meeting her on Saturday and would tell her everything then, explain the whole online thing.

"I should have told her already. I want Sharon to be the public face of the Shargrays, I want her to be completely involved in it, I want everything to be in her name. I don't think people would want to see me as the creator, and I'm not, not by myself."

Graham took two phones from his satchel, opened one to check something, and started typing rapidly with his thumbs on the other. It was a strange sight. A slightly dowdy adult, with thumbs that danced over a keypad with the dexterity of a twelve-year-old.

Hollie's phone pinged immediately. There was a new message, from a previously unknown number, obviously Graham's second phone, as it was identified as belonging to the Shargrays. A blush crept up Graham's neck as she looked at him. He reminded Hollie of strawberry and vanilla ice cream as the flush of blood blended with his otherwise pale complexion.

I've included links to our social media feeds too. They're sort of transcripts of the conversations Sharon, and I have, and a few simple animations I've drawn."

"I suppose I should have the agent's name," Hollie said, "just for the records."

Graham's thumbs performed a quick jig on the screen and Hollie's phone pinged again. A name, and a phone number, appeared in her messages. She voiced the name out loud as she read it.

"Erica Whitely."

"Do you know her?"

"I've heard of her, in another context." Hollie wasn't sure what else she could, or should, say.

Graham checked his watch and said he really ought to be getting back to work, as he only had an hour for lunch.

Hollie realised she had no idea what Graham did for a living, but it didn't feel like the right time to ask, and it didn't seem to be that relevant. When he left, she reached for her drink, only to find it was cold, she drank it anyway. Listening to Graham had given her a thirst. Before heading back to the offices, she sent another message to Stella, even though the first two still hadn't been answered.

CHAPTER 23

Sharon was on a call when Hollie returned from her lunch meeting. She had one hand half covering her mouth and the microphone of her headset. She was speaking almost in a whisper. Hollie only caught a few repeated goodbyes, and possibly a kiss sound, as she walked over to Sharon's desk.

'Was that Graham by any chance?"

"Er, yes. I'm not really supposed to take private calls, but it's been very quiet today, and I didn't think it would matter this once. You won't tell Stella, will you?"

"Of course not. Is she in her office?"

Sharon said that she hadn't seen her all day, or any of the other partners, that was probably why it was so quiet. Hollie asked it any of them specialised in contract law.

"That's a strange coincidence. Graham just asked me the same thing. I think he must have a friend at work who needs some advice. He said he couldn't tell me any details right now, but that he'd explain it all at the weekend. We're able to meet on Saturday, his wife's going to see her mum and taking the children, so we can have some time together, Graham and me that is, not me and his mother-in-law."

Sharon's explanation was so convoluted that she had forgotten the question by the time she had finished. Hollie had to ask her again about contract law before she said Mr Wilkins was probably the best one to talk to.

"Would you like me to see if he's free tomorrow? I could leave him a message; he usually checks his voice mail first thing."

"No. It will keep until next week. It might be better to leave it a few days, and I have a couple of phone calls to make first thing tomorrow."

Hollie smiled, raised a finger to indicate she was going upstairs, and started to back away from Sharon's reception desk. But escaping her on what was obviously a dull day was not that simple. Sharon was intent on sharing overheard gossip about a row Taylor and his boyfriend had had over his obsession with trying to sort out everyone's life except his own.

"How did you overhear that?"

Sharon put a finger to her lips and pointed to her headset with the other hand.

"Sometimes I forget to turn off my link when I put a call through. Accidentally of course. I never do it on purpose."

Hollie shook her head and told Sharon she was a very naughty girl. She pressed the button to summon the lift, remembered the mirrors, and told Sharon she might take the stairs as she needed the exercise.

Once alone in her office, with the door closed, she rang Erica Whitely, choosing this time to use her official work phone. While it was ringing, Hollie realised she couldn't mention Graham as he wasn't a client of theirs yet, so she shouldn't know about his potential contract. A voice said hello, and Hollie pressed red to end the call.

"Idiot," she mumbled, and held the button down to turn her phone off completely.

She stared at the now dark screen, wondering what she could say if the elusive Erica Whitely called her back. She could always mention Jonas, as his agent she would know about the Comtesse's murder and the resulting bad publicity if the police leaked Jonas's name as a suspect. No newspaper would dare print it yet, but word would spread, and his career would probably be in jeopardy.

Hollie turned her phone back on. There were no messages, no missed calls, no texts. She breathed a sigh of relief and felt her adrenaline levels subside. Her heartbeat gradually returned to normal, and the tension eased from her shoulders. Hollie enjoyed less than a minute of tranquillity before the screen on her phone lit up and it trilled cheerfully. She checked the number. It was Erica Whitely returning her call.

"This is where you earn your keep," Hollie muttered to herself. She answered the call with all the confidence she could fake.

"Hi, you must be Ms Whitely? I'm sorry, I pressed the wrong button when I called just now and accidentally cut you off. So stupid of me."

After explaining who she worked for, but not precisely in what capacity she was employed, Hollie said she was trying to help Jonas Moon in this difficult period. The woman was polite, well spoken, and said she would, of course, do anything she could to help.

"If only we hadn't had to postpone our meeting I could have vouched for the dear boy. But I'm sure the police will find whoever was responsible. I expect such a wealthy and influential woman as the Comtesse would have any number of enemies."

Hollie tried to arrange a meeting with her, but Erica apologised and said she had a rather full diary for the next several days, appointments she simply couldn't break. She had insisted on first names, explaining that her business was all about personal trust, but reaffirmed that she just couldn't see how she could help. A meeting with Hollie was obviously not going to make an imminent appearance on her to-do list. Hollie asked if she would ring her if an opening did appear in her diary and thanked her anyway.

There was no connection Hollie could see between Jonas and Graham. The fact that Erica Whitely was an agent to them both, must be a simple coincidence. She wandered out of her office in search of Taylor. He was, as always, staring intently at his computer. Although, on this occasion, he was slumped in his chair, pinging rubber bands at the screen.

"Would it be foolish to ask what you're doing?"

Taylor shrugged and swivelled his screen round to face Hollie. There was an animated cartoon face of a teenage girl. Behind her was a similar illustration of a boy with scruffy, spiky hair.

"Who or what is that, or them? And what have they done to deserve your passive aggressive anger?"

"There's nothing passive about my anger. And they are 'The Shargrays', or someone is. And whoever is behind it is a social media phenomenon. And my idiot boyfriend thinks they're amazing. "

Hollie didn't say anything. She couldn't reveal what she knew, even though Taylor would find out very soon.

"So, why do you have a problem with her, them, whatever?"

Taylor said he didn't have a problem with her, or them, specifically, but with the rumour that whoever was behind it was about to secure a gold-plated book deal.

"It's not like they have any special talent. And it's just a stupid cartoon, not even a very special one. It could be anyone. It could be some creepy old man, a pervert."

"Well, they must have something going for them, and I can't see a publisher giving that sort of deal to a pervert. Tell me," Hollie asked, pointing to a figure at the top of the screen, "is that the number of followers they have?"

Taylor nodded. Even with his undoubted skills, he hadn't yet discovered the identity behind the Shargrays, or maybe he hadn't bothered to look. Hollie wondered how he would react when Graham Dankworth became a client, and his identity was revealed. Taylor turned his screen back to face him and pinged another rubber band at it. She decided to have a word with Stella and suggest the real identity of the Shargrays might be restricted to as few people as possible. Obviously, Sharon would know, and with her capacity to chat it would be unlikely to remain a mystery for long. Maybe it would be wasted energy, it might be better to make a formal announcement and deal with any fallout.

Hollie's body felt drained of energy. She had another Parkrun, and now an award ceremony to attend on Saturday. The supper with Kendra and Ben had somehow slipped her mind. She texted Peter to ask if they were free on Sunday, for a barbecue, rather than Saturday for supper. Sent a similar message to Kendra and Ben and cursed again at her lack of organisational skills. Marcus and Peter would understand, but Kendra and Ben were a complete unknown. There was no way she could avoid the awards ceremony, and she didn't want to, it sounded like fun. A smile crept over her face at the idea of being in disguise again, being blonde again. The whole subterfuge thing was much closer to what she had originally signed up for.

"What are you smiling about?" Taylor asked.

Hollie told him she had just remembered something. She backed away from Taylor, mumbling about a party and having lots to do. At the top of the staircase, she heard another rubber band hit its target and a big sigh from Taylor.

Sharon was still at her desk, examining her nails, when Hollie returned to reception. Sharon held up the fingers of her left hand.

"I just broke a nail. So annoying."

"Do you know where everyone is? I've been trying to contact Stella all day, but she hasn't replied to any of my texts or messages.

"Well," Sharon said, staring into space as if the answer might have been projected on the wall opposite her. "Mr Patterson is in court; he'll be there tomorrow too. Mr Wilkins is probably in his office, hiding. He rarely comes out of it. I think the poor man is a little bit of a recluse nowadays."

"What happened to the thing about being on first name terms with everyone?"

"To be honest, I've never really felt comfortable calling the partners Rupert and Stephen. I don't mind calling Stella by her first name; she's different, but not Mr Patterson and Mr Wilkins."

Hollie reminded Sharon that she was looking for Stella.

"She was here first thing. Sort of in a fluster, not really like her at all. Then she went out, about twenty minutes after I arrived."

When prompted for more details, Sharon confessed that she had no idea where Stella was, and she had been a bit vague about when she might be back.

"There was nothing in her diary, maybe it was something private."

When they were friends, in the school holidays, and even at university, Stella would often not be in contact for days, occasionally weeks, but since Hollie had started working for her firm, they had spoken every day.

In her car, before driving home, Hollie checked her phone again. There was still no word from Stella. She sent her yet another message, just two question marks, and her fingers hovered over Jeremy's name. But what if she asked him, and Stella was doing something she didn't want Jeremy to know about, like having an affair, or covering up a murder.

Hollie couldn't imagine a motive for Stella to have murdered the Comtesse, but that didn't mean there wasn't one. She started the engine and pulled out of the underground car park. On the way home, she thought about the job and how Stella had been so keen to recruit her. Hollie's simple, steady, teaching career already felt like a lifetime ago. But it could probably be easily rekindled. Gordon would almost certainly take her back if he hadn't yet found a replacement. And there was always Jean Carpenter and Pirton Lane.

When Hollie arrived home, she was surprised to hear the television already on and the commentary from a cricket match coming from an open window. She found Oliver ensconced in the lounge with a bottle of beer and a large bag of crisps.

"What are you doing home at this time? And watching cricket?"

"Relaxing. What does it look like?"

She positioned herself between him and the television, hands on hips, head tilted to one side, waiting.

"Okay," he said, "we had to evacuate the building, five fire engines arrived with sirens going, very exciting, but it turned out to be a false alarm. Now, any chance I can watch the next over?'

"And I've had a very stressful day too. Thank you for asking."

Oliver put his beer down and turned the television to mute. But he didn't relinquish his crisps or turn the picture off.

"Okay, I'm listening, what's happened?"

It was tricky to describe how a lunch meeting with Graham Dankworth, aka the Shargrays, could be described as stressful. So Hollie focussed on the other oddity of her day.

"Stella's disappeared."

"Kidnapped? I hope she treats them gently."

Hollie sat heavily on the sofa, next to Oliver. She rested her head on his shoulder. Oliver turned off the television.

"Okay, tell me all about it."

"I'm probably being stupid. Jumping to conclusions. And I have absolutely no justification for what I've been thinking."

Oliver told her he always trusted her intuition and to tell him exactly what was worrying her. But there was nothing Hollie could put into words which would accurately reflect her unease.

"Stella's not replying to any of my messages, nobody seems to know where she is, and I'm nowhere nearer to proving Jonas is innocent. And I don't know, maybe he isn't."

"Well, Stella has an alibi of sorts. She was with us when the news came through. I know she's a pretty cool sort, but I can't see her murdering someone, then turning up to a barbecue as if nothing had happened. Anyway, what would her motive be?"

Hollie didn't reply. She knew Oliver must be right. At least, she hoped he was. He suggested she take a day off, just like Stella had probably done.

Friday morning, long after Oliver had left for work, Hollie managed to drag herself from her cosy bed. She shrugged a dressing gown round her shoulders, even though it wasn't at all cold, and trudged downstairs.

The coffee machine gurgled and spat while she watched it, bleary-eyed, and still half asleep. Ten minutes staring at the garden, plus a decent caffeine hit, gave her brain time to come out of its comatose state.

She had decided she wasn't going to go into the office, but she couldn't waste the whole day staring at a lawn now lacking its familiar stripes. Hollie wondered just how well she really knew her best friend. They met frequently for coffee, chatted about old friends, new friends, and work colleagues. But Hollie didn't enquire too deeply about Stella's private life. Her involvement, however tenuous, with a serving police officer had come as a complete surprise.

Stella was one of the most intelligent people she had ever known, but she was also a free spirit, capable of acting spontaneously, impetuously, even rashly. Was an affair with a client impossible? A wealthy, influential, charismatic, older woman might have appealed to Stella. But surely, she couldn't be capable of murder. Hollie's phone trilled. The unexpected sound made her jump, and the dregs of her coffee leapt out of her mug and onto the arm of her dressing gown.

"Stella?"

"Why sound so surprised? Sorry I missed you yesterday, but I'm here all day if you want to drop in for a chat?"

Hollie hesitated. She wasn't sure that she would like the truth, even if she could find out what that was. Worse still might be lies. She checked the time.

"I could be there by twelve, if that's okay?"

"Perfect. See you then."

Stella hung up immediately and Hollie's phone went dead. She threw her dressing gown in the washing machine and set it on rinse.

CHAPTER 24

Hollie took her time to eat a leisurely breakfast of toast and peanut butter, accompanied by a large mug of tea. She was in no rush to see Stella and there was some research she wanted to do before she left for the office.

Whilst nibbling on her fourth slice of toast, smothered in a thick layer of butter this time, the jar of peanut butter having been exhausted, she found and began to explore the Shargrays online presence. With occasional restorative sips of tea from a second mug, Hollie was drawn into the short videos posted by Graham.

He had constructed complex histories for his fictional couple, the details of which were only gradually revealed through casual asides. Even though they only appeared as animated characters, both with larger-than-life eyes, the Shargrays were both interesting and amusing. They were made with sketchy, freehand line drawings, which came to life remarkably well. There was an abundance of frizzy hair on the female character, called Shar, and a comb-over on the man, called Gray. Hollie had only the vaguest idea how animation was made. The shaky lines and apparent simplicity probably disguised some quite sophisticated and laborious production techniques.

All the characters did was discuss what was going on in their lives, presumably inspired by Graham and Sharon's real-life conversations.

The main voice was that of the young female, but the vocabulary, syntax and language was not typical of the teenage girls Hollie had taught. The Shargrays were extremely articulate and most of the content was them discussing books, films, and whatever was in the news. But they avoided contentious issues like politics, gender, and international disputes.

The posts and content were eclectic, but charming and honest. She could see how the Shargrays could appeal to a broad audience.

In an introductory video, which Hollie had to track back to find, the site's authors claimed not to be photogenic, and to be rather shy. Having met Graham, she wouldn't dispute either of those claims in regard of him, but Sharon was both photogenic and quite outward going.

Hollie was still surprised that Graham had gathered such a large following, until she realised that she had just spent more than an hour listening and being amused by his characters. She was in danger of being late for her meeting with Stella.

The washing machine started to bleep persistently, demanding her attention. Hollie was convinced it must have been designed by a man, as a woman would have invented an audio warning which was far less irritating. Hollie bundled the damp washing into the tumble drier and set it going. She tucked her notebook and pen into a capacious shoulder bag and rushed out of the house to get to her meeting with Stella.

When Hollie arrived at work and climbed the stairs from the carpark, she found the door to reception area wedged open. It was probably against fire regulations but must have provided a welcome cooling draught in reception on a hot day.

Sharon obviously didn't hear Hollie arrive due to her gum shoes making no noise on the stairs. She was staring intently at her computer screen and jumped when Hollie said hello.

"Oh my God. I didn't hear you come in. Are you practising sneaking up on people?"

"Sorry. I didn't mean to make you jump. What were you looking at?"

"Oh, just this thing online that all my friends are talking about. They're not even real people, the ones in the posts, well, probably not, but not anyone you can recognise. Although they do talk about the same stuff that Graham and I talk about."

"It's not the Shargrays you're watching, is it?"

"Yes. Are you following them too? Of course, you taught English didn't you, so it's probably your sort of thing. And their names are almost a mash-up of ours, Sharon and Graham, and they call each other Ess and Gee, which we did on the writer's course when we first met. Someone noticed that everyone's names started with a different letter and ours stuck."

Hollie wondered whether she should have revealed that she was familiar with Graham's online presence.

"Sort of," Hollie was blustering. "But not really. I don't follow them. Do you know if Stella is in yet?

"Yes. She said, if you came in early, to send you straight up to her office as she's not doing anything special."

Before Sharon could ask her anything else about the Shargrays, Hollie sought refuge in the lift. As soon as the doors closed, she remembered the mirrored walls and cursed.

Stella's office was situated in a corner of the building. It had two windows, one looking across a side street, the other with a view of the leafy square onto which the main façade of the offices faced. You might not be able to see Mulberry Park, but the room was larger than the bed-sit they had shared for a year at university.

Stella came out from behind her capacious desk and pointed to one of two facing sofas.

"Let's make ourselves comfy. Coffee? Tea? Too early for wine, but I have some chilling it you fancy being a bit naughty. It is almost twelve?"

Hollie had the sensation that she was about to be interviewed, given bad news or pressed into keeping a secret. She hoped this wasn't a gentle way of telling her that the job wasn't working out. She opted for tea, green, no sugar. The offer of wine was tempting, but she needed a clear head if she was going to successfully navigate whatever Stella had planned, and maybe mine her for answers to some other questions. Assuming this wasn't the goodbye speech, Hollie decided to get in the first punch.

"Where were you yesterday? I was trying to reach you most of the day."

Stella had her back to Hollie, but she could see it stiffen slightly. Was it the sign of an impending lie, or bad news? Stella's shoulders had relaxed by the time she brought two cups and saucers over and placed them on the low table which separated them. She was a professional lawyer of course, and quick to adjust.

"I was with Maryam, trying to determine what stage the police are at, vis-à-vis Jonas."

"And that took a whole day?"

"Maryam didn't want us to be seen consulting with each other. I do have a rather high profile and she, of course, has many colleagues in the area. People might have recognised us if we'd loitered around town, and word could have got back to her superiors."

She went on to explain that they had decided to meet at her and Jeremy's seaside retreat.

"But that's miles away. You do mean the one at Burrows Sands?"

"We only have the one holiday home, my dear, in this country anyway. We simply thought we'd make a day of it. You know that little seafood restaurant on the harbour. Well, we had the most amazing lobster salad for lunch. We must take you and Oliver there again. Next time you come down with us for a weekend, we'll book it, to be sure of a good table."

Hollie recognised something in Stella's voice, or maybe it was the speed she was talking. She was, without doubt, concealing something. When you have known someone for a long time you get a feel for their patterns of speech, and Stella was being exceptionally formal.

"You two are only friends, nothing more than that? I did get that right the other day, didn't I?"

Stella fidgeted with some papers on the table, squaring them up, then standing to put them on her desk. She also found several other things to adjust once there.

"We're still friends," Stella said, with her back turned to Hollie. "Maybe," she hesitated, "a little more than friends."

Once she had let her guard down, Stella admitted that she and Maryam had enjoyed a mutually beneficial exchange of information and opinions, which included an update on DI Gilroy's plans and a quiet afternoon in the cottage.

"Which didn't involve the bedroom?"

"Do you have to be quite so direct, Hollie, so intrusive? But yes, if you must know all the details, we may have had a little rest and relaxation amid the more professional exchanges."

Hollie didn't need or want to hear any more of what had gone on. She picked up her teacup, but it was too hot to take more than the tiniest sip, a token break in the conversation, allowing Stella to switch the emphasis.

"What I can tell you is DI Gilroy is planning to arrest and charge Jonas on Monday. He is only being held back by the reservations of the criminal prosecution service, which fortunately gives us a little breathing space. Hollie wondered how far Maryam and Stella's friendship had rekindled, and whether it was going to impact on her own, much more mundane, relationship with Maryam. She looked down at her own hands, debating whether it was pertinent to pursue details of their relationship, or whether it was simply her own prurient curiosity.

"I presume you two weren't seen together?"

"Absolutely not."

"Then I suppose that side of things is not really any of my business.

Stella sat on the sofa opposite Hollie and leaned back into the cushions. She mouthed a 'thank you' as their eyes met.

"So," Stella said in a brisk, let's change the subject tone. "Tell me how that meeting went with Graham. Has he agreed to heed our advice regarding the delicate situation with Sharon, and reconsider the focus of his affections?"

"Actually, he wants our advice in a professional context, as a client."

Stella's eyes, already large, widened even further as Hollie recounted the details of the Shargrays, and the tsunami of online followers she/he had gathered, and Graham's honourable plans for his future with Sharon.

"And Sharon knows nothing at all about this Shargrays business?"

Hollie nodded. They both shared some reservations about what Sharon's reaction might be when she found out. Hollie thought she would take it in her stride, being so besotted with Graham and believing in him so wholeheartedly. Stella voiced some doubts, but Stella was a cynic who considered love no more than another four-letter word. Stella suggested that a man pretending to be a couple online might carry some rather awkward PR repercussions.

"They will have to be very careful how the reveal is handled. Nothing stays secret forever. But I presume that's the publisher's responsibility."

They both shared the same opinion, and neither was confident that crediting the whole concept to Sharon would prevent the true origins from emerging. Hollie's cup was cold when she finally remembered she was thirsty. Green tea was not a favourite of hers, but she was determined to shed a few pounds, no matter what Oliver said. She had decided that a change of career was also the right time to change her dietary habits. She grimaced and put the almost full cap back on its saucer.

"Coffee?" Stella asked. "Cream and sugar, and a biscuit maybe?"

"Milk, and just half a spoonful of sugar please, but no biscuit. And am I that transparent?"

Stella made her a fresh coffee and, when she sat down again, leaned forward, bringing her to within whispering distance of Hollie.

"Oliver hasn't developed a wandering eye, has he?"

"Of course not. It's just me. Oliver would never cheat on me."

"Shame," Stella said, grinning. "I thought I might be in with a chance."

Hollie closed her eyes but smiled too. Stella could never remain serious for very long. How she managed to stay calm and negotiate some of the huge divorce settlements she handled was a total mystery.

"Are you never serious about relationships?"

"Only where money is involved, not about sex.

Stella grabbed her hand and dragged Hollie to her feet. She said she wanted to see the Shargrays website or blog or whatever it was that was so popular.

"We need to do it on your computer. I don't want anyone knowing I've been looking at things like that."

"There's nothing risqué about it, and you do know you can delete your browser history, don't you?"

Stella picked up Hollie's coffee and led the way out of her office, still talking as they walked down the stairs.

"I've never trusted those things. You'd be amazed at what Taylor can find when we need him to."

They settled themselves in Hollie's cosy office. Ten minutes later, Stella said she was singularly underwhelmed with the Shargrays, what they had to say, and what she called very childish and amateurish cartoons.

"Who reads this stuff?" she asked.

"Close to five million people, at one time or another."

Stella abandoned the computer and went over to the window. She was obviously still very enamoured by the view.

"We could swap offices if you'd like," Hollie suggested. "I could probably make do with all that space you have."

"I do actually envy you," Stella said wistfully. "Maybe not your office, but the simplicity of your life, and Oliver, and your pretty little house."

"Like I said, we could swap. I don't mean Oliver, of course. He's mine."

Stella didn't respond. Hollie knew she wasn't serious, just having one of her 'Stella' days, as she used to call them when they were younger.

"What about tomorrow? "Stella asked without breaking her thousand-yard stare."

"You mean, the award ceremony? It's all sorted. I have my disguise ready, tried and tested. I just hope Jonas doesn't recognise me."

Stella asked if she had bought a wig, and when Hollie described it, she demanded that Hollie wear it to work one day so they could all see her as a blonde. She also gave her a more detailed description of the wayward man she was going there to observe, and a name for the co-writer.

"They'll all have name badges, I suspect, or there will be a table plan or something like that. Anyway, we need a detailed report, the odd picture wouldn't go amiss, and make a note whether the couple in question leave together and at what time."

Stella was still staring out the window, as though part of her mind was somewhere else.

"Are you okay? You don't seem to be yourself today."

"Sometimes I wish I wasn't me; I mean not this version of me. It would be so much easier if I could start life all over again and get rid of some of the complications."

"Like Maryam?"

Hollie thought she heard a very quiet 'Mm', but then Stella pointed at something through the window.

"Are they doing it, in the park, in public? Surely not."

Hollie went to see what Stella had spotted, but it turned out to be a couple helping each other with stretching exercises before they started a run. Stella was disappointed.

CHAPTER 25

When the alarm clock rang, only a few inches away from Hollie's ear, she groaned, reached out without opening her eyes, and pressed the 'snooze' button. She was certain another five minutes in bed wouldn't do any harm.

"Morning, sleepy head."

Oliver's voice was coming from the wrong side of her. She opened one eye to see him place a mug of tea on her bedside table.

"What are you doing up already? It's Saturday, isn't it?"

"I thought I might join you on the Parkrun this morning. Give my legs a bit of a stretch."

Hollie groaned again and wriggled up until she was sat, back propped against the headboard.

"Okay. But why?"

"I thought it might be fun, and you're not the only one who thinks they could do with a bit of exercise and body toning."

With her mug of tea clasped firmly in both hands, Hollie closed her eyes again and took a sip. She had been dreaming when the alarm went off, but only had the vaguest memory of what it was about, something to do with shoes and red wine. She blinked her eyes a few times. Oliver was already dressed in shorts and a lightweight hoody.

"You are actually serious, aren't you, about running today?"

"I was reading yesterday about someone who went from couch potato to marathon runner in under six months."

Hollie groaned and closed her eyes again. Once Oliver had an idea in his head, it was unlikely to go away, but she wouldn't mind his company and encouragement. The Parkrun had initially been a means to an end for her; she never intended to become an exercise freak. And now that she had mentally ruled out Kendra, and probably Ben too, as a potential murderer, there was no reason to even go on the Parkrun.

"You do know you need to register and get a barcode?"

Oliver held up his hand to show a wrist band with a barcode on it. He was, as always, more organised than she had been.

Thirty minutes later she was up, showered and dressed. And a plate of scrambled egg on toast, prepared by Oliver, had been cut into pieces small enough that her stomach might not reject them that early in the morning. Hollie had slightly over-indulged on wine the previous evening and wasn't sure she should be driving, never mind running.

"Can we take your car, please? I'm not sure I'm sober enough to drive."

They pulled into Mulberry Park's main entrance and found a spot to leave Oliver's car. Almost as soon as he had turned the ignition off, Kendra and Ben pulled into the space next to them.

Kendra was driving, and waved to Hollie as though they were old friends. Once introductions had been made, Kendra drew Hollie to one side, whispering to her.

"I have no idea what you must have thought last week. I hadn't realised those scratches and bruises showed quite so clearly. They don't usually, and I noticed you looking at them.

"I didn't think anything about them," Hollie lied. "But how did you get them? They looked painful."

Kendra explained that in her role at Pirton Lane, she specialised in helping some of the children with more complex needs.

"Between you and me, they can be a bit of a handful at times. An occasional bruise or scratch comes with the territory. Sometimes, I blame anything like that on Ben, it's my warped sense of humour, and he goes along with it just to see how people react. But I usually know not to do that with people who don't know me. It gets sort of awkward talking about work sometimes. Confidentiality and all that."

Ben had overheard the end of the conversation and interrupted, saying that was why he married her. He quickly added that he was referring to her sense of humour, not the fact that bruises weren't so obvious with her colouring. Ben was stammering when he realised his explanation could have been misinterpreted.

"In reality, Kendra's much more likely to leave the bruises on me. Physical or emotional." He closed his eyes and sighed. "And I'm not serious about that either. Maybe I should just keep my mouth shut for a while."

"And, of course, that's how he learned to run so fast," Kendra added, before she hugged him and kissed him on his cheek.

Hollie wondered if they had put on this sort of performance when interviewed by the police. It would explain Maryam's conviction that the marks on Kendra's arm were not connected to the Comtesse's murder.

The four of them made their way towards the start point and agreed to meet at the end of the run for a coffee.

"My God," Ben exclaimed." Look at those two. They have to be raising money for a charity dressed like that."

It was Peter and Marcus, both at their second meeting were dressed in lurid matching outfits. Marcus was effusive in greeting them. Peter hung back a little, possibly embarrassed by their apparel.

"Do not say a word about my outfit! Peter muttered. "The way I suffer for my love."

"Oh, shush, Peter," Marcus insisted. "You know you have that flamboyant alter ego budding inside you. I'm just helping you blossom."

Kendra greeted them both like old friends, until Ben reminded her they only had a few minutes until the start of the run. When they both started on stretching exercises; Peter and Oliver joined in. Hollie could see the competitive edge creeping in between her husband and the more experienced runners. Part of her wanted to join in the exercises too, it did make sense to avoid unnecessary injury, but she now felt embarrassed about her lack of flexibility. Marcus sidled up to her, nudged her gently with his elbow.

"There's nothing very flattering about these warmup routines. I think I will risk a torn muscle rather than display my body in that sort of pose."

Hollie knew exactly what he meant. She felt at least eight pounds heavier when she had looked at herself in the mirror that morning.

There was a whistle, followed by a PA system producing an agonising screech of feedback. A man with a microphone started to explain to newcomers how it worked. At the end of his introduction, he said there would be a brief countdown before the run started. There followed a repeat of the numbering and recording procedure for registering times, and the more eager entrants clustered around the start to set off almost together.

The run itself was uneventful, other than Oliver taking off as though there was a cup for the fastest newbie. Hollie jogged around keeping Marcus company. There was no way she was going to race against anyone, and she didn't want to pick up an injury as she would be working at the awards event that evening.

"So," Marcus said, after the field thinned out and they couldn't be overheard. "What about those photos you were going to show me?"

Hollie had forgotten her promise to show him the scene of crime pictures. She was not sure how she thought he might help but wondered if there was a clue somewhere that everyone had missed. And it might be in the detail of those images.

"I have them on my phone, my work phone. I don't have that with me, but I'll show you tomorrow, at the barbecue. I don't think I ought to email them to you as I'm not sure that I'm legally supposed to have them. You are coming tomorrow, aren't you?"

She had left all the arrangements to Oliver. Her new job had dominated Hollie's brain to the extent that the cancelled dinner and substitute barbecue had almost slipped her mind until that moment.

"When have you ever known me to miss a party. Especially one with murder photographs."

"They are a bit gruesome. Are you sure you want to see them?"

"If you had seen some of the stuff that's been emailed to me over the years, you would know that nothing shocks me any longer."

Hollie said she might try to catch up with Kendra, just to check on the barbecue and apologise again about tonight. Marcus said he believed there might be an ice cream with his name on it. He slowed as the route brought them close to the dam end of the lake and made a half-hearted effort to run on the spot, pretending to warm-down, before seeking a convenient bench. His face was pink from exertion, and it clashed with his outfit, a disaster far greater than being unfit in Marcus's world. He held Hollie's elbow while he recovered his breath.

"Go on, my dear, run like the wind," he panted. "Leave this ageing pouf to recover his dignity."

"You are not old, Marcus. Peter told me you're younger than him and he's two months younger than me."

"I am an old soul, my dear Hollie, carved by the winds of time from ancient stone, but I need to sit, these shoes are definitely not me."

Hollie smiled as Marcus turned his head to one side as though weary of life.

"Give a boy the right shoes and he can conquer the world."

"Marilyn Monroe?"

"She is my spiritual sister."

Hollie laughed as Marcus once again had tweaked a quotation to fit his own situation. As she set off running again, she wondered if he hadn't inadvertently said something significant. She felt there was something about that red shoe, something so obvious they had all missed it? Her immediate plan though was to catch up with Kendra, but she proved to be both too far ahead and probably much too fast for Hollie to chase. She jogged the remainder of the course by herself, still trying to grasp what they might have missed.

Hollie was still running easily, still feeling surprisingly fresh, when she approached the finishing gate and was handed a token. Oliver, having tried at first to keep up with Ben, then Kendra, had only finished a handful of places in front of her.

He was still doubled over, trying to catch his breath when she joined him. Hollie rested a hand on his shoulder and bent down to whisper in his ear.

"Not so easy, is it?"

"It's my shoes, I don't have proper running shoes."

"You don't have proper running legs either, but I quite like them."

She patted Oliver's bottom, leaving her hand in place somewhat longer than necessary. If anything, his face was an even deeper shade of red when he pulled himself upright.

"There you are," Kendra said as she appeared from behind them. "How was your first Parkrun?"

"Brilliant," Oliver responded, almost too eagerly.

When Peter and Ben joined them, Hollie checked that they were all coming to the barbecue the next day.

"What was the problem with tonight?" Kendra enquired. "If it's okay to ask."

"Just work, something came up, an event I had forgotten I had to be at."

"I thought you were a teacher, English, so Peter said."

Oliver, having regained his composure, took up the explanation.

"My wife is now a trainee investigator for a law firm."

"Not so much an investigator," Hollie said, not wanting to reveal too much. "More a fact checker, for pending cases, but it is a bit of a career change and a steep learning curve."

Kendra was fascinated and wanted to know what she was investigating and whether it was dangerous. Hollie told them about the awards dinner that evening and how she would be there to observe someone who might be cheating on his wife.

"Now you have to tell us who," Kendra insisted.

"Which law firm?" Ben asked.

Hollie said she really ought not to be talking about it, that she was still, technically, a teacher and that her new job was more like work experience than a real job.

"Who knows what I'll be doing come the new school year. I may even be at St Edmund's."

Hollie wasn't sure how to change the subject but was saved when Marcus appeared, grasping the back of his thigh.

"Oh, my God, my leg."

He was hopping on the other leg and whimpering with pain. Ben reacted first, getting Marcus to lay on his back and straighten his leg. Ben lifted it onto his own shoulder and pushed Marcus's heel up and his knee down. The expression on Marcus's face was a mixture of surprise and admiration.

"Goodness, Ben," he said. "I never knew you felt that way or swung that way either."

"Shut up and try to relax."

"Exactly what my first boyfriend said."

"A little more pressure," Ben said, "and I might do some serious damage."

Marcus was about to respond, but Peter told him not to say anything more.

Hollie took Oliver's arm, turning him towards where their car was parked.

"See you all tomorrow," she said, over her shoulder. "About three o'clock, no need to bring anything."

Marcus made a miraculous recovery as soon as he deemed Hollie to be a safe distance away and not susceptible to any further questions. He waved from his prone position and Hollie heard him asking Ben if he had ever thought about taking up physiotherapy professionally.

CHAPTER 26

While Oliver was driving them home, Hollie took a phone call. It was the friend of Stella, the one whose company was providing the catering for the awards ceremony that evening. She introduced herself as Kate and apologised for not having been in contact earlier, saying she had been a bit busy arranging everything.

After running through how Hollie should dress, basic black skirt or slacks and black shoes, flats were better as she would be on her feet all night, she told her what time to arrive and gave her directions to the rear entrance of the building.

"There's not much parking for staff, so much easier if you can get someone to drop you off or get a taxi. Message me when you get here, and I'll get you badged up and cleared through security. They're very fussy about these things nowadays."

The outfit wasn't a problem. Hollie had a black pencil skirt and suitable shoes. Kate apparently would supply her with a blouse and an apron upon arrival.

"I've told the rest of the staff that you work for a production company and you're doing research for a new reality television show. That was Stella's idea. She's a mad-crazy woman, but you can't help but love her."

Whenever someone said they loved Stella, Hollie always wondered in what context they were using that word.

After a quick lunch and a long bath to ease some aching muscles, Hollie got ready for her first proper under-cover assignment. Flat shoes had been standard workwear as a teacher, so she had several pairs to choose from. The blonde wig came out of its box for a second outing, and after a little thought, she opted for simple stud earrings and minimal make-up. Nothing that would cause her to stand out from the other staff.

Late that afternoon, Oliver drove her to the rear entrance of the hotel, making her promise to wait inside until he arrived to pick her up. She rang Kate to say she was there, gave Oliver a quick kiss on the cheek, and got out the car. She had to gesture at him to make him leave. Oliver mouthed 'take care, I love you' before he drove off. She took a deep breath and turned towards the rear door of the hotel as she heard it open.

Kate was a tall slender woman, not much older than her, but with lines showing at the side of her eyes and a generally busy demeanour. Her hair was tied in a ponytail, and she wore a baseball cap with her company branding on it. After introducing herself to Hollie, she bustled her into the building.

"Sorry, we've not much time to chat, I need to keep everyone on their toes."

Kate took her to a changing room, and gave her a choice of three blouses to find one that was a fit, all black, all with the same red logo Hollie had noticed on Kate's cap.

"I'm not really sure what you're doing, or what you need, but I thought you could just wander round, filling up people's glasses, as long as you don't get in the way. Does that sound okay?"

Hollie apologised in case she was being a nuisance and promised to try not to ruin the evening. "I worked as a waitress when I was studying, so I should be able to manage okay without pouring wine over anyone."

"Please don't. There are going to be some expensive gowns on show." Kate didn't sound amused. She left Hollie to change and shouted instructions to someone before she was halfway out of the room. Hollie only reacted after the door had closed and she was alone.

"Remind me not to take up working in catering if this investigator gig doesn't work out."

With her new blouse buttoned up, and a black apron tied round her waist, Hollie checked her wig in a mirror, never confident it was on straight. Taking a deep breath, she opened the door and found her way into the main auditorium. Kate and another woman were making final adjustments to the place settings and checking name cards against a clipboard her assistant was carrying. She looked up and saw Hollie, checking the names on one table.

"When you're done, why don't you pop into the kitchen and introduce yourself to everyone. I would do the honours myself but as you can see, I have my hands full right now."

Hollie nodded but didn't say anything as she didn't want to distract Kate from her task. Behind the scenes, in the kitchen, were a dozen or so people. A handful were busy prepping dishes, but most were chatting, taking it easy before the onslaught of guests. Hollie expected a frosty reception, but the back story Stella suggested made her instantly popular, everyone relished to chance to appear in a new television series. Hollie maintained a denial of any details which only seemed to convince everyone of her authenticity.

Some ten minutes later, to Hollie's relief, Kate reappeared in the kitchen. The atmosphere became more serious, champagne was poured into tall flutes on circular trays, and four servers were dispatched with them to greet the guests. Hollie followed them out and took a position to one side of the auditorium which gave her a clear view of her target, a man called Mathew Frost. Kate appeared beside her with a large white napkin and an opened bottle of champagne.

"Here you go, your first task," she said. "You now have a reason to circulate. They're a thirsty group, this lot, always are. Chauffeured cars and taxis give them an excuse to drink until they can't hold the glass any longer. It will only be a minute before some of those are empty. There's red and white wine on the tables already. Keep it flowing, if you can. We make a good profit on every bottle consumed."

Hollie moved randomly around the tables, keeping half an eye on her target and the two women either side of him. The other writer, that his wife suspected him of having an affair with, was seated directly opposite Mathew Frost. She couldn't see how anything compromising, or revealing, was likely to happen until they left.

Spotting a guest with an empty glass, Hollie approached him from the side. He was talking to the woman next to him and didn't see her.

"More champagne, sir?"

He put his hand over his glass and turned towards her.

"I'd like some fizzy water if you have any?"

They both recognised each other at the same time. Graham had seen her in her blonde wig before, but she had never seen him, or could have imagined him, in a dress suit and bow tie.

"Are you still spying on me?"

"No, absolutely not. This is just a coincidence. I had no idea you'd be here."

"Is your presence to do with the Comtesse. Sharon told me all about that business. Jonas is over there, with his agent, well, she's my agent too. Is he a suspect?"

Hollie had noticed Jonas's name on the table plan but hadn't realised that his agent, the elusive Erica Whitely, might also be there. She asked Graham to point her out, and he said it was the woman on Jonas's right.

She had the appearance to Hollie of a well-preserved forty-something. Either Jonas had a taste for older women or, more likely, a penchant for women with influence and power.

"She has very expensive taste in shoes," Graham said. "Not much change out of two thousand for that particular pair."

"I didn't know you were an expert in shoes?"

"I recognise Louboutin when I see them. Most people are familiar with that brand, if only for the red soles."

Hollie was staring at the agent's feet, trying to get a clear view of her shoes. They looked very similar to the pair the Comtesse had been wearing when she was murdered. It couldn't be a coincidence. Erica Whitely must have chosen them on purpose, maybe to attract the attention of Jonas.

Graham touched her elbow to get her attention. Hollie's thought process was interrupted.

"I presume you're double tasking," he said. "But is there any chance you could get someone to bring me some fizzy water. I don't want to drink too much wine, just in case I have to say something later."

Hollie apologised and asked Graham if he was nominated for an award for the Shargrays. He laughed and told her he was there for his day job, for his work in an animation studio.

"Well, good luck anyway. I'll see if I can do something about that water."

Slipping back into the kitchen area, Hollie asked whether there was fizzy water available and was told it should be on the tables already. When she said there wasn't any on table eight, Karen overheard, thrust a couple of bottles at Hollie, and asked her if she could check all the tables for both fizzy and still water.

"I know you're not really here to work but it will help me and give you another reason to circulate."

After supplying Graham's table with both fizzy and still water, Hollie checked all the others. It was only that one table which had been missed. She lingered for as long as she dared near Mathew, the man she was there to observe, but didn't see or hear anything relevant or incriminating, but she supposed they would have to be careful not to reveal themselves in such a public arena and with so many cameras around.

To avoid being recognised, even though her wig gave her a very different look, Hollie approach Jonas's table from directly behind him. He was subdued, certainly not the life and soul of the party, and hardly gave her a second glance. On closer observation, Erica was maybe only in her early forties or even late thirties. Her skin was in poor condition for her age, possibly from too much sun, but her husky laugh also suggested a long and unhealthy relationship with cigarettes. Hollie made a mental note to do a little more research on sunscreen products for herself. It was impossible to get a close look at Erica Whitely's shoes as her feet were tucked neatly back under her chair.

Hollie took a position at the side of the auditorium where she could keep an eye on Jonas, Erica, and the possibly errant husband. Mathew Frost didn't appear to be at all interested in the women at his table, and Hollie was beginning to think she was going to have nothing to report.

The supper went on for over an hour, only ending when a couple appeared on stage and a round of applause broke out amongst the guests, rather loud and accompanied by whistles and cheers. A long introduction was followed by jokes, which Hollie assumed an insider would find funny, and eventually the first award was announced, and the winning names read out.

Four of the people on the table where Mathew was seated, rose, and made their way to the stage. Her suspect also stood, but only to move three places to his left. He leaned in close to a woman with very short hair and large round glasses who had been poured into a plain, black trouser suit. The plunging neckline of her jacket left little to the imagination, but there didn't appear to be very much of her to reveal. Hollie tried not to stereotype students at school but sometimes those thoughts crept into your head uninvited. The woman didn't look as though she was trying to appeal as any typical male-fantasy stereotype.

Whatever Mathew Frost said to her, possibly about the interminably long acceptance speech, made her giggle. Hollie moved slightly closer, to give herself a better view of them, and saw the woman's hand slide across his thigh. They were both looking at the stage and the presentation, but their minds were obviously somewhere else. Hollie took her phone out, carefully zoomed in on the critical action, and took a couple of photos.

She felt like a cross between a voyeur and a paparazzi, and hoped the white cloth over her arm was doing its job of concealing her phone from general view. Pretty much every guest had been snapping away during the evening, but it was probably frowned upon for staff to do the same.

She was just in time. A ripple of applause accompanied the winners back to their table and, although her target remained in his new seat, all hands were now above the table and above suspicion.

The presentations continued, one obscure award after another, most of them meaningless to Hollie. Even Graham, along with two others from his table, were called to the stage and came away with a small silver microphone on a solid wooden base.

Jonas Moon was nominated for an award for providing the most creative voice-over. Hollie had never heard of the short film that was cited and, while Jonas was making his acceptance speech, her attention drifted back to Erica Whitely.

The agent had taken a phone from her bag. Hollie assumed she was going to take a photograph of Jonas's moment of triumph. But she began to type a message instead. It was a slow process as she used a stylus rather than her fingers and thumbs. She stopped typing, her lips moved as she re-read the message. She tapped the screen again, presumably sending it on its way.

Her behaviour became even more intriguing when she produced another phone, checked it, smiled, and put it back in her bag. The first phone was then wiped carefully with a napkin and left, face down, on the table.

Hollie remembered her primary reason for being there, but kept an eye on that phone, now residing between Jonas and Erica. It stayed there for the remainder of the evening. Over the next half hour, she managed to photograph a couple more inappropriate moments between Mathew Frost and his strange paramour.

The event wound to a raucous conclusion. There was little

more to observe regarding the illicit couple who had tactfully separated at some earlier point. The phone Erica had been using was still on the table, exactly where she had left it.

Jonas noticed it after Erica had stood up, her attention turned to the other guests in their group. He picked up the phone, tapped the screen a few times and it lit up. He frowned, shook his head, and grabbed Erica's elbow to stop her moving further away.

Hollie edged as close as she dared, trying to catch their conversation, but she only heard Jonas's last comment.

"It's not happening Erica. It's done, finished."

Erica stared at him, no emotion showing on her face. She opened her bag and Jonas dropped the phone in it. Hollie realised that only Jonas's fingerprints would be on that phone but had no idea what significance that might have.

CHAPTER 27

Hollie was exhausted by the time Oliver arrived to collect her. As a thank you to Kate, she had helped with the clearing up, but only after loitering near the main exit and getting a photo of Mathew and his co-writer getting in a cab together. Sharing transport could have a perfectly innocent explanation, but not so innocent when combined with the evidence of their earlier intimacy.

"So, did the evening go according to plan?" Oliver asked.

"I suppose so. But it's a strange affair if you'll excuse the pun. I don't feel like celebrating my role in the possible break-up of a marriage."

"It's not you who is having the affair, and what you're doing is helping his wife. She's the one that's being cheated by him not being able to keep it in his pants."

"You would never do that, would you?"

"And risk losing the best wife I've ever had?"

"You mean the only wife you've ever had – unless you have something to tell me."

Oliver said she could follow him to the ends of the earth and not discover anything that would shock her.

Hollie wasn't sure whether she should be pleased that Oliver was laying claim to eternal fidelity, or disappointed that he wasn't more dangerous or adventurous. But there was no way she would ever want to share him, so she decided, if Mo ever conked out, she would buy him a new ball of string.

"So," Oliver asked. "What exactly did you manage to achieve this evening?"

Hollie told him about Mathew Frost and the elegant but strange woman he was obviously involved with, and about Graham being there and winning an award, and Jonas's agent too, and the outrageously expensive shoes she was wearing. Oliver dismissed the possibility of the shoes being a coincidence and suggested she was trying to copy the Comtesse's style, now she had departed the scene.

" I'll worry about it tomorrow. Right now, I just want to go to bed."

"I like the way you think."

"And go to sleep," Hollie added.

When Hollie woke on Sunday morning, she reached out her arm to wake Oliver and found she was alone in bed. Oliver had already got up and let her sleep in. One section of the newspaper was on the bed beside her, but when she saw the time, she cursed and threw the covers off. It was already gone ten.

She found Oliver in the garden, cleaning the barbecue, which didn't need cleaning because he would have made sure it was spotless after the last time they used it.

"You should have woken me up."

"Why?"

"Because we've got people coming and there's food to prepare."

Oliver told her to have some breakfast, get a coffee, and relax; he had it all in hand. But she couldn't relax. The coincidence of those shoes Erica Whitely had been wearing, being a match for the ones the Comtesse had been killed with, wouldn't leave her head. It nagged at her all through the morning and she only managed to tuck it out of sight when Peter and Marcus arrived just after two o'clock.

She had told Kendra and Ben to come at two-thirty. Hollie didn't want them to be the first to arrive, she needed backup. She no longer had Ben in her mental suspect list, but he was still an unknown quantity, as was Kendra.

Marcus managed to get Hollie alone before the others arrived and reminded her about the crime scene photos.

"Do you really want to see them? They are not very pretty."

"My dear Hollie," Marcus said with a grimace. "If you'd seen what I've seen backstage of a fashion show, you would have a new definition of what that term 'not pretty' encompasses!"

Hollie fetched her work phone and explained again she couldn't send them to him as she shouldn't really have them, and for him not to tell anyone about them. She opened the picture app and told him to ignore the ones she had taken the previous evening.

"That's another case. A quite different affair – literally."

Marcus flicked through the images, making no comment, and showing no reaction to the blood and brutality of the scene. He went back over them, expanded one, and stared at it, frowning.

"This was a Sunday morning, wasn't it?"

He observed that the Comtesse was somewhat overdressed, but speculated she was off to church, last bastion of hope for the wealthy he said.

"But it is strange that such a woman would be wearing knockoff designer shoes, even to a provincial church. I mean, I've seen her at fashion shows, and I can't imagine she would be seen dead in those shoes, yet there she is, dead in those shoes."

Hollie asked what he meant by knockoffs, even though she was sure she understood.

"Knockoffs, fakes, imitations, copies. Call them what you will, but they're not genuine Louboutin.

She asked how he could tell, and Marcus pointed out that, even on such an amateurish photograph, one could see the uneven stitching, that the back of the heel was too low, and the tip of the toe was poorly formed.

"The colour looks dull too, but that could be the lighting. Mind you, the blood has come up a lovely deep shade of red."

Marcus looked up at Hollie, offering her the phone back, but she was staring over his shoulder. He turned to see what had caught her attention, but there was only an apple tree and a hedge.

"Do you looking for apples?" he asked. "I don't think they'll be ready for another couple of months."

She had almost gone into a trancelike state, but Marcus's question brought her back to the present. She shook her head and blinked a couple of times.

"I should have photographed them, got a close-up."

"Sorry, you've lost me. The apples?"

Hollie explained that Erica Whitely, Jonas's agent, was wearing almost identical shoes last night. She thought again for a moment or two, and asked Marcus whether, if she could get a photograph of another pair of Louboutin shoes, would he be able to tell her if they were genuine?

"If there was sufficient detail, I would imagine so. It would help if you had shots of the inside of the shoes too, if you want a definitive answer."

Kendra joined them and asked what they were talking about. Hollie said shoes and Marcus said murder, both spoke at the same time. Hollie slipped her phone into the pocket of her jeans. Marcus improvised an answer.

"We were discussing how imitation fashion items have murdered the market for the genuine article."

She mentally thanked Marcus for digging her out of a hole and let the ensuing conversation drift over her head. Hollie tried to imagine a scenario where she could get close enough to Erica Whitely to get a photograph of her shoes - assuming she would be wearing them. After sipping her drink, she made an excuse and retreated to the bathroom. Sitting next to their bath on a small pine chair acquired at a sale when she and Oliver had started dating, Hollie tapped a number on her phone. It answered after two rings with a curt, 'Hello'.

"Is that Grace?"

Hollie couldn't think of a way to pose her request, other than being direct.

"I want to ask a favour. But it's not strictly legal."

"Go on." Grace sounded cautious.

She took a deep breath and covered her mouth with her hand, not that anyone was likely to overhear her where she was.

"I want you to gain entry into a house for me."

There was long pause before Grace answered. She asked what was in it for her, and what precisely did Hollie want her to liberate from the property.

"I don't want you to steal anything, just take some photographs."

Hollie explained what she wanted photographs of, and that there was only the one occupant in the house, so it should be possible to judge when it was empty. Her stomach lurched and Hollie leaned across and lifted the toilet seat, fearing she was about to be sick. She decided she didn't have the making of a criminal mastermind, and reminded herself that she was doing this to try to solve a murder - although she still wasn't sure what it would prove if Erica Whitey's shoes were genuine. She described the shoes in some detail so that Grace would recognise them.

"If you find them, make sure you get close up photos of the stitching, and the heel, and the inside of them, and what size they are."

"You are one crazy woman. You do know that, don't you?"

Hollie knew she sounded mad but had a gut feeling she was onto something. She also had a gut feeling that she needed to end the call quite quickly. She said she would text the details over in a few minutes, made an excuse that someone was coming, and broke the connection. Within seconds, there was a tentative double tap on the door. It was Kendra.

"Are you okay? Oliver was worried that you'd been up here for a while."

"Just a bit of an upset tummy. I'm fine. I'll be down in a minute or two."

"Do you want a drink of water or anything?"

"No, honestly, I'm fine."

Kendra left, after promising that she'd pop back with a glass of water if Hollie didn't reappear in ten minutes.

She made it back to the barbecue with a minute to spare, having texted Grace the address, repeated her instruction not to touch the shoes and said that anything else was up to her. She offered her a hundred pounds for obtaining the photos, not having any idea what the going rate for organising a burglary might be.

Grace replied with the single word, 'cool'. A few seconds later, she texted again.

"I'd have done it for free, just for the buzz, but I can always use some spare cash."

Oliver asked if she was feeling all right and Hollie said it was probably just the excitement of the previous evening. He asked if she was sure, and did she want to go and take a break for half an hour?

"No, I'm fine. It's just that I think I might have crossed a line."

"Taking those photographs last night?"

Hollie didn't want to involve Oliver as an accomplice in a burglary. If Grace was caught, she might cite Hollie as the instigator of the offence. But she told herself again that the cause was right, even if the method was suspect. Her phone pinged.

"Yes," she said to Oliver. "Something like that."

"Are you going to see who that is? "Oliver asked.

"Probably just junk," she lied. "It will keep."

Hollie chatted to Kendra about her work, trying to keep her mind off Grace, until Oliver declared the sausages and burgers were just about ready.

Marcus and Kendra offered to help her ferry salads, plates, and cutlery from the kitchen to the garden table. But they soon took over the task completely and made Hollie sit on a seat in the shade with a glass of fizzy water.

It had only been thirty minutes since she had spoken to Grace. Hollie didn't expect the message to be from her. But when she sneaked a peek at her phone, under the table, the message could only have been from Grace.

"Scoped the place. Looks simple enough. Owner in residence. Will keep an eye on it and check in with you later."

The afternoon and evening passed without further communication from Grace. Hollie ended up drinking a little more than she intended. By the time everyone had left, Oliver had to guide her indoors and instructed her to go to bed. He said he would clear everything up.

"Do you want me to wear a wig for you tonight?" she giggled. "I have one you haven't even seen yet. Have you ever imagined me as a sexy redhead?"

"I think a large glass of water, bed and a good night's sleep is a better plan."

Hollie giggled again and asked when he was going to join her. Oliver didn't give her a direct answer. By the time he got her up the stairs, undressed, and in bed, she was almost asleep.

"You are going to have the mother of all hangovers tomorrow morning," he said as her eyes closed. "And, in that weakened state, I shall make you tell me exactly what you've been up to."

He pulled the covers up and drew the curtains. Hollie moaned, turned on her side, moaned again, and fell asleep.

CHAPTER 28

When she woke on Monday morning, Hollie turned her head towards Oliver, and moaned. It felt as though someone was banging a large bass drum inside her head.

She remembered commissioning Grace to commit a crime, and subsequently drinking several glasses of red wine to numb the guilt. This was her payment for the alcohol-based anaesthetic. Oliver must have put her to bed, but she had only vague recollections of the barbecue after the phone call to Grace. She lifted one hand to her head, half expecting to find herself wearing a red wig. The details of that Sunday afternoon and evening were a little muddled to say the least. She was aware that Oliver was sleeping peacefully beside her, and nudged him, cursing that she had to move her head in the process. He woke immediately, pushed himself up on one elbow and massaged his eyes with the fingers of his free hand.

"How are you feeling this morning?" he asked, yawning.

"Horrible."

Oliver grunted, pushed the cover back, got out of bed, and stretched.

"I'll just shower, then I'll make you a mug of tea."

"Coffee, please."

"That bad?"

Hollie tried to nod, as her throat was too sore to speak again, but it was a bad decision. She winced as her head throbbed again.

"Coffee, a cold flannel and two paracetamols coming up."

She smiled and whispered, 'Thank you'.

The shower thrummed. It sounded like bumblebees battling through heavy rain to attack her. Hollie managed to drift off to sleep again and was only woken by a cool flannel being draped over her forehead.

She must have drifted off again as the next thing she was aware of was Oliver, dressed for work, replacing her coffee with a fresh brew.

"What time is it?"

"Just gone eight. Do you want me to call Stella and tell her you're not well so won't be in today.

Hollie struggled into a sitting position and took the pills he had left on her bedside table. She washed them down with the glass of water Oliver had also provided.

"No. I'll be okay. Don't bother her, there's stuff I've got to do, things to check."

It was gone ten-thirty when Hollie finally made it into work. She was still feeling fragile and not sure what she was going to do; everything now depended on Grace and her assignment. The illegal activity Hollie commissioned had undergone a rebranding in her head as research.

"Morning," Sharon chirped, far too cheerfully.

"Hi, is Stella free?"

"As far as I know. But she has a meeting scheduled with Graham, his agent and Mr Wilkins at eleven o'clock."

Hollie checked her watch. Erica Whitely could be here in the next twenty minutes, just possibly wearing those shoes. She looked around reception, wondering if she could hide somewhere and spy on them. There was nowhere she could physically hide, but there was a sofa, two armchairs, and a low table with a few magazines on it, provided for the convenience of clients.

"I might just sit here for a while. I don't want to disturb Stella if she's preparing for a meeting."

"Would you like a coffee?" Sharon suggested. "I could get you one."

It sounded like a good idea to Hollie, even though it would be her third that day. Not only might it make her feel a little more human, but it would look natural, like she was a visitor. Once settled with a coffee, a small packet of complimentary biscuits and an open magazine, Hollie checked her phone. There were no messages. She opened the camera app in readiness for Erica Whitely's arrival, and placed it, face down, on the sofa beside her.

Both biscuits and her cup of coffee had long gone by the time Erica led Graham through the front doors. A second cup had been half consumed, by which stage Hollie decided she should maybe avoid any more caffeine for the rest of the day. She left some in the cup so that her presence on the sofa looked realistic, and because she didn't want to have to rush to the toilet and miss them.

But Hollie's plan, to get a picture of Erica's shoes, failed. The agent arrived dressed in a trouser suit and her feet were comfortably clad in low-heeled, black patent loafers.

Sharon called Stella and relayed the message to Graham that she would be down in a minute or two. She offered them coffee, which they both declined, and Erica Whitely came over to sit on one of the armchairs, only a few feet away from Hollie. Graham was chatting with Sharon and hadn't even glanced in her direction.

"Do I know you from somewhere?" Erica asked. "Your face seems familiar."

"People say that sometimes. I do have a twin sister who works in catering."

Erica Whitely smiled, seemingly pleased with her observational skills. "Did she happen to be working this Saturday, at an awards ceremony?"

Hollie confirmed her sister had, as far as she could remember, been working at that event. She excused herself, mouthing that she needed the ladies' room. The excuse was genuine, but it also meant Hollie could avoid a possibly tricky face-to-face with Graham. After hiding for ten minutes, she cautiously eased the main door open a crack and scanned the room to ensure that the reception area was clear, before emerging completely. Sharon was staring out the window, oblivious to Hollie's return.

"Have they gone up to see Mr Wilkins?"

"Yes, and how come you didn't say anything to me about all this? Graham said he told you everything on Thursday when you had lunch together. And why did you arrange to have lunch with him anyway?"

Hollie told her that Graham wanted to tell her himself and she had promised not to spoil the surprise. As for the reason they met, Hollie gave the vaguest of explanations about identifying the right partner for advice on his offer of a publishing contract. Somehow, Sharon accepted her account and forgave her for keeping 'mum', as she put it.

Sharon also said that Stella had left a message for Hollie to go straight up to her office as soon as she wanted to. Stella had said she wouldn't be long as she was only introducing Graham to Mr Wilkins, who was sometimes a little nervous with new clients. While in the lift, Hollie's phone pinged. Taking the stairs had been out of the question in her current condition, but her plan to keep her eyes closed was interrupted by that sound. Several pictures from Grace had arrived, all were of Erica Whitely's shoes and included close-ups which revealed every detail, from every angle. Grace had been thorough in carrying out her assignment.

Hollie's heart was beating so fast it threatened to burst out of her chest. She mumbled 'gotcha' and gave a silent prayer that Grace wouldn't be caught in the act. She had forwarded the images to Marcus before the lift stopped. Mr Wilkins must have felt at ease quite quickly as the door to Stella's office was already open when she got there.

"Come in. Shut the door. I've got some bad news. Though, to

be honest, it's not unexpected. Jonas has been arrested and charged with the Comtesse's murder."

Hollie swore under her breath, not something she often did, but events were moving a bit too quick for her to prove her theory. Stella continued her briefing.

"Rupert's on his way over to the police station right now, so we should know more details soon. I confess, I'm not sure how much of their evidence the police will reveal. It's not my area of expertise."

Knowing how many missing pieces there still were in her jigsaw puzzle, Hollie hesitated before expounding her shoe theory.

"I may have some good news, well, possibly good news, but it's complicated, and I haven't quite worked it all out yet."

Stella said that Rupert and, of course, Jonas would welcome any kind of straw to grab hold of. Hollie showed her the pictures of Erica's shoes, which Stella instantly recognised as being the same was the ones that were used in the Comtesse's murder.

"But that's the point," Hollie said. "They may not be quite identical. The Comtesse's shoes were fakes. It doesn't make any sense why she wouldn't be wearing genuine designer shoes, and that Erica Whitely had just happened to be wearing an almost identical pair of shoes on Saturday night."

Stella asked how she had obtained the photographs, but Hollie told her it was probably better if she didn't know. While Stella was half smiling and looking at her enquiringly with raised eyebrows, Hollie's phone pinged again. She took the phone back from Stella. It was a response from Marcus.

"Those are the real deal. No change out of 2k for them."

She looked up at Stella and said it was pretty much confirmed. The Comtesse had been wearing fake designer shoes and Erica Whitely had genuine Louboutin shoes in her wardrobe.

"I am going to guess," Stella said slowly and quietly, "that this new information is not going to be admissible in court?"

Hollie's phone pinged again. It was another text from Grace. She said she had found something else, something that was curious, and was Hollie free to take a call.

"I've got a call coming," she told Stella. "I ought to take it, and you might not want to be party to the conversation."

Stella nodded, guessing that her friend could be operating in a legal grey zone. What she didn't guess was just what depth of grey the zone was, into which she had drifted.

Hollie texted Grace a thumbs-up. Her phone rang straight away. She checked the number and told Stella this was it.

After being unceremoniously bustled into the corridor, Hollie answered the call. Stella whispered, 'Tell me later', before closing her door. Hollie stood in the corridor and covered her phone with a cupped hand in an attempt at privacy.

"Hi Grace, sorry. I was in the middle of something. Hang on a second."

There was a toilet at the end of the corridor. Hollie ducked in and checked both the cubicles were unoccupied to be certain she was not overheard.

"Okay, all good now. What is it you've found?"

"It's probably nothing. A key to a storage unit. But I recognised it because..." There was a long pause, followed by a sigh. "Well, I may have a unit there myself, just for a few odd things I'm keeping safe. You know what I mean? I don't particularly want to spell it out."

After being reassured that Hollie had no interest what she kept in her own storage unit, Grace said she was on her way there now, and that in five minutes she should have some answers. She said the key was hidden, unlike the costume jewellery, which was in plain sight and wasn't worth the trouble to liberate. Hollie was worried that this mission was getting out of control, but Grace had certainly fulfilled her primary task.

"By the way, the photos are perfect. Thanks."

"No problem. I'll call you if there is anything interesting at the lockup."

Twenty minutes later, Hollie was back in her own office, staring at the pictures of Erica's shoes and wondering how the wrong person was in possession of the genuine Louboutins – and could the wild theory that was forming in her head be right. But, of course, Erica might be a very successful agent and she may well have splurged out on shoes that were ridiculously expensive. But that still wouldn't explain why the Comtesse would be wearing knockoffs.

Hollie's phone pinged again. It was another message from Grace, asking if she was free to take another phone call. Hollie sent a thumbs up again.

"I've found something else, but I don't know if it's significant or just a bit weird."

Hollie asked her what it was, and Grace said it was a car. The only thing in the lock up was a sports car with two flat tyres and a damaged front wing.

"I don't know much about cars," she said, "but it must be worth a bit, and it's strange to keep it hidden here. At least, I reckon it's worth something. It's a Porsche."

"A sports car? What colour is it?"

"Green, sort of pale apple green, but it's covered in dust, it must have sat in here for years."

There was the sound of a car door opening.

"There's even keys in the ignition," Grace said, sounding surprised.

"Don't touch them," Hollie almost shouted into her phone.

"Okay, okay, don't lose it. Anyway, I can't drive, or to be more accurate, I don't have a license."

Grace promised to take some photos and send them to her.

"When you've done that, are you able to put the key back in the house, exactly where you found it?"

"As long as the owner hasn't come back. I don't know how long she's going to be out for."

Hollie assured her that the owner wouldn't be back for a while yet, and that she could give Grace plenty of warning when she might be expected. While she spoke, Hollie was descending the stairs to check with Sharon that Erica Whitely and Graham were still with Mr Wilkins. Hollie was planning to stay in reception and act as an early warning system for Grace. It was the least she could do.

Sharon organised tea for her this time, along with more biscuits, which Hollie didn't really need, but ate anyway. Within a few minutes, a whole series of photographs arrived from Grace. They ranged from a wide shot of the lock-up with the back of the car showing, to details of the damaged wing and several shots of the interior. Hollie had no idea what the car might be worth so sent a couple of the pictures to Oliver, hoping he could help.

Ten minutes past with no word from Grace, and Hollie was starting to feel anxious. But then Oliver rang and told her he had looked up the car using its registration plate. It wasn't taxed and would need a test certificate but even in that condition it was still worth twenty thousand, maybe more. Hollie thought that was a lot of capital to leave hidden in a storage facility, even if Erica Whitely was running a very successful talent agency. When Grace sent her a brief message saying, 'mission accomplished, key back in place', Hollie headed back up to Stella's office. The door was open, and Hollie stood, leaning against the frame, until Stella looked up and noticed her there, smiling.

"I know who killed the Comtesse. I can't prove it yet, but I think I might be able to with a little help from Jonas."

"Well, don't just stand there, come in. Tell your Auntie Stella all the good news. I presume it is good news?"

Hollie closed the door, sat down opposite Stella, and took a deep breath.

"It's the same person who killed Jonas's first wife. It's Erica Whitely, his agent."

CHAPTER 29

Stella asked Hollie to explain her theory in detail. How Jonas's fingerprints were all over the shoe used to kill the Comtesse was still an unexplained detail, but a very important one, as Stella pointed out.

"We can't take your theory to the police if we can't provide a reasonable explanation, one that will exonerate Jonas. At the moment, it's all conjecture. And that's apart from the fact that we can't explain how we know some of this without admitting being accomplice to a crime ourselves – assuming I'm right about how you sourced this information."

"The car is not really hidden. Anyone might have seen it there."

"Only if the lockup had been open when they were passing. But we can't even reveal that, unless we can also explain how we know about it. And I doubt claiming to have x-ray vision, which enables us see through the lockup's doors would be believed."

"I might be able to fill in some more details if I can speak with Jonas?"

Stella rang Rupert and asked when he was going to see their client next, and whether it would be possible for Hollie to be present. The way the rest of the conversation went was difficult to follow, but it sounded positive. Rupert had wanted to interview Jonas by himself on his first visit but agreed to Hollie going with him on his second visit.

"Best I could get," Stella shrugged. "But he also wants to know why. Maybe you could be vague about your methodology as it doesn't quite fit with the remit of the firm."

"Tomorrow then," Hollie said, and Stella nodded."

"There's someone else I need to talk to first."

"Anything I should know about?"

"Probably not. If you speak to Rupert again, tell him I'll explain it all tomorrow, or as much as is possible, before we meet Jonas."

Hollie stood to leave. Stella said nothing more until she was almost out the door.

"Hollie, take care. If you're right, and she's killed twice already, Erica Whitely could be dangerous."

"I don't plan to slay the dragon myself. But you did send me on that self-defence course, so maybe she ought to be the one worrying."

Hollie messaged Maryam as soon as she was back in her own office.

"Can we meet? I'm available any time today."

Staring at her phone, she willed Maryam to respond. The message was doubled ticked, so at least she had received it. Hollie knew she must have other cases she would be working on, and now Jonas had been charged, they were probably taking priority.

She skipped lunch, being far too nervous to eat, but had drunk so much coffee that her stomach was beginning to imitate the sounds of a percolator. Hollie tapped in several more messages to Maryam but deleted them before pressing send. Eventually she jabbed at the screen so hard she broke a fingernail.

"I know the identity of the real killer – for both murders! Contact me! Please!"

Although Hollie abhorred the use of exclamation marks, she decided they must be justifiable on this occasion, if only to grab Maryam's attention. Even with those added, it was still twenty minutes before she received a reply.

"5pm, same place."

It was the longest two and a half hours of Hollie's life, and she arrived at the café far earlier than the appointed time. Grace was nowhere to be seen. An older woman took her order for a black coffee and a Chelsea bun. She needed something stodgy to mop up all the fluid she had ingested that day.

Maryam arrived at a quarter past five. She wasn't the habitually prompt type. Hollie was making her coffee last, but now had a slice of chocolate cake too. She had convinced herself that nervous energy would be burning up the calories.

"I haven't got long," Maryam said as she took a seat opposite Hollie. "And you must know now that Jonas Moon has been charged with the murder of the Comtesse. It's pretty much in the hands of the crown prosecution service now."

"But he didn't do it. And I know I can prove it."

Maryam sighed, as though faced with explaining to a child why the adults knew what was best and that the case was effectively closed.

"It was Erica Whitely," Hollie blurted out. "Jonas's agent. She killed the Comtesse and Mei Ling. Probably out of jealousy in both cases."

"And you know this how?"

Hollie showed her the pictures of the car Grace had discovered, and the damage to its front wing. She explained about the fake shoes and the real shoes, being on the wrong people, and how she was sure that was the explanation for Jonas's fingerprints being on the murder weapon. Maryam listened, but showed no reaction, no hint that she might agree with Hollie's theory.

"How did you get the photographs of the car? And where did you find it?"

It was common knowledge, even to an ex-teacher turned private investigator, that the police would need a search warrant to enter Erica Whitely's house. And for that, they would need some sort of reasonable cause. Hollie slumped in her chair, the last piece of chocolate cake on her plate held no attraction for her now.

"Look," Maryam said. "I can see where you're coming from, and a part of me wants to believe you. But we have no reason to search her house or any private garage. We can't go hammering on someone's door because we fancy it, and because some ex-schoolteacher has formulated a bizarre theory which solves two murders."

"It's not in a garage, it's in a lock-up. And you do think Mei Ling was murdered, don't you?"

"Maybe. But just how did you come across this lock-up with a car hidden in it?"

Hollie was about to mention Grace by name but checked herself just in time. She spoke carefully and slowly.

"Someone, an acquaintance of mine, might have found a key to the lock-up in Erica Whitely's house."

Maryann stared at the table, not saying anything, not moving a muscle. Hollie realised she had, in effect, admitted that she was an accomplice in a crime, trespassing at the very least, but more likely burglary as they had borrowed the key. Also, a few other items might have been relocated, knowing Grace's inclinations.

The door of the café opened. The bell above it tinkling several decibels louder than usual and sounding to Hollie like a warning. She was facing the door. She had specifically chosen her position so she would see Maryam the moment she arrived. But the person breezing through the door now was Grace. Not the best timing.

Grace looked at Hollie, obviously recognised Maryam from behind, grimaced, and snuck quietly down the side of the room and into the kitchen, apparently unseen by Maryam.

"That was Grace just came in, wasn't it?"

Hollie wondered if they issue police with special backward facing surveillance cameras as part of their standard kit.

"It was, yes. I suppose she's come in to help clear up when the café closes for the day."

"I meant, it was Grace who..." Maryann paused briefly,

"effected an entry into the Whitely residence on your behalf."

"I didn't say she did." Hollie added defensively.

"And I would prefer you didn't tell me anything about that. I would prefer not to know the details. And I'm beginning to think it's better never to know all the details where you're concerned – I'm coming to understand that. What was it you said you taught?"

Hollie ignored the sarcasm in Maryam's tone. She had assumed she would take the information Grace had discovered, accept its significance, and Jonas would be cleared.

"What do you need from me?" Hollie asked.

Maryam explained that they could only search Jonas's residence, his person, and his car. She said they couldn't randomly search the premises of his friends and business associates. All the evidence Hollie had found so far wouldn't sway her DI, as it wasn't admissible, and he was convinced of Jonas's guilt, and he had the evidence of Jonas's fingerprints on the shoe embedded in the Comtesse's neck, and his lack of an alibi, and a motive – namely money. All Hollie had so far was a theory.

Hollie realised she had most of her jigsaw completed, but the last few pieces wouldn't quite fit, and without those, it was impossible to persuade Maryam to investigate further.

"What can I do?" Hollie asked.

"Give me something solid, something I can run with. Gilroy isn't as confident as he pretends to be. The prosecution service had to be serenaded to get this far. Find me a reason to search Erica Whitely's place, one that will stand up in front of a judge for a warrant. We simply can't act on hunches. And if you could explain just how those fingerprints came to be on the murder weapon, other than the obvious, one that would exonerate Jonas Moon, then don't hesitate to tell me."

The older woman came out from the kitchen and picked up their empty cups. "Have you finished with your cake, dear?"

Hollie nodded. Her stomach rumbled its approval at her

decision. Maryam half stood, pushing her chair back a few inches.

"Let me know if you get something I can act on. A part of me doesn't believe Jonas Moon is guilty, but I don't know why, it's just one of those gut feelings, but I have to go with Gilroy as things stand."

Maryam left the café, but Hollie didn't move. It was like someone had misplaced the last few pieces of her jigsaw puzzle. She could see most of the picture, but it wasn't complete. While she was staring at a few crumbs on the table, the last evidence of her chocolate cake, the chair opposite her scraped against the floor and Grace slid into it.

"Weird, that car, right?"

Hollie blinked twice. The jigsaw puzzle broke up in her head. There were no pieces missing, it must be that she just hadn't put them together the right way. Grace sitting there reminded her that she had promised payment for services rendered. She wondered what the going rate was for commissioning a burglary and if the hundred she had offered was enough.

"What do I owe you? You know, for..."

"Nah, forget it. I had fun. And I sort of collected my payment anyway."

"You stole something?"

"That woman has more jewellery than my mum. Mind you, most of my mum's stuff looks like it came from a fairground. What do think of this?"

Grace angled her head towards Hollie and held a finger behind her earlobe. Alongside numerous silver studs and rings was what looked like a sizeable diamond.

"Is that real?" Hollie asked, leaning forward.

'Half a carat I reckon. Nice cut too. She only had the one and it was tucked away under a load of junk. She's unlikely to spot it's gone for ages."

Grace told her exactly where she had found the key to the lockup and asked what the significance of the car was. Hollie explained her theory while Grace listened, only interrupting occasionally. When she finished, Grace nodded, grinning.

"That is so cool. We make a great team."

Hollie had no intention of them becoming a team. This venture was never meant to be any more than a one-off arrangement, but having someone to call on with Grace's particular skills might, of course, be useful in a future case.

"How did you actually get into that house? Did you have to break a window or something?"

"Easy." Grace hesitated for a moment. "Stupid cow leaves her back door unlocked. The house backs onto the park and there's a big brick wall. I suppose she never imagined anyone could climb it."

"But you did?"

"Nah. I balance-walked along it from the end of the terrace. Piece of cake."

Hollie wished she hadn't mentioned cake. Her tummy rumbled again as though demanding more, or maybe less.

"So, you're going to nail the old witch now?

"Hopefully. Look, I need to get back to my office. There's some research I need to do for a meeting tomorrow."

Grace asked that she keep her up to date on 'their' case. Hollie winced inwardly as to how she could break it to Grace that they were not actual partners.

"Funny woman that Whitely. You know she has an Oscar, one of those Hollywood awards."

"I didn't know they gave them to agents."

Grace said it wasn't a real one, but a good fake, even the right sort of weight, not a plastic copy. And she said that the plaque on it was even weirder, probably a joke. It was inscribed to the best supporting agent in the industry.

"There was something else about it too," Grace said. "I reckon it's been used as a weapon. It's been wiped clean, but there's a trace of blood on the edge of the base."

Hollie left the café after thanking Grace profusely and made her way back to the offices of Patterson Wilkins.

Taylor was at his desk, no longer flicking rubber bands at his screen, but still frowning at it.

"Am I interrupting you?"

"Nothing important."

"I wondered if you could do some digging for me, online."

She explained that she was curious about the relationship between Jonas Moon and Erica Whitely, his agent.

"I doubt she posts much on social media," Hollie said, having checked already. "But are there other places she might show up?"

Taylor grinned, saying there was no place to hide in a digital world. It might have sounded more promising if he hadn't tried to use an American accent and a deep voice - neither of which sounded remotely genuine.

"I was hoping you'd say that, but maybe not in that accent."

Hollie also hoped he hadn't taken offence as he was no longer grinning.

"Is there any chance you might be able to dig something up by tomorrow morning? I have a meeting with Jonas and Rupert. It would be really helpful to be prepared."

Taylor's frown returned. He said it was his date night with Simon, and that Simon always found his accents amusing. When Hollie looked blank, he explained.

"Simon. My partner. Anyway, what time is your meeting?'

Hollie said she wasn't sure. Taylor tapped a few keys and told her it wasn't until after lunch.

"How do you know?"

"Well, I could pretend it's a special extra sensory mind-reading ability. But the truth is, the partners all have their diaries on the intranet system."

Hollie looked at him blankly again.

"Like an internal internet. Didn't you have one at your school?"

"Not that anyone told me about."

"Well, I'll start digging now. I should have something for you by lunchtime. No promises though, little lady."

Hollie tried to smile when the terrible drawling accent returned. She checked her watch and decided there wasn't much else she could accomplish that day. She thanked Taylor and made her way down the staircase to her car.

When she got home the house felt unnaturally quiet. It was still August, but the temperature had dipped below sunbathing levels and there was a threat of rain in the air. She needed to stop thinking for a while.

Putting on her favourite album, Hollie turned the volume up high, then cranked it a bit more, took flour and eggs from a cupboard and started to make fresh pasta for Oliver's supper. He deserved a treat with all he'd had to put up with.

CHAPTER 30

Hollie was on her second glass of white wine by the time Oliver came home, and had prepared a pesto sauce, having found just enough fresh basil in their small greenhouse. She was beginning to wonder if their supply of wine was decreasing a little faster than was healthy. The dough had rested and had been run through the spaghetti machine. As there was nothing else to do until he arrived, she had retreated to their study, and was staring at her home-made incident board, trying to find the missing pieces of her puzzle.

From somewhere in the back of her brain, she remembered a mantra which must have been repeated on several television crime shows. Motive, opportunity and means. The three main questions for which she needed answers.

The opportunity was simple enough to explain. Erica Whitely knew the Comtesse would have been alone because she had arranged a meeting with Jonas, only to cancel it at the last moment. She would possibly have been able to see Jonas walking in the park from her bedroom window; he had said it was a habit of his.

Motive, Hollie assumed, would be jealousy. Either she and Jonas had been in a relationship in their early years, or it was a fantasy which had been shattered when he married, maybe on both occasions.

Means was the slightly trickier one. Jonas's fingerprints on the murder weapon were difficult to explain. He had said he and the Comtesse used separate dressing rooms, so they could only have got onto her shoes if he had handled them. The weapon which had stunned her, and left her vulnerable to such a gruesome end, might well have been the replica Oscar – if Grace was right about the blood and if Erica Whitely had taken it with her to taunt the Comtesse.

Hollie picked up her phone and started to write a message to Maryam, but hesitated, not wanting to land Jonas deeper in trouble. She stared at the screen and decided it was worth the risk.

"Were there any other fingerprints on the Comtesse's shoes, or was it only Jonas's that were found? What about the Comtesse's own fingerprints?"

She pressed send and waited. The message wasn't read immediately. The front door opened, clicked back into its frame, and Oliver's muffled voice drifted through to her.

"Hi, where are you?" he called.

"In here. Working. Sort of."

In a few seconds, Oliver had found her hiding place and was standing directly behind her, looking at her makeshift incident board over her shoulder.

"I see Cruella De Vil is still very much a person of interest."

Hollie had stretched pieces of blue hair ribbon from her cartoon to a picture of a shoe. She was also linked to Juliette du Colbert, a newly added picture of a green Porsche, a picture of an Oscar, and a printout of a newspaper cutting reporting Mei Ling's death.

"It's her. I know it's her. But I didn't have any red ribbon, so I had to use blue. I must get some."

Over supper, and rather too much wine, Hollie explained all the pieces of the puzzle which made sense and the one piece that didn't. That was how Jonas's fingerprints came to be on the murder weapon.

By the time Hollie fell into bed, exhausted, Maryam had read her message, but had still not responded.

Hollie was driving into work the next morning when her phone pinged. She couldn't wait until she was in the car park before she could check it, so pulled into a parking bay.

"Fingerprints on both shoes? Significant? And you were right about one oddity, none of the Comtesse's fingerprints found. Not sure how we missed that peculiarity."

Hollie replied. "I'll contact you later. Have an important meeting with Jonas first."

In reception, Hollie said hello to Sharon but didn't linger. She wanted to know if Taylor had uncovered anything interesting or useful.

He was on the phone when Hollie arrived at his desk but ended the call quickly.

"How did your date night go?" she asked.

"Total disaster, as usual. I don't know why we do it. Simon chose the restaurant, Greek. I had the oiliest Moussaka known to man, even Greek men, and he ate far too many olives, he knows they don't agree with him. I won't go into the details in case you're planning to eat today."

"I'm sorry it didn't go well."

"But I did come into work early today, Simon was still out like a light, and I've found a few snippets which might be of interest."

Hollie pulled a chair up next to Taylor and took her little black notebook out.

"He lived with her for a couple of years, Jonas that is. There's no specific evidence that they were in a relationship, but he did accompany her to a lot of functions, as her plus one, I assume. If she had a cleaner, we could always try to trace her; there's nothing escapes their notice. Anyway, I have sent you press clippings of various events and some pap photos. Jonas was only a B-list celeb in those early years, so not that many pics."

"When was all this happening?"

"They must have met before his first wife's hit-and-run accident, and he lived with her until he met the Condon Queen. He moved out soon after that, and rented a flat in the centre of town until they and married. I have to say, that Comtesse has a very curious history."

"I know. She told me all about it herself."

"Anyway. He is still named as a co-owner of Erica Whitely's house, the one on Clarendon Avenue."

"How did you find that out?"

"When he married the Comtesse, it was included on the legal documents we hold for the Colby Group. I did a search through our digital archive, just on the off chance. But that's about it. Erica Whitely is nowhere on social media, other than in her professional capacity."

Hollie told Taylor that might be just what she was looking for. She said to give her best wishes to Simon and hope he feels a bit better soon.

"That man deserved everything he got. He's an idiot, but he's my idiot. So, thank you. I'll pass on your condolences.

Once in her office, Hollie closed the door. She needed time to think about how to approach Jonas. If she was too confrontational, he might clam up. It was possible he might still harbour feelings for Erica Whitely and consider himself obliged to defend her. Hollie started to scribble her questions on a fresh page of her notebook, crossing some out, rephrasing others.

It was almost lunchtime when the phone rang. It was Rupert asking if she was ready to leave. He also asked if she was appropriately dressed. When she asked him to define that term, he hesitated for a moment.

"It's not advisable to turn up to a prison in a short skirt or revealing too much cleavage. You must know what I mean without me spelling it out further."

"In case the prisoners get excited, you mean?"

"You'll only be meeting Jonas, not the whole prison population. It's also the wardens you have to watch out for, and not just the male ones."

She met Rupert in reception. He gave her a top-to-toe glance and nodded his approval. Prisons are probably not that different to boys' schools, Hollie thought. Lots of testosterone laden males with very few opportunities to exercise their desires.

The journey to the prison took a little over thirty minutes, during which time Rupert explained the procedures and formalities they would have to go through. She knew she shouldn't find it exciting, but the butterflies now holding a party in her tummy had not been part of her lunchtime sandwich filling,

The room they met Jonas in had only a table bolted to the floor, and three plastic chairs. It hardly seemed likely that a prisoner and his lawyer might initiate a riot, but it was both reassuring and worrying that they were prepared for such an eventuality.

Hollie remained silent while Rupert went over the facts with Jonas, trying to elicit any discrepancies which might help his case. She wasn't paying full attention, or making notes, even though she knew she should have been. Hollie was rehearsing the few questions she wanted to ask, the answers to which might complete her jigsaw puzzle.

After fifteen minutes, Rupert turned to her and asked if she had any questions for Jonas. She was taken by surprise and stumbled to get her notebook open to the correct page.

"Sorry. Um, Jonas, is it alright to call you Jonas rather than Mr Moon?"

He nodded. Rupert had avoided personalising their conversation, and he coughed discretely to show his concern for her doing so.

"When you were living with your agent, was it an intimate arrangement?"

Jonas stared at her. Hollie had rarely seen that neutral look on a student's face, but they were very bad actors and Jonas was a professional. He asked exactly what she was implying. Hollie decided that if he wanted her to speak plainly, it wasn't a problem.

"Did you have an affair, sleep together, shag, bonk, make the beast with two backs? Is that clear enough?"

At the quote from *Othello*, a hint of a smile had snuck onto his face.

"You are not a lawyer, are you?"

"I was an English teacher. Quite a good one, I think."

"I did indeed lie between that maid's' legs. Is that plain enough for you."

Rupert was frowning, possibly trying to locate the quote, while Hollie was unconvinced that the term 'maid' was appropriate for Erica Whitely, but she let that pass.

"And I presume your affair ended when you met the Comtesse?"

Jonas's head dropped. He studied the fingernails of one hand before looking up and answering in a far quieter voice.

"Erica is not a woman who accepts rejection lightly." He shrugged. "Maybe that is what makes her such a good agent. But it was never more than an arrangement as far as I was concerned. A convenience of mutual benefit."

"So, she accepted the situation once you and the Comtesse were married?"

His face returned to its status as a blank canvas. "

"Not entirely," he replied, offering no specific details.

"This may seem a strange question, but please believe me, I'm not trying to pry unnecessarily into your private life. Would you have had occasion to handle Erica's shoes during your... shall we say occasional liaisons?"

Jonas bristled. Hollie had never seen anyone who could do that outside of dramas on television.

"I have no idea what may feature in your fantasies, but shoes do not have any sort of roll in mine – or Erica's for that matter."

Hollie apologised again and said she was only trying to establish the circumstances in which his fingerprints might have come to be on her shoes. Jonas frowned and narrowed his eyes.

"Surely it is how they came to be on Juliette's shoes which

should be concerning you?"

"Or, more precisely," Hollie explained, "the shoes which were used to murder Juliette."

Both Rupert and Hollie watched as the import of her words, and their implication, became apparent to Jonas. He looked her straight in the eye, thinking for several moments, before he answered.

"I did help her put her shoes on some few days before my wife was murdered. Erica had pulled a muscle in her back. It seemed a small request, a duty which I could perform as a friend, nothing more than that."

"When exactly did this occur? It might be important."

"It will be in my diary, which I don't have, of course. The police took it into their possession. But it was the day we were meeting with the producers of my new show."

Hollie made a note in her book. Jonas asked why it was so significant. His eyes still alert as though he already knew the answer. Hollie ignored his question.

"Can you remember what type of car Erica Whitely drove when you first met?"

Jonas's frown morphed into a look of bewilderment.

"I don't drive. I take no interest in cars. I do remember it was green, sporty, uncomfortable, noisy."

When Hollie asked what happened to it and whether she had sold it, Jonas looked blank.

"I have no idea. I assume she must have got rid of it. She didn't have a garage and taxis were often a much easier option. She must have sold it."

A look of realisation slowly crept over Jonas's face. His mouth opened and his eyes looked like they might take leave of absence from their sockets.

"You think Erica..."

Hollie interrupted him, explaining that all she had so far were theories.

"But you do co-own her house, don't you?"

"Yes. Why? It was a gesture, nothing more. I paid off her mortgage from my television contract. It was an extremely lucrative deal, which was down to her negotiating skills, and my talent, of course."

"I can't explain it all right now," Hollie said, as she still didn't trust Jonas not to warn Erica Whitely. "But I assure you, if my theory can be proved, we will let you know immediately."

"When I get out of here, I am going to kill that woman."

Rupert warned him to guard against such language, and in the event of Hollie being correct and the police confirming her theories, Ms Whitely would be behind bars, for many years.

"If I don't, I will at least murder her reputation."

Jonas thanked them both profusely before they left, despite Rupert repeating that they were not out of the woods yet.

On their way back from the prison, Hollie checked with Rupert that the records they held would confirm Jonas as a part owner of Erica Whitely's house. He assured her that if Taylor had checked the documentation, it would be so.

"That young man doesn't make mistakes. Even though he's not trained in law, he is most thorough."

Hollie messaged Maryam from the car, telling her about the house and asked if shared ownership was enough for a search warrant. Maryam replied with three thumbs-up emojis.

"Can I be there for the search?"

"No way."

Hollie hadn't expected her to agree. But after a couple of minutes, another message pinged on her phone.

"You know the neighbour, don't you?"

"Yes."

"I can't stop you visiting her on the day?"

Hollie smiled when she read it.

"Good news?" Rupert asked.

"I think it might be."

"Be sure to keep me informed." He quickly added, "When appropriate, of course."

CHAPTER 31

When Oliver got home that evening, Hollie was pacing round the garden, phone in hand, constantly checking the screen.

"Waiting for a call?" he asked from the back door.

Hollie explained about how the missing pieces in her puzzle had almost all turned up, the way Jonas's fingerprints came to be on Erica Whitely's shoes, how she must have planned the murder, even the object she probably struck the Comtesse with before finishing her off.

"In that case, I think my amazing gumshoe wife deserves a large glass of wine."

"Maybe a small one. But I haven't heard from Maryam yet. I think I've given her enough evidence to get a search warrant, but I don't know whether her DI is going to act on it."

Oliver suggested they go out for a celebration supper. He said it was up to the police now, she had done everything she could. Hollie wasn't sure she could eat or drink anything. But he persuaded her to stop pacing and sit down on one of the sun loungers while he fetched two glasses. Although it was still August, the evenings were already beginning to feel cooler, and Hollie sat with her knees together, both hands and her phone resting on them. She kept staring at the screen, willing it to bleep.

It complied with her wishes at precisely the same time as Oliver offered her a glass. Hollie ignored the wine as she stabbed impatiently at the screen.

"They're going to do it," she shouted at Oliver, jumping up from the sunbed and almost knocking one of the glasses out of his hands. "Tomorrow morning, six o'clock."

"That's good then. All the more reason to celebrate."

"I've got to sort out what I'm wearing," she said.

"To go out?"

"No. For tomorrow morning."

Hollie headed off towards the house leaving Oliver with two glasses of white wine in his hands and a confused look on his face. She turned back to him in the doorway.

"Do you want to order pizzas. I could eat an elephant."

Oliver took a sip from one of the glasses, then from the other.

"Two jumbo pizzas coming right up," he said to Mo, who was quietly minding her own business, huddled in her docking station.

Hollie set her alarm clock for four-thirty. There was no way she was not going to be in the vicinity when the police raided Erica Whitey's house. Oliver stirred, rolled over, and went back to sleep.

The sky was a clear pale blue, and the birds sounded like they were having an argument when she left the house. Hollie was sure her car made more noise than usual, but thankfully, it started at the first turn off the key.

At that hour in the morning, the air had a chill to it. She had decided to give her second wig an outing, a pageboy cut, and an almost purple red, not very natural, but surprisingly warm. To add to her disguise, she had opted for leggings under her shorts and a loose sweatshirt. She hoped Maryam didn't recognise her and ask her to leave, but she had given her the time of the raid so must be expecting her to be loitering close by.

Hollie left her car in Mulberry Park, walked round the edge of the lake, and took the path which eventually led to Clarendon Avenue. She checked her watch. It was fifteen minutes before the action was due to start. But, just in case they were early, she decided to casually jog past the house. She had run the length of the avenue four times, wondering what Erica Whitely had been doing with that phone on Saturday night. It was the one piece of the puzzle she couldn't quite fit.

When they arrived, the police were not using sirens or blue lights. There was only one marked car, a police van and two plain cars in the cavalcade. Hollie was disappointed that there was no dramatic revving of engines, no squeal of brakes, no shouting and hammering their way through the front door. The only noise was when one policeman banged on Erica's front door with a gloved fist and announced their presence through the letterbox.

Curtains were drawn back in Erica's house at the sudden noise, as well as both her neighbours' bedrooms and two houses across the road. Hollie slowed as she got near to the action and one of the policemen stopped her.

"I'm sorry, madam, but could you either turn around or use the other side of the street."

"Why? What's happening officer?"

As she asked, trying to sound as innocent as possible, Maryam emerged from one of the cars. She didn't appear to register Hollie's presence, but on reaching the front door, she turned, looked straight at her, and winked.

A slow shake of the head from Maryam told Hollie not to cause a fuss. Not wanting to get on the wrong side of her, but slightly disappointed, Hollie turned around, ready to return to her car. The day was already warming from the rising sun, and she took her wig off. The policeman could think whatever he wanted.

There was also no point in pretending to jog. But before she had taken more than a couple of steps, she heard her name being called. It was Wendy Mordant, standing at her open front door, wearing a long pink dressing gown and fluffy slippers.

"What are you doing here at this time of day?"

"I was just out jogging. Then I came across all this."

"Have you any idea what's going on? I saw you talking to that policeman."

Hollie glanced at the policeman. He was not taking any notice of her or Wendy; he kept staring at Erica Whitely's house, probably wishing he had a more important role. She climbed the four steps to Wendy's front door, so she didn't have to shout.

"I think it's some sort of raid. I'm not sure what it's about though."

"It will be drugs. Those creative types all use drugs. I do hope this doesn't affect the house prices."

The policeman, who had spoken to Hollie, decided to take an interest in the two women watching the proceedings.

"Could you both go indoors, please. We don't want any more of a disturbance than necessary. There's nothing to see here."

He was polite but firm, and probably correct in that Hollie would find out nothing by standing on the pavement. Wendy took Hollie by the elbow and pulled her into the hall.

"Those policemen ought to have more consideration for law-abiding citizens. We pay their wages, so I think I have every right to know what's going on in my own back garden," she said, closing the door with more force than was necessary.

Hollie told her that, from the little she had overheard, the police raid next door was somehow related to a murder enquiry. Half-truths and lies were coming far more frequently from her lips, and she was slightly concerned whether she had always possessed this talent.

"Well," said Wendy. "We will just have to see what they are talking about."

She strode into the kitchen and returned a few moments later with two glass tumblers.

"Here, take one of these."

Hollie followed Wendy into the lounge and watched as she put the tumbler against the wall and pressed her ear to it.

"Does that actually work? " Hollie asked.

Wendy shushed her. Her eyes looked up towards the ceiling as she remained with the glass sandwiched between her ear and the wall. Hollie was not convinced but followed suit a few feet away, facing Wendy.

Voices could be heard from the adjoining house, muffled, but clear enough for Hollie to follow the gist of the conversation.

"Where were you when I reported a burglary yesterday?" Erica Whitely demanded.

"I don't have information on that report, madam. What was stolen exactly?"

"A diamond earring. A valuable one. Maybe more, but I haven't had time to check properly."

"Just a single earring, madam?"

"Yes, just one, but it was a one point two carat diamond. I don't presume you have any idea of the value of such a stone."

"Anyway, madam, that would not have come through to my department."

"Who are you then, the thought police?"

"Major crimes. My name is DI Gilroy. I assume you are Ms Erica Whitely?"

There was no audible answer. Hollie imagined that she was either nodding or panicking, possibly both.

"We are investigating a murder, and I have a warrant here to search your property."

There was another silence following that announcement. It was interesting to hear the infamous DI Gilroy at last. He sounded more cultured than Hollie had imagined. She hadn't yet heard Maryam's voice, although it was difficult to identify all the background speech through a wall, using a glass tumbler as a listening device.

Another voice, a younger one, male, Hollie thought, said that he had found and bagged the shoes.

"What do they want with her shoes?" Wendy asked, sounding puzzled."

"I'll tell you later. Just listen."

DI Gilroy was arresting Erica Whitely and cautioning her. He spoke more slowly than the way they rattled through it on television, but her response was typical.

"I want my lawyer. I'm not saying another word until I have my lawyer present."

Maryam's voice, also muffled, but unmistakeable, had a note of excitement to it.

"I found a key, boss, at the bottom of a dirty laundry basket. Looks like it belongs to a lock-up, one of those storage places, judging by the key fob it's attached to.

"It never had a fob on it," Erica protested." You've just put that there."

Grace had never mentioned a key fob; she had said she recognised the key itself. It dawned on Hollie that she must have added the fob to make the key easier to identify. That girl was more devious and far-sighted than any recalcitrant student she ever had to deal with.

Wendy took her glass away from the wall and gave Hollie a long stare.

"You know exactly what's happening next door, don't you. So, I'm going to make us both a coffee and you are going to tell me what on earth is going on."

Hollie felt obliged to comply with Wendy's demands and, over a very welcome coffee, freshly brewed, explained her change of career, which might not be permanent, her involvement with the Comtesse du Colbert and that the police had suspected Jonas Moon of her murder. She omitted her special relationship with DS Maryam Chandra and the role Grace had played in her investigation.

"And I assume your mother is not interested in buying a property in this vicinity?"

"I'm afraid my mother died."

Wendy was shocked, and apologised profusely, assuming it had only happened in the last few days. Her face turned red and, as she put her coffee down her hand shook. A few drops spilled onto the table. Flustered, she grabbed several tissues from a nearby box to mop it up. Hollie realised Wendy's mistake.

"It's okay. My mother died almost eleven years ago."

Wendy looked up. Her eyes narrowed and her mouth hardened into a thin straight line.

"I now understand why my son took so many wrong turns if he was taught by such devious role models as you. I think it's time you left. And if your mother makes a miraculous recovery, you can tell her that my house will never end up in the hands of your family."

Hollie saw no point in trying to offer her own apologies and decided to leave as graciously as was possible, before Wendy could lay her hands on a sharp knife, heavy ornament or even a stray stiletto shoe.

The police van remained in the street with one uniformed officer guarding the front door and what Hollie presumed were a forensic crime team in unflattering white coveralls. The policeman, who had earlier directed Hollie to move away, recognised her. He turned towards her as she skipped down the steps and onto the safety of the pavement. She looked at her watch. It was only just gone seven o'clock. She waved to the officer and jogged down the street, back towards Mulberry Park.

Hollie decided a pot of tea and a bacon roll would be a well-deserved reward for nailing Erica Whitely and, presumably, freeing their client. Grace's café' might be open by the time she got there, especially if she did a couple of laps round the lake first. She was dressed for a run and the breakfast would then be doubly justified.

She had just taken a second bite from a large white bap, encasing three rashers of bacon and a generous squeeze of ketchup, when her phone rang. It was Maryam. She swallowed hurriedly at the same time as answering.

"Hi Maryam. How did it go?"

"You probably know already. One of my officers noticed the

two of you through next door's window with your makeshift listening devices."

"Yes, well, that was Wendy's idea, not mine. But it worked surprisingly well."

Maryam said she would have to remember that trick. She also warned Hollie not to celebrate too soon. Could she see the bacon sandwich? Had she got a secret camera in the café? She said they had to wait for forensics to finish with the car and to check what other fingerprints they might find on her shoes, but she was hoping Erica Whitely slipped up on those details and the Comtesse's would be found on them. Maryam said she seemed to be the kind of arrogant bitch who might make those sorts of mistakes, and immediately apologised for her choice of language."

Hollie said she understood but hoped that Maryam could let her know when the results came through.

"We also took that replica Oscar and I think you were right, or someone was right, about the blood on the base. I'll get back to you as soon as we have the results. Gilroy's here. Have to go."

Maryam had finished the call abruptly. Hollie assumed she was still at the station and wary of being overheard, especially by DI Gilroy.

Ketchup was oozing from one side of her bacon roll. She licked it off before it dribbled over her hands and finished her breakfast. She smiled with the slightly smug contented warmth of someone who had just solved her first case.

CHAPTER 32

Hollie enjoyed a feeling of success for almost thirty-six hours and was congratulated by both Stella and Rupert when the news reached them. Stella praised her highly, told her she always knew she was a fit for the job, and promised to take her and Oliver out for a celebration dinner. Rupert was less effusive, saying that it was now in the hands of police and that they sometimes took a more nuanced view of evidence they hadn't discovered themselves.

She took the remainder of the day off, as Stella had suggested, and spent the afternoon in the garden, drinking tea and reading a book. When Oliver came home, she related the morning's events to him, but left out the reason for her abrupt departure from Wendy's house.

She gracefully accepted Oliver's offer to take her to the same Italian restaurant where her adventure had started.

When Hollie arrived at work the next day, a little late due to a minor hangover, she found Sharon staring into space, apparently unaware of her presence.

"Are you okay?" she asked.

Sharon sighed and her head turned to acknowledged Hollie.

"Yes, sort of. It's just that Graham's agent has been arrested."

"Yes, I know, for Juliette du Colbert's murder. That's good news, isn't it? Jonas will be released."

"But she was negotiating that deal for Graham, for us. Now it might all fall through, all his plans for us were based on that contract."

Sharon dabbed at her eyes with a tissue, which was already smeared with mascara. She looked at it, sniffed loudly, and threw the offending item in a bin. She vigorously blew her nose on a fresh tissue. The bin, Hollie could see, was already half full.

"I'm sorry," Hollie said, not having thought about the consequences of her own success.

"It's not your fault Erica Whitely is a bitch and a murderer."

"There must be other agents who would be interested. After all, she's already done all the groundwork for them."

"I suppose so," Sharon sighed. "But who, and how do you find them?"

Hollie made an excuse about tidying up some paperwork and escaped to the solitude of the staircase. Even after such success she didn't want to see herself reflected a thousand times, smaller in stature with each iteration, but the same basic shape. Her balloon of joy had been somewhat deflated, but Taylor tried to puff a little more air into it when he applauded her as she passed his desk. The effect was minimal.

She sat in her office, wondering how she might restore equilibrium in Sharon's world. After a few minutes, and with no solution in mind, Hollie took the stairs to Stella's office, knocked on her door and entered without waiting for a reply.

"We have to help Sharon and Graham. I forgot that bloody woman was his agent and now I've screwed up their plans."

Stella was on the phone and indicated for Hollie to take a seat and hush for a moment. After mouthing an apology, Hollie went over to the window, leaned on the ledge, and stared at the leafy square which the building fronted. A couple of young mums were sharing a bench, watching their children play on a wooden climbing frame. She wondered if that should be her, but Oliver had never shown any enthusiasm for starting a family, and she hadn't pushed for it either. Maybe they were not natural parent types.

By the time Stella finished her conversation, Hollie had calmed down a little. She told Stella they had to solve Sharon and Graham's problem as she had almost single-handedly created it. Stella steepled her fingers, elbows on her desk, and looked directly at Hollie, making a little 'hmm' sound as though she wasn't too bothered by the problem.

"I don't know any literary or theatrical agents," she said, smiling. "But I definitely know a man who does."

"Can you ask him please, pull in a favour, just explain the situation, blame it on me."

"I shouldn't need to explain it, he's only next door and he already has all the details."

Hollie must have looked confused, she certainly felt it. Stella picked up her phone and tapped a couple of buttons.

"Stephen. We have a small problem which I think you may be able to help us with."

Stella explained that Stephen, known to Sharon as Mr Wilkins, had acquired a reputation in his younger days for negotiating lucrative contracts for artistes in the creative industry.

His office was right next door to Stella's. When they entered, Hollie was surprised by the book-lined room. It had a polished wood floor and Persian rugs scattered across it. Old, worn leather armchairs gave it more the aura of a gentleman's club than a cutting-edge lawyer's office. The effect of entering from a bright white corridor made Hollie feel like she ought to have brought a torch. Even the light from the window was muted by half-closed, grey, roller blinds.

Mr Wilkins himself, Hollie could see why Sharon couldn't call him Stephen, was warm and welcoming. He indicated for both Hollie and Stella to sit and, after getting them both to recap the problem, told them that he thought he knew just the right people to put Graham in contact with. It was a larger agency he said, with many more fingers in the publishing world than Erica Whitely was likely to have enjoyed.

"I admit I was not taken when I met her, more a one-woman assault force than an elegant negotiator. I'm sure we can sort out Graham and Sharon's little hiatus."

"Would it be all right if I told Sharon? She is rather upset about the whole thing."

"It might be better if we leave Graham to tell her," Stephen suggested. "Once it's all sorted out, he can explain the details. But I suppose you could tell her that we are handling it, and not to worry too much."

Back in Stella's office and with a welcome cup of coffee in her hands, Hollie sank onto one of the comfortable sofas.

"I guess that's it then, onto the next case. Tell me, what's happened with that writer who I got those compromising pics of at the awards ceremony?"

Stella told her not be so impatient and that some processes took far longer than she might imagine.

"Our object is not necessarily to break up marriages, sometimes it is a matter of renegotiating, but also being prepared in the event that those negotiations break down."

She suggested Hollie might take a few days off, promising to contact her if something urgent came up, something that required her special abilities.

"Oh, and by the way," Stella added, "a small sum should be deposited in your bank in the next couple of days. Regard it as a sort of signing on fee. It shouldn't cause a problem that way if you're still under contract with the education department."

Hollie had been so involved in the case that she had forgotten about being paid. And she hadn't given any thought of returning to teaching, or precisely when her contract ended in that respect.

Taking Stella's advice, Hollie had a brief chat with Sharon, before heading home. She told her not to worry, and that Mr Wilkins had everything under control .

It was mid-afternoon, and Hollie was enjoying some well-earned personal sunbathing time when her phone pinged. She thought about ignoring it, but couldn't. It was from Maryam.

Probably just saying thank you she thought.

"Four o'clock, same place? Important we meet."

Hollie frowned. She thought the case was wrapped up. But her phone pinged again, this time it was Stella.

"Jonas has not been released yet. We might have hit a small problem."

As if on cue, the sun hid behind a cloud, the temperature dropped, and Hollie shivered. Something had obviously gone wrong, and she had no idea what it could be. She checked the time on her phone. It was already gone three. A quick reply to Maryam with a thumbs up, a slightly longer one to Stella to tell her she might know more later today as she was meeting a mutual friend, and Hollie rushed upstairs to change out of her bikini.

CHAPTER 33

Out of breath, flustered and panicking, Hollie managed to change, drive to the library car park, pay for parking her car and still arrive at the café ten minutes early. Maryam was twelve minutes late. Hollie's tea was cold because she was too nervous to drink it and suspected she had put at least four spoons of sugar in it by mistake. She had also ignored the tempting array of cakes at the counter as her stomach might have rejected any solid food.

The one consolation was that Grace didn't appear to be working today. She wouldn't have known what to say to her about their joint project until after she had seen Maryam.

"Sorry I'm a little late," Maryam said as she settled on a chair facing Hollie. "It's all a bit chaotic at the station. I'll tell you about it in a minute."

Maryam had curtailed her explanation as the older lady, who Hollie now knew was Grace's aunt, the café owner, came over to take her order.

"Something to drink, dear? Cake? I think we've got some Chelsea buns left, and some nice scones."

"Just a coffee, please. Large, black, no sugar."

"Sugar is on the table, dear. Suit yourself whether you have any or not."

Hollie asked if she could have a fresh pot of tea and a fresh cup too. The woman looked at her as though she had asked for a line of cocaine, but shrugged and said, 'no problem', once she was out of earshot Maryam held up her hand.

"Please, let me explain where we are before you say anything.

I'll answer any questions you have, once you know all the facts."

Maryam told her that everything had worked out exactly as Hollie had suspected. The shoes they retrieved from Erica Whitely's house had Juliette du Colbert's fingerprints all over them. And they were waiting for DNA results for both pairs of shoes and the blood match for the trace found on the trophy, but preliminary results looked positive. She suspected they would be confirmed in the next day or two. We can't get full DNA tests done overnight, no matter what you might have thought.

She also said that Hollie's theory that Erica Whitely carried out the murder, knocking out the Comtesse with the Oscar, then dealing the fatal wound with a stiletto heal, was spot on. That she switched the shoes at the time of the murder, while the Comtesse was unconscious, was also correct. And she has even confessed to the murder, but it's not quite that simple.

Maryam paused as their drinks arrived. Hollie was wondering where the problem was, or even if there was one.

"She claims she had taken the Oscar with her to show the Comtesse that Jonas loved her, and he was only using her wealth and position to further his career."

"So, it was basically what I thought?"

"So far, so good," Maryam said.

"Jonas has been cleared?"

"Not exactly."

"What do you mean? You just said that Erica Whitely killed the Comtesse and has confessed."

Maryam hesitated and looked past Hollie to check that nobody was within hearing distance.

"The phone, the one that sent that strange message to the Comtesse, it was turned on again."

Hollie guessed bad news was coming.

"We managed to locate it this time. It's strange but makes sense. The phone had been found by a cab driver. He turned it on in case the owner had one of those 'find my phone' functions switched on and would come to claim it."

When Hollie pressed her, Maryam told her it had been found in the taxi, slid down the side of a seat. The driver had no idea how long it had been there as he only found it by chance when someone was sick on Sunday night, and he had to strip all the seating out for a deep clean.

"But how does this affect Jonas?"

"Our tech guys had no problem opening it. Jonas used the same code as he does for his main phone. Rookie mistake."

Hollie was thinking back to the award ceremony and the phone she had seen Erica Whitely using. It had to be the same one.

"You said you located it 'this time'?"

"It had been turned on a few days ago, but for less than a minute. Not long enough to get a location. But a text message was sent at that time, Saturday night. It was from Jonas Moon to Erica Whitely. When we arrested her, we found it on her phone. She actually directed us to it once she knew we had her for the murder."

"What did it say?"

Maryam hesitated and then said there was only so much she could tell Hollie, and she had probably overstepped the mark already. She hesitated, breathed a long sigh, and said all she could say was that it positively identified Jonas as an accomplice in the murder of the Comtesse. She pushed her chair back, stood, and spoke very quietly.

"Sorry."

Hollie watched her leave the café, wondering how she had got Jonas so wrong, and still didn't want to believe that he and Erica Whitely had planned the whole thing together.

Grace came out of the kitchen, probably when she saw Maryam leave. She sat opposite Hollie who was still staring at the door.

"Bad news?"

"Confusing news and, yes, very bad."

Hollie explained what she knew to Grace who pursed her lips, nodding slowly.

"She framed him, didn't she."

"I'd like to think so, but how, and more importantly, how do I prove it?"

"Not my department. Shame you didn't take a picture of her doing that thing with the phone at the awards ceremony."

"But I did."

Grace asked if she knew anyone who was good at tech stuff, and Taylor instantly sprung to mind.

"There's some extra data captured on every pic you take," Grace said. "I had a boyfriend who was into photography."

Hollie checked the time. Taylor might have left the office already, and she didn't have a contact number for him.

Oliver had to listen to the whole story again that evening, which he did without any complaint.

"She did it while Jonas was on the stage?" Oliver asked. "While he was collecting an award?"

When she confirmed his query, Oliver said the solution was simple.

"The event was filmed, I presume?"

Hollie confirmed that it was, as far as she knew. She had been aware of the cameras and had tried to stay out of shot as far as was possible. But she couldn't avoid them entirely as two of the cameras were constantly trained on the audience.

He suggested that, if the police got hold of the coverage, there might even be a shot of Erica Whitely sending the text to her own phone from the one supposedly belonging to Jonas. He thought again and asked if she could have sent that original strange email to the Comtesse.

"You're right. That's what must have happened. And I bet they record everything at those events, for reaction shots and fill-ins."

Hollie was hoping Taylor might be able to establish the time her own photos were taken from the data on her phone.

"But I don't know when that original text was sent, and I doubt Maryam would be able to give me that sort of detail."

"Surely she is bound by legal procedure to disclose it to Jonas's lawyer?"

Hollie hoped Oliver was right but was disappointed that she couldn't fit that last piece of the jigsaw herself and would have to leave it to someone else. It was always the most satisfying piece to fit, even better than finding the last edge piece.

The next morning, Hollie was waiting at Taylor's desk over half an hour before he arrived. She had even arrived before Sharon.

After a garbled explanation, which Taylor had to keep interrupting to ensure he understood the whole story, he took her phone, found the picture of Erica Whitely sending the message, and swiped up on the screen. He handed the phone back to Hollie, who could see a table of data. The location, time, date and even the settings on her phone when she took the pic.

"It's called metadata," Taylor said, "or EXIF data when it's a picture, if you want to be pedantic. All phones and cameras record it unless you disable it for privacy reasons."

Hollie thanked Taylor and took a screenshot of the data. She went to her office and sent the original pic and the data to Maryam, explaining how she suspected Erica Whitely had set out to frame Jonas in case she ever got caught. She sent the same message to Stella and Rupert, walked over to the window, and stared out at Mulberry Park. The teachers' group would be running there every Wednesday during the summer, but she wondered if she could still identify as part of that cohort. She now felt more qualified to describe herself as an investigator, less so a teacher.

It took four days for the police to gather the data from the video production company which had covered the award ceremony. Four nail-biting days for both Hollie and Stella. Four days during which Oliver crept around their house as if it had land mines buried in every room. They had also wanted Hollie's phone to check the data from her photos was accurately reported and not tampered with. Maryam had confirmed with Rupert that they found a partial fingerprint on Jonas's second phone which belonged to Erica Whitely. After those four days, all charges against Jonas were dropped. And after forensics had matched paint samples from Mei Ling's bike against the marks on Erica Whitely's car, she was also charged with a second count of murder.

Another strangely quiet week passed before Sharon handed her a plain white envelope when she arrived at the office. There was a credit card inside it and a hand-written note.

"I understand that you and your husband enjoy Italian restaurants. This is a corporate card issued by the Colby Group. Use and abuse it at your will, in perpetuity, for dining in any Italian restaurant, or any other restaurant for that matter. Nothing will bring back Juliette or Mei Ling, but I'm sure they would both consider this a small gesture to thank you for your services."

Hollie went straight to Stella's office and, waving the card in front of her, demanded to know whether she knew anything about it.

"Why don't you and Oliver take myself and Jeremy out to supper, and we can see if a risotto con funghi and a nice bottle of Valpolicella can jog my memory."

Printed in Great Britain
by Amazon